The Pirate Davy Jones

Scott D. Williams

ISBN: 979-8-9853749-0-2

Printed in the United States of America
Suggested Retail Price (SRP) $14.95

The Pirate Davy Jones is printed in Calluna

Layout by KingsizeCreations, LLC www.kingsizecreations.com

Acknowledgements

I first conceived of writing the backstory for Davy Jones after my last deployment in my Navy career in 2005. It was just after we'd crossed the Equator and observed the time-honored tradition of the Crossing the Line ceremony that I realized there was very little information about the mythical Davy Jones and I knew I had to give him a life before he became the legend.

After countless stops and starts, it was my lovely wife, Rasha, who convinced me I could do it. There were others, too, who urged me along, including Joe, Sarah, Doug, Colorado Pat, and Corporate Dave, to name a few.

This book is dedicated to my children: Alex, Michael, and Emily – all in the uniforms of the United States Navy and Army – and Ephemeral and Ryan. Special thanks to all of the Trusty Shellbacks, Polliwogs, and members of His Most Royal Majesty's Court of King Neptune. We are all part of the Ancient Order of the Deep.

Most of all, this book is for My Love, Rasha.

The Pirate Davy Jones

"Roll out the TNT, anchors aweigh!
Sail on to victory, and sink their bones to Davy Jones,
hooray!"
– Excerpt from the song of the US Navy

L ife is a fragile, insignificant thing when the sea god unleashes his mighty wrath. Sailors pray to him for salvation, often in vain, for he is implacable in his vengeance – especially when he is betrayed.

The object of his fury was a terrified mother with her unfortunate baby.

The howling storm arose from an otherwise beautiful evening. Sailors aboard the vessel gasped in horror as mountains of black clouds raced over the horizon, the wind turned from a gentle breeze to a howling demon, and the once placid sea boiled like a witch's hateful cauldron.

Even as the sails were hurriedly taken in, the ship was thrown backward, as if smacked by a huge hand, hurtling it toward the deadly teeth of rocks that suddenly appeared as if summoned. There was nothing they could do but brace for the impact of their doom.

Below in the hold, the woman held her precious infant.

She heard the awful crack of the main mast giving way before the storm's onslaught and the screams of the men as they were blown overboard. One of the sailors shouted a warning that they were going down, then he too disappeared as the sea god claimed another soul.

The ship heeled sharply over, broached by a towering wave. The woman sobbed and clutched her baby even more. A tremendous shudder reverberated through the timbers of the vessel as the dismasted hulk was driven onto the sharp rocks. The impact threw the woman against the bulkhead. The sea rushed through the side, hungrily gobbling up the all that stood in its way.

The woman quickly removed her necklace and looped it twice around the infant's neck to keep it secure. Then she took a deep breath and plunged into the cold sea, trying to find a way out. She fought to keep her baby's head above water as she struggled against the strong flow, kicking with all her strength. The darkness, combined with the choking salt water, forced her to feel her way along the now submerged deck. Her lungs ached for air as she tried in vain to find an opening to the surface, but she couldn't tell which way was up. Hopelessness stole upon her as she realized she couldn't hold her breath any longer. Her mouth opened in a voiceless, angry scream and the relentless sea invaded, choking the last of her life. Arms limp, the baby floated away.

Soon, the baby felt arms around it again. The tumultuous swirl of the shipwreck was gone, replaced by a rhythmic forward motion. A high voice singing a beautiful lullaby greeted its ears. Invisible fingers stroked a strange medallion hanging from the baby's necklace. The little child fell asleep, feeling safe once more in the dark depths.

Wales, 1683

"There are many fish in the ocean, Davy – big fish, little fish, and very, very strange fish – but the only one that matters is the one you're about to hook." It was his father's favorite saying, one he was to remember for the rest of his unnatural life.

Davy Jones was a young lad on the cusp of manhood, perhaps twelve or so, living the impoverished life so typical of Welshmen of the times. Most days he arose early, before the weary sun crept over the horizon and cast its dull light through the sole window of the tumbledown, one-room shack he shared with his father near the rocky beach. The cries of the gulls and the steady roar of the surf were his constant companions, indeed, his only friends. This was because his father, Wyn, chose to lead a secluded life, away from "prying eyes and curious looks" he told him. Davy didn't question his father. It was all he had known and he was satisfied to spend his days learning the fishing trade and earning his keep.

Their time was spent on the waves in their small, dilapidated boat. It had a single lugsail, stained gray with salt and sun, but most of the time they simply rowed their way about, Davy at the oars and Wyn guiding the tiller. When they at last found a good spot – chosen by Wyn's practiced eye and innate sense – his father would order him to "avast sculls" and heave the anchor over the side. Then they would cast and tie off their nets and take up old poles to drop their lines into the murky depths.

Wyn was a man of few words, so after some time had passed Davy would beg him for a story, or failing that, a swim. The outcome depended on Wyn's mood. Sometimes, if the fish were plentiful, Wyn would rub his grizzled jaw, crack a wry smile, and tell Davy tales of adventurous mariners, or dark monsters of the deep. These were the good days. Davy loved to listen, and he never interrupted his father.

Other times, when the "sea god were sour on them" Davy was allowed to slip over the side and swim for a while. Before he departed, his father would always caution him not to take too long, and if he pounded on the deck he was to "light along" and come up immediately. Today was one of those days.

He found the salt water refreshing. He dove under, eyes open, and pushed away. The keel of their small boat receded quickly as the sea swallowed the world above. It was a magical, wonderful place, full of interesting creatures and features. Webs formed between his fingers, helping him power through the current. As he reached bottom, he scanned the rocky bed for clams. Breathing was no longer troubling, as the gills that opened on his neck took over and allowed him to breathe with ease. His dark eyes grew larger and the pupils dilated until the white disappeared altogether. A filmy, blue cast came over them, enabling Davy to see well in the dark depths. Davy had experienced this transformation for as long as he could remember, when he first slipped into the ocean that seemed to beckon him as a mother opens her arms for her child. Here he felt at home. But only he and his father knew.

He was studying the cautious movement of a crab as it

felt its way along a rock when he heard the familiar thumping of the oar. He stroked the crab and then turned toward the surface.

Wyn heard the splash and turned to see Davy grinning and waving. The boy swept aside his stringy wet hair, his eyes returning to their normal shape, and filled his lungs with a big gulp. Wyn motioned to him to climb aboard with a grunt. It was time to haul in the nets and head back to land.

Davy was mending a net behind the shack when he heard a distant rumble of approaching riders. He turned his head in time to see Wyn's face poke the lone window.

"Git yerself hid!"

He dropped his work and darted behind a thick gorse shrub. The yellow flowers filled his nostrils with a coconut scent and provided excellent cover for his small frame.

Four riders came up the narrow path from the field of heath, the horses snorting as they trotted along in file. Wyn stepped outside, arms folded. The men halted their mounts a few paces away and climbed down. They were armed with rude cudgels and their leader sported a sword. He stepped forward, eyes scanning the shack, surrounding area, and finally rested on Wyn.

"His Lordship has sent us to take census and collect taxes," he said. "How many souls live here?"

Wyn observed the colorful coat of arms on his jerkin, which signified the office of the magistrate for the Duke of Beaufort, who occupied Oystermouth Castle a couple of miles away. "Jest me," he replied. "Me wife passed on some years ago."

"That so?" the man replied, peering over Wyn's shoulder at the open door. "Then you won't mind if we inspect your...humble abode." He shoved Wyn aside and strode inside.

Aside from the glow from the fireplace, it was fairly dark inside. The magistrate's man peered into the gloomy corners, noticing little but a rough, low bed, a small table with no chairs, and fishing tackle. A lidless pot bubbled over the fire, filling the room with a combination of smoke and fish. The man studied the contents for a moment and straightened up.

"You eat well for one man," he loudly remarked. He went back outside and confronted Wyn. "Where are the others?"

Wyn spat. "As I said, I'm alone here."

The man jabbed his finger at Wyn's chest. "Do you think me a fool?" His question was met with stony silence.

"Search the area, just in case this peasant has forgotten his kin."

The magistrate's men fanned out. Davy saw them approach and crawled backward through the tall grass toward the cliff.

"Ye won't find naught," called after them.

"While my men are looking for your long-lost relatives," the magistrate's deputy said to Wyn, "you can show me your earnings."

"I ain't got two coppers to rub together," Wyn replied, restraining himself from glancing at the men thrashing through the heath.

"Well then, I suppose you'll need to provide our Lordship with payment in kind." The deputy stepped back inside and examined the room for something of value. Wyn dashed around the shack.

Davy reached the edge of the cliff. He held on to the tough grass as he lowered himself over the side and found a foothold. He flattened himself against the rough rock and silently prayed to the old sea god that his father often mentioned in his stories. He heard a rustling in the grass above him.

"You there," Wyn called at the magistrate's man peering over the cliff. "Avast! Yer about to go overboard! The grass grows over the cliff."

The man jumped back and swore at him. Satisfied, Wyn returned to the doorway.

"See anythin' ye like, ye goddamned swab?"

The deputy glowered at him. "You are the poorest, meanest wretch in His Lordship's entire county," he declared, tipping over the table. He shoved Wyn again and called to his men.

As they mounted their horses, the deputy magistrate pointed at Wyn. "We'll be back in a fortnight. I expect you to have your taxes ready for collection, or you'll be rotting in His Lordship's cell."

They spun their horses around and departed, leaving a cloud of dust.

Wyn watched them until they were specks in the distance. He turned to find Davy behind him. "That was a close shave, lad."

The next day Wyn decided it was time to find work.

"Stay close to the house," he warned Davy. "Anyone comes, you make yerself scarce. Hear me, lad?"

Davy nodded and watched his father trudge down the hill. It would take him a few hours to reach the docks at Swansea.

Meanwhile, he reasoned, the sea was calling. Wouldn't hurt to take a little dip and perhaps find some mussels or crabs for dinner.

He found the salt water refreshing, as usual. He dove beneath a roller and skimmed the bottom as he stroked his way against the current. After a short time, he was a good league from the coast, exploring the nooks and crannies of an underwater rock formation. He discovered the remains of a wrecked shallop, its mast long gone. Many a ship had met a similar fate in storms that wracked Bristol Channel. Swimming through the open door of a small cabin, he paused to let a squid pass. He smiled as it gazed at him for a moment before pushing away. He turned his attention to exploring the contents of the derelict. Little of interest, other than a rusted set of calipers and soggy, unreadable charts, remained. Davy exited the boat and headed to the top to get his bearings.

He passed a school of mackerel and reminded himself to pick up dinner before it got too late in the day. Sunlight filtered down into the depths, guiding his way to the surface. He wiped the water from his eyes and pushed back his black hair, squinting as his eyes adjusted. He'd been down for so long that he'd lost all sense of time. It was about noon, he reckoned, and he was miles away from shore. He sighed and dove, knowing he'd make better time underwater.

He plucked a pair of red king crabs he found along the way and waded ashore. He picked up his clothes and climbed the bluff. It was still hours from sunset, the summer light not fading until late this time of year. He stoked the fire and filled the old cooking pot with fresh water from a nearby brook setting it to boil.

A few wild potatoes might make for a good stew, he decided. There were many growing in the local area, and a short walk down the hill would put him among them. He grabbed a rusty old knife and the fish pail.

He'd already dug up a half dozen when he heard a strange whistling. He turned back toward the shack and glimpsed the figure of a man emerge in the shadow of the shack's door. Davy shielded his eyes from the glare of the setting sun and called out. The man glanced his way. It wasn't his father.

Frozen with fear, Davy dropped the bucket and thought furiously. Unable to come to a decision, he opted to duck into the tall grass. When he looked again, the man had vanished. He waited for several minutes and then decided it must have been some wanderer. He cautiously crawled forward, keeping his eyes locked on the shack. Finally, he arose, gathered his potatoes, and walked home.

He paused at the door, gathered his courage, and peered through the crack. The darkness revealed nothing. He slowly pushed the door open. "Who be there?"

Silence greeted him. He ventured inside, tiptoeing on the

dirt floor. The shack was empty of intruders. He exhaled loudly, realizing with a smile that he'd kept his breath the whole time.

Wyn came home to a pleasant aroma. "What's this? Ye made a stew, lad?" he grinned.

Davy beamed and pointed to two steaming bowls on the low table. They sat down to eat and Wyn announced he would return to town the next day. "Got me some work with the longshoremen on the docks in Swansea," he said.

"What will ye do, da?"

"Oh, handlin' lines, offloadin' cargo and such," Wyn replied.

"I didn't know ye knew anythin' about ships," said Davy. "And it's so far away, in the big city."

"Aye, yer old man knows a thing or two about the sea," Wyn sniffed. "I ain't always been a landsman."

"Really, da? Tell me about it! Did ye sail the seven seas? Is that from where ye got all yer stories?"

Wyn cleared his throat and his brows furrowed. "That ain't nothin' to gab about," he answered gruffly. "Now, wash out these here bowls and git yerself to bed."

Wyn arose well before dawn the next day and set off at a brisk pace for the long journey to Swansea, leaving Davy asleep. After a couple of weeks of this daily ritual, he could clink together a few coins in his rough hand. Then the day came when the magistrate's men were seen approaching the shack.

Wyn gave Davy a nod and the lad climbed through the back window to go hide in the underbrush. Wyn stiffened his upper lip and walked outside to wait for his unwelcomed guests.

The deputy magistrate climbed down from his horse. "We've come in the name of our lord to collect the taxes you owe – as I promised we would."

Wyn set his hands on his hips and spat. "On church day, no less."

The deputy scoffed. "You don't strike me as the kind of man that observes the holy Sabbath." He held out his hand. "Pay your share. Two shillings, six pence."

"Half crown ye say? I jest got me some work," Wyn said. "All I gots is..." he fumbled the coins in his pocket, "jest shy of a bob. A man can't live on fish alone."

The deputy glowered at him and snatched the coins from Wyn's outstretched hand. "See here man, I'm only collecting for this month. You'll need to do better than that."

"Ain't got that much. Mebbe you can visit again when the moon turns and I'll have the rest." He spread his arms. "Can't give what I don't have."

The deputy glanced over his shoulder at his men and drew his sword. "Perhaps he needs help finding the rest of what he owes. Shake it out of him."

Wyn edged back as the men approached.

Davy, watching the scene unfold from his hiding spot, took a deep breath. He thought about jumping out and running away to distract the magistrate's men when something else caught his eye.

Eight men emerged from the heath to his left, not more than twenty paces away. They looked grim and threatening. They advanced on the startled deputy, quickly covering the distance in long strides. Battered cutlasses were in their fists.

"Leave off," one bellowed. "This one is ours."

The magistrate's men backed away. "You are interfering with His Lordship's business," the deputy cried.

"Stopper that gob," one of the strangers ordered. "Or we'll gut ye." The others growled in assent.

The magistrate's men quickly mounted their horses and fled at a gallop. Two of the newcomers quickly grabbed Wyn's arms and their leader pointed his blade at him. The strangers wore the garb of seamen, and their ill intent was clear in how they howled like wolves and swore like devils.

Davy saw a strange expression on Wyn's face, one he'd never seen before. Fear.

2

"Take us back to yesterday, Morgan, or there be no t'morrow for you."

Davy was confused and frightened. Who were these rough men, and why were they threatening his father? Why did they call him Morgan? He stayed hidden, uncertain as to what he should do.

"Ye have the wrong man," Wyn replied. "I'm just a poor..."

"Enough with the games, Morgan Gwynn," the man with the sword retorted. "We know you, *quartermaster*. You remember your old shipmates, eh?" He dug the point of his blade just a bit into Wyn's chest, causing him to wince.

The men guffawed. Davy saw Wyn's face harden as he spat at his accuser.

"Ye won't get squat from me," he declared. "Sheer off, ye grass-combing buggers!"

The man with the sword, clearly the leader of the vicious

group, swore as he wiped the spittle away from his face.

"Now, now, Morgan. That's no way to treat your friends," he said, regaining his composure. "We're all gentlemen of fortune. There's no need for insults. Just give us what we want and we'll be on our way. You can get back to your...humble life," he sneered.

Wyn was silent. He swept his eyes over the shack and the spot where Davy was hiding before he turned his attention back to the swordsman.

"Aye, I'll give ye what ye want."

"By thunder!" the leader exclaimed. "There's the old quartermaster we all know! Take us to it!"

"Nay, it'll take me some time," Wyn said. "I've hidden it."

The man chuckled, lowering his sword. "Of course you have. Well, we'll just help you, shipmate."

Wyn lifted his chin in defiance. "It ain't here. Like I says, it's hidden. Ye can't go with me, or ye will be discovered."

"Those sheriff's men will be back soon," the man said. "Don't you try to make amends by selling out your old shipmates, Morgan."

"I never been no songbird," Wyn snarled. "If'n any o' ye swabs knows that, it'd be ye, Shipwreck Tom. I'll bring it to the beach at midnight t'morrow and light a lamp."

"Aye, and don't think of strayin' too far," Tom warned. "We'll be keepin' a weather eye on you." He nodded to his men and they departed on a path that led to the shore.

As Wyn watched them go, Shipwreck Tom turned back. "Remember this, Morgan. We found you once, and we can find you again. There's nowhere you can run. Nowhere in this world. You can lay to that."

He turned away and they descended the cliff, leaving Wyn to ponder his fate and Davy to wonder just who these men were, especially the one he thought he'd known all his life.

Davy quietly watched as his father sat by the fire. The burning questions struggled to escape, but he choked them down at the sight of Wyn's furious countenance. Finally, the old man arose and turned to him.

"It's a right shame ye had to see that," said Wyn. "No matter. We ain't got much time now, so I needs ye to do what I says, ya hear?"

"Yessir," Davy answered anxiously.

"Gather up what victuals and crockery we 'ave and fill up this 'ere seabag," he said, pointing to a dusty lump in the corner. "Then put on yer coat. We weigh at sundown."

Davy moved to obey. He understood his father's command, but where they would sail was a mystery. As he grabbed a few items, he furtively glanced at his father, who was busy prying off a plank in the corner of the rafters. His groping hand found an old dirk, which be shoved into his belt. Then he withdrew a roll of something in oilskin and stuffed it down the inside of his jerkin.

"Da," said Davy, mustering his courage. "What's that?"

Wyn turned and glared at him. "Never ye mind!"

Davy filled a small water cask from the nearby spring at the bottom of the hill. His hands shook as he remembered the threatening promise of the man named Shipwreck Tom.

In all the stories his father had told him over the years, he'd never claimed to be a member of a ship's crew, much less in company with the foul-tempered lot that had just visited them. His suspicions grew. He weighed the cost of confronting the old man. Was his curiosity worth alienating the only family he'd ever known? Perhaps when they'd escaped the present danger Wyn would confess all, Davy reasoned. No need to press him when he was clearly anxious.

He returned with his load and sat down on the floor of the shack. Wyn was sitting by the fire, staring into the flames. Together, they waited for the fateful dusk to fall.

Wyn finally broke the silence.

"Listen here, lad," he said, removing something from his pocket. It was a medallion on a necklace made of some kind of metal. It shimmered dully in the firelight.

"This here is yers," he said, handing to Davy. "Don't ever show it no one, not a soul."

"What is it, da?"

"I don't know, but I reckon ye should have it. Methinks it's got value, more than gold."

Davy studied the medallion. Strange runic marks ran along the circular edge and a large sapphire was set into the middle of a raised, eight-pointed star. He turned it over to find a trident engraved on the smooth surface. He began to ask another question, but Wyn shook his head.

"Don't bother lad, I don't know. But someday mebbe ye will find out." He leaned closer. "Keep it hidden."

Davy put it into his pocket and turned back toward the fire. His mind raced with questions, but he knew his father would answer no more.

A beautiful sunset bathed the cliffs of Gwyr in a warm, orange glow that on any other day would have brought cheer, but Davy felt only dread. He watched the fiery disk as it quickly sank, until the top rim winked its last farewell and withdrew. Twilight commenced and Davy turned to Wyn, nervously expecting his next command, but it did not come. He closed the shutter and then moved to the door. Before he could open it, he heard Wyn's low voice.

"Avast."

Davy meekly returned to the fire and sat down.

Twilight is a time of wonder. Shadows of the earth compete with the vivid colors of the fading sky, playing tricks on the eyes of unwary men. It was Davy's favorite time of the day for that very reason. He often stole along the rabbit trails in the heather and marsh, straining to see the game that emerged during this magical time. He would imagine himself as a famed hunter, prowling for the king of the rabbits, who lived in some secret warren, if only he could track him down. He had many fictional fights with the armies of the Rabbit King, always ending in glory as he triumphed over their furry leader and returned home with his invisible pelt slung over his shoulder. The soft fur would bring him luck and protection, he'd declare to himself.

Now he longed for that enchanted pelt and all its charms as the dreadful dusk took hold of the cliffs. The long shadows of twilight had consumed all, and the creeping things of night were coming out to stalk their prey. Only the last dark blue and purple patches remained, retreating in haste before the ominous black host of the Lord of Night. A sliver of crescent moon dared to peek through the heavenly curtain and shine its feeble light down upon the shack on the cliff, but Davy was not comforted. This was the witching hour, his father had once told him, and dire fate awaited those who were tempted to tread among the shadows. Of course, it was only his way of convincing the lad to stay inside and not cavort around the dangerous rocky crags, but for Davy it took ahold of his mind like some dread warlock and unlocked his fears.

Wyn stirred. "Time to shove off."

His father led the way, cautiously glancing this way and that, as Davy followed, mimicking his movements. The water cask was heavy under his arm and the seabag slung over his back bore him down, but Davy wasn't thinking of his burden. Every insect chirp, every cry of an unseen bird, every rustle of some creature of the night camouflaged in the grass and rocks set his mind racing with fear. In his head, be quietly donned the invisible pelt of the Rabbit King.

Wyn led them down a path to the beach. The cool sand brought a measure of relief to Davy as the familiar crashing of the enduring surf penetrated the darkness. They escaped the clutches of the witches and their phantom minions, he told himself, thanks to the Rabbit King. The sea, even at night, was something he could embrace.

Together, they pushed the skiff off the beach and climbed aboard. Wyn ordered Davy to take the sculls as he guided the tiller to bring the bow into the oncoming surf. The little boat easily crested the first small roller before it broke into a frothy mess behind them. The looming cliffs of the Gwyr peninsula began to shorten as they steadily pulled out into the Bristol Channel.

There was no question of raising the lugsail. Even Davy knew it would only serve to increase the visibility of their low profile in the water to watchful eyes. He continued to quietly pull at the oars as Wyn guided them on a westerly course. The old man quietly damned the faint moonlight, but they had no choice in the matter. He glanced up at the dark gray clouds, which in their stubbornness, refused to obscure that white beacon.

Perhaps it was a lapse in concentration, or maybe Davy was just nervous, but his stroke was suddenly uneven, and in his attempt to correct his mistake he slapped an oar flat against the water. The smack resounded like a breaching whale.

"Avast sculls," Wyn growled in a low voice filled with disgust. He spun around, scanning the dark void for any sign they'd been detected. And there it was, a faint creak of metal and the shutter of a lamp was raised, not a cable length away. A cry went up and then the sound of oars splashing indicated the chase was on.

Wyn leaped forward and shoved Davy behind him as he grabbed the sculls. "Hold our course!" he commanded.

Davy took the tiller as Wyn began pulling with long, powerful strokes. There was no need to be silent now. The little skiff leapt forward in short, bobbing movements against the current. A musket ball whizzed overhead, causing Davy to hunker as low as he could while still keeping a grip on the handle of the rudder. He peeped over the gunwale and saw their pursuers, silhouetted against a river of reflected light cast by the moon on the water behind them. Eight men were crammed in a jolly boat, six manning the oars, one steering in the stern, and one propped up in the bow, reloading a long musket.

Wyn knew he couldn't outrun them, so he ordered Davy to change course. "Make yer heading sou' by sou'west." Davy understood they were bearing for Morte Point at the head of Rockham Bay. This was an area Wyn particularly favored for catching mackerel. He clearly intended to lure their chasers into the infamous bay with its dangerous surf and craggy reefs that had sent many an unwary boat and even ships to their doom. *If only we could get there before we're overtaken or shot*, Davy thought.

As if on cue, another shot rang out and whizzed past Davy's ear, striking their bare mast and sending chips of wood flying. He saw the man reload and noticed how the adversary was gaining. He put the tiller over, pointing the bow almost due south. Now the wind was on their starboard beam and Wyn ordered him to put up the sail.

Davy secured the tiller with an eye-spliced line and then set about the task of attaching the boom to the mast. He feverishly passed boltropes through the grommets in the sail and hoisted it up the twelve-foot pole. The little skiff heeled sharply to port as the brisk westerly caught the sheet. They immediately surged ahead, gaining speed and leaving a creamy wake.

Shipwreck Tom howled in frustration and shouted at his oarsmen to pull harder.

Wyn again traded places with Davy and told him to keep

pulling at the sculls while he focused on navigating the upcoming Rockham Bay. Still on the starboard tack, he steered as close to the wind as he dared while simultaneously trimming the sail to avoid luffing. As they approached the dangerous waters, he kept a close eye on their leeway to avoid the infamous hidden shoals and eddies known to local mariners.

The chase went on for another hour. Davy kept up a torrid pace, but his sore arms were betraying the signs of fatigue. It was now difficult to see their pursuers and Davy sighed in relief. "We did it, Da!"

"We ain't done nothin' yet, lad," his father said grimly. "Lookee yonder, two points windward."

A vast shape, barely visible, emerged from the darkness. Davy's heart sank as he recognized it as a brigantine, the kind Wyn had often mentioned in his stories as the favored rig of pirates. It was less than three cable lengths away and closing.

"Da, what do we do?"

Wyn glanced at the boat trailing them and the ship ahead. He took a deep breath.

"We goes on, lad," he said. "If'n we can get to the shoals, we stand a chance."

The southern shore was barely a nautical mile away, but it could have been a thousand in Davy's mind. A lamp appeared aboard the brigantine and he could see figures at the beakhead of the approaching ship. One of them pointed at the skiff and shouted. A swivel gun was aimed in their direction as the ship changed course slightly to cut them off.

A loud crack followed by a puff of smoke announced the ship's intentions as a small projectile skipped across the water in front of the skiff. Davy looked at a downcast Wyn and realized it was over. A voice shouted to them.

"Heave to and stand by to be boarded!"

"It's no use, lad," Wyn sighed. "Avast sculls and lower the sail."

Davy complied and the little boat drifted to a halt. They waited, bobbing with the waves as the ship tacked into the wind and reefed its sails, resting within pistol shot of them. Wyn withdrew the roll of oilcloth from his shirt and gave it to Davy.

"Stuff this down yer trousers and don't let them see it," he said. "No matter what happens to me, keep this safe!"

The boat behind them soon caught up and Davy saw the men ship their oars. Shipwreck Tom hailed them.

"Halloo there, shipmate! Kindly take our line." He threw it over and Wyn reluctantly tied it off to a cleat. The pirates heaved on the line and brought the two boats together, their larger craft bumping the skiff roughly as their sides met.

Two pirates trained muskets on Wyn and Davy as Shipwreck Tom stepped over the side.

"Out on a late-night excursion, I see," he sneered. "I told you there weren't nowhere you could run that we wouldn't find you."

Wyn glared at him.

"This here your lad?" the pirate inquired.

"Nay, jest a boy from the village," replied Wyn. "It's his boat."

Shipwreck Tom laughed. "Well, that's bad luck for you, lad."

"You let me Da be!" Davy shouted at the pirate.

A moment of silence passed as Shipwreck Tom digested this new information. "I see," he drawled. "That changes things, don't it, Morgan?"

"This here business is between you and I, Tom. He ain't got no part in it," said Wyn desperately. "Why don't we leave off and let him go home?"

The pirate scoffed. "You know better than that, Morgan. We can't have any witnesses."

Wyn stood up and one of the pirates leaned closer, leveling his musket at Davy's chest. Shipwreck Tom lifted his hand to halt his crewman.

"No need to be hasty," he said, looking at Wyn. "Let's get down to business. I believe you have something for us."

"Didn't have time to fetch it," said Wyn.

Shipwreck Tom stepped forward and grabbed him by the shirt. "Don't play us for fools, quartermaster! Where is it? Give it up!"

Wyn smiled and tapped his forehead. "It's in here."

The pirate cursed and spat. "Take him," he ordered. Two pirates grabbed Wyn by the arms, roughly shoving him into the jolly boat.

Davy leapt forward. "Da!"

Shipwreck Tom quickly drew his dirk and clubbed Davy over the head. The boy tumbled overboard and sank.

"Ye son of a whore!" Wyn snarled. "I'll send ye to hell fer that!"

The pirate spun around and held his blade to Wyn's throat. "I'll meet you there someday," he hissed. "But first, you're going to have a nice little chat with Captain Tew. Secure him."

As the pirates bound Wyn, Shipwreck Tom loosened the line holding the two boats together. They pushed off and manned the oars. Soon they were pulling for the brigantine, leaving the empty skiff to drift on the black waves.

When Davy came to his senses, he found himself flat on his back staring at the starless night sky. He sat up and rubbed the aching lump on his head. Even as he registered the sand below his palms, he realized he was alone. The skiff was gone and so was Wyn. He looked around and took his bearings. The familiar outline of the Gwyr cliffs greeted him.

How did I get here?

He shook his head, trying to clear away the fog that had settled in his mind like the mists that so frequently visited the local coast. Had he swum all the way home? It didn't seem likely to him. The tide would have carried him to the beach in Rockham Bay, if anywhere. And why hadn't he drowned?

No matter, he decided. *My da – whatever his name – was taken by those pirate bastards.* He scanned the sea and saw nothing. No lamplight, no ship. What to do now?

He trudged up the path back to the shack and sat down inside. There were a few smoldering embers left and he idly stirred them with a stick. The magistrate's men would be back soon, he surmised, so he couldn't stay here. His father was in the hands of an enemy that was probably gone for good. He had only one choice.

He took the medallion out of his pocket and put it around his neck, then fished into his trousers and withdrew the oilcloth. He examined it for a moment, but there wasn't enough light to make out the scrawled marks on it. He shrugged and stuffed it down his shirt, pulling the laces together at his throat to hide his two secrets.

The little shack on the cliff disappeared behind him as a determined Davy Jones marched through a sea of tall grass toward Swansea.

3

Noise, confusion and a pot of piss carelessly thrown from a window greeted Davy as he staggered into Swansea. The baleful sun, attempting to pierce the reluctant coastal haze of the late morning, cast a dull glare upon the mass of humanity as it went about its business, like so many ants.

A life of solitude with his father hadn't prepared Davy for this. His eyes darted nervously as if he were seeking a way to escape the madness, but he knew he had to find the docks and somehow figure out a plan to board a ship. Wyn, or Morgan, was now out there, somewhere at sea – and surrounded by enemies. He had no idea how he was going to convince a captain to take him aboard, but he did have a destination.

Hours earlier, he was on a dirt path headed to the town when the sky brightened enough for him to see better than the feeble moonlight. It was then that he plucked the oilskin from his shirt and unrolled it, revealing what appeared to be a map. He didn't understand the places or names scrawled on it, but they were clearly far away over the sea. One place in particular was marked with an X. He'd have to find out where it was and then find a ship headed in that direction. That had to be where those pirates were taking his father. He'd figure the rest out later.

For now, he was lost. The narrow streets and tall buildings of Swansea made him feel trapped as he dodged trading carts and bustling passersby. Then he caught sight of a tall church spire in the distance. He considered going inside and taking a view from the height of its bell tower, where he might be able to locate the waterfront. Davy's mind worked furiously. Perhaps the local – what was he called? Parson, that was Wyn had called him. Davy smiled as he remembered how his father had mentioned a parson in one of his stories. Although he detested religion in general, he believed that the clergy were basically good people, if not misguided. Maybe the local parson could tell him if there were any good captains that might take on a boy for a voyage around the land the map described as "Africa" into the ocean beyond.

He was mulling this over when he bumped into something rather hard. That something turned out to be someone. A tall, muscular youth grinned with evil delight and grabbed Davy by his shirt, pinning him to a slab-sided tavern wall.

"Well, wot 'ave we 'ere?" he asked, leaning into Davy's face. His dark eyes narrowed below his blond mop, and he bared his brown, crooked teeth. His breath was overwhelming, and Davy looked away in disgust and fear.

"Tis a wharf rat, looks like," his skinny companion sneered in a whiny voice. His greasy, tangled red hair was crowned with an equally appalling cap that appeared to have been plucked from the muck of a pigsty. His numerous pimples contrasted his pasty white pallor.

"Mo' like...uh, yeah, hee, hee, hee," tittered a third adolescent, his ample belly jiggling. His pear-shaped frame, topped with a pointy shaven head, seemed enormous on his stumpy legs.

The first boy towered over Davy, glaring at him with contempt. "Well boys, wot does we do with stinkin' little wharf rats?"

"I catches em' and eats 'em," the fat one replied proudly. "Mos'ly roasted, or sometimes when dere's no fire, I..."

"Shut up, you bleedin' idiot," skinny one ordered his odious companion. He turned to face Davy, his sallow face twisting to a grin. "Nah, we drowns 'em!"

"Well dat's a plum ideer, but I prefers to stomp 'em," the tall one said. "Makes fo' a pretty sight."

He viciously threw Davy to the ground and promptly kicked him in the ribs. Davy cried out, curling to protect his wounded side.

The other two joined in kicking and stomping on the helpless Davy. He rolled from side to side with each strike, howling with pain. "Avast! Leave me alone! Please," Davy begged, "jest stop."

"Well, da rat speaks!" the leader of the tormentors announced. "Say mo', rat. Ask me fo' mercy. An' call me *sir*," he added with a smirk.

They halted their abuse and waited for Davy's reply.

"S-sir, if you please, please let me go."

"Aw, dat's proper, nice like," the skinny one laughed. "Dat rat knows 'is place."

The fat one trumpeted his agreement with a loud, greasy fart. His skinny pal glanced at him and shook his head in amused disgust.

The leader of the motley trio put his beefy hands on his hips. He drew a deep breath and smiled. "See boys, dat warnt so 'ard. Ya beat a rat enough 'an he learns 'is place."

He squatted next to Davy. "Now rat, now dat ya is trained all proper, be off wit' ya!"

Davy scrambled to his feet and turned to go.

But the bully had one parting shot. "Ya bastard!"

The bullies burst into laughter. Davy halted and turned red. He felt a surge of energy leap like a bolt of lightning and flash throughout his body. He wheeled around and struck the bully full in the mouth with his little fist. The brute staggered backward, holding his jaw. He spat blood and a tooth flew to the dirt.

Momentarily astonished, the bully regained his composure and said, "Why, ya little shit!" He lunged, but Davy spun on his heel and took off like a hare.

He bolted around the corner, a few steps ahead of his pursuers. Davy glanced at the tavern sign and shot through the open door. Before his eyes could adjust to the dim light, he ran smack into a barstool and tumbled into a heap on the floor next to a table with three men. He scrambled to his feet and looked straight into the eyes of a black-haired youth standing with an amused expression on his square jaw. He looked about Davy's age, but was better fed and clearly confident. He wore a barman's apron around his chest, his breeches were worn, with holes in the knees, and a short cap adorned his head. He stood a full head taller.

Before the boy could speak, the bullies rushed through the doorway. Davy whirled around and met his aggressors, who stopped short, panting. Their leader glared at Davy, then glanced at the tall boy next to him, who coolly regarded him.

"What's goin' on here?" the lanky, muscular boy demanded.

"None o' yer bizness," the bully answered hotly.

"Ya lubbers is in my place, so that makes it me bizness," the boy replied. He drew a cudgel from behind the bar and slapped it against his hand. "I don't likes the look of ya, so why don't ya be on yer way befo' I rouse out yer brains and make a mess on the floor."

Davy looked at the boy in wonder.

The bully was taken aback, but he regained his composure after glancing at his two pals. "Well, looks like we got two rats to squash, boys," he announced. He advanced toward Davy and the boy, somewhat hesitantly.

"Yeah, squash 'em," the fat one growled.

The bar boy roared and charged, swinging his club. The leader ducked and the club struck the fat boy in his heavy jowls. He fell to the floor with a heavy, wordless thump. The leader tackled Davy and brought him down like a sack of grain.

While Davy and the bully leader rolled around the wooden floor, the skinny one gave a yell and charged the dark-hair youth, knocking him into the bar. The boy twisted and shoved him away, then brought his cudgel down on the leader, whom had Davy pinned. He grunted with pain and rolled off Davy. The skinny one struck the bar boy with a right cross, but he just glared at the redhead and kicked him in the gut, sending his thin frame backward. Davy sprung to his feet and chased after the scraggy bully, who, fearing a poor outcome, sprinted for the back door.

The leader of the toughs regained his feet and threw a chair at the bar boy, who ducked and brought his cudgel in a sweeping overhand arc on his shoulder. Crying out in pain, he was unable to avoid the next blow aimed at his temple. He fell to the floor in a heap, unconscious. An elderly man sitting nearby guffawed and returned to his cup.

Meanwhile, an emboldened Davy caught the skinny boy's ankle with a flying tackle. He grabbed his greasy red hair and repeatedly pounded his enemy's face into the floor until his nose broke and blood poured out.

The bar boy watched in silent fascination as Davy rained blows down on his helpless victim. Enraged, Davy beat his fists into the boy's back and head until he exhausted himself and sat on the floor, panting.

Weeping, the scrawny youth crawled out the back door, leaving his pals behind.

Davy looked at his savior and said, "Much obliged. Name's Davy."

"John. John Roberts," the boy answered. "Help me get these lugs outta here."

John talked his father into giving Davy a job sweeping floors, clearing tables and serving ale to the patrons in exchange for room and board. The Red Dragon tavern served only one meal a day, and Davy soon learned the only 'room' available was in the back with casks of ale. Nonetheless, he happy to have a place to stay in Swansea while he looked for an opportunity to get aboard an outbound ship.

When business was slow, Davy and John discussed just about everything. John was a year older than Davy and he yearned to see the world. When his family went broke from the bad economy in his hometown Little Newcastle in Pembrokeshire, they moved to Swansea to make their fortune. While it kept them fed, it wasn't exactly the kind of life John wanted. He told Davy how he became enamored with the tall ships and came and went from the harbor. Davy listened attentively as John told him tales he overheard from the seamen who came in and out of the tavern with the tides. Together they agreed to one day leave Swansea and partake of daring adventures on ships bound for exotic foreign lands. John said he wanted to see the Far East and the New World. Davy had only one destination in mind, but he went along with his friend's fantasies.

"Why, there's sea monsters, pirates, mermaids and such too," John declared. "I heard them sailors say so."

"No!"

"Yep," John nodded solemnly. "And there's riches beyond yer wildest dreams."

"How come ye ain't gone to sea yet?" Davy asked.

"My da won't lemme leave this place. Says there's too much to do here and I canna believe everything they says."

"Even if it were part true, I can't wait to see it," Davy answered firmly. "Don't get me wrong, I'm in debt to your da. Still, wouldn't it be grand?"

John nodded. They were quiet for a while, before Davy spoke again. "John, let's go have a looksee at them ships t'morrow."

"Aye, we can go afta sunrise."

They ambled through the streets of Swansea, taking in the sights. John talked about the time he saw an English man-of-war anchored out in the bay. It must have had a hundred guns, he declared. Davy said that was stuff; no warship had that many guns. Nonetheless, John went on to describe the swarm of sailors that climbed the rigging and scurried about the decks, and of the tall officer that must have been the captain.

"Then this fellow comes across in a barge with six men rowin'," he said excitedly. "They was all dressed the same with blue jackets an' such. What a sight!"

"Was he carryin' a sword?"

John bobbed his head. "Aye, a big ol' saber. I bet he killed pirates with it."

"Pirates!" Davy spat in disgust, recalling the men who took his father. "Such mean bastards. Only a low-life scoundrel would be one of them."

"I don't know mate," John answered slowly. "I hear they have adventures, steal gold, and get to lay with fereign women..."

"John! Yer awful!" Davy shook his head vigorously. Then they both burst out laughing.

John smiled. "Let's get a drink. There's a tavern I know just 'round the corner."

They rounded said corner and noticed a knot of sailors gathered in the alley, shouting and swapping money as they watched a game of dice. Davy and John exchanged smiles and headed toward the boisterous group.

"All right boys," cried a burly man in the middle. "Place yer bets!" Several sailors exchanged coins in side bets and a ginger-haired young man slapped his shilling down on a sailcloth mat with six crude symbols in charcoal and picked up three dice.

"Feelin' lucky, lad?" taunted the burly man with a leer. He wagged a fat finger at the sailor. "I already cleaned out yer mate."

"Aye, the luck o' the Irish is with me. Watch an' weep, fat man," the redhead declared in a sing-song voice. He cast his dice and an anchor showed on two. "Ha! Doubles! Pay up!"

The burly man grunted and tossed two shillings, as the other sailors passed coins back and forth.

"What are they playin?" Davy asked John.

"Oh, that's crown 'n anchor," he replied. He went on to explain the rules.

"Looks fun. Wish I could play," Davy murmured.

The Irishman rolled the dice again and the crowd erupted in applause as he again raked in winnings.

"Take that, fat man!" he crowed. The banker grumbled and anted up again.

The game proceeded several more rounds and Davy watched enthusiastically. It finally ended with the Irishman taking his earnings, somewhat less than what he gained at the top of his game. He turned and noticed Davy and John with their hands in their pockets. He grinned and flipped a coin at Davy. "Here boyo, light along into the tavern and tell the bartender to draw me a mug." He turned to his mate, a short, dour, Welshman. "Let's go Cad, drinks are on me."

"O-k-k-kay, Malachy," his friend answered.

Davy and John sprinted around the corner and informed the barman as instructed. A moment later, the two sailors sauntered into the tavern, the Irishman all smiles. The barman pulled two pints of beer and slide them over the long wooden bar.

Malachy eyed Davy and John. "Well now, lads, ye look like a fine pair. I see ye eyein' me quid back there like hungry foxes. Why don't ye come over here with me mate. This here is Cadfael Hywel. I'm Malachy Maceachthighearna, but most fellas just say Ahearn. We is on the *Henry*, that fine Indiaman ridin' pretty in the harbor. What ye two do around here?"

"Nothin' much," Davy began.

"Other than hard work," John interrupted. "We is lookin' fer adventure, mebbe on the high seas."

"That so?" Malachy grinned. "Well then, mebbe ye'd like to see the ship," Malachy said. "We go all around the world, ain't that right Cad?"

Cadfael grunted into his glass of whiskey and turned away.

"Pay him no mind, he's not sociable, but he's a good un," said Malachy. "Now lads, join us fer a drink." He motioned to the bartender. "Pour these lads a round, Bart."

The bartender set a heavy mug before Davy and glanced at him with a shrewd eye.

"Here's mud in yer eye," Malachy said, tossing back his ale.

John grinned at Davy and took a swallow. "See? We is already havin' fun!"

Before Davy could answer, Malachy turned to him. "So, lad. Ye ever been to India?"

Davy shook his head. "What's India?"

Malachy roared with laughter and Cadfael sighed.

"Why lad, it's Paradise! We takes our load o' broadcloth an' iron, an' we comes back with spices an' such. An' then she pays off an' we're rich! But first," he paused with a low voice and a wide grin, "we gits ourselves some o' them women o' questionable morals," he cackled. "Ye prob'ly don't know what to do with them, seein' as ye is just pups, but ye keep with Cad an' I, an' ye'll figger it."

John grinned at Davy and asked Malachy, "When does we fight pirates?"

"Oh, now lad," Malachy began.

"We don't," Cadfael interrupted. "An' don't ye wish fer it neither."

"My mate has it the right way," said Malachy. "Pirates is a bad lot, an' they will kill ye as much as look at ye. We aim to steer far away from them."

"Bah," John shrugged. "I ain't afraid o' pirates. Anyways, it sounds like a great adventure, don't it, Davy?"

Davy was uncertain, but reminded himself he needed a ship to find his father. He nodded.

"Ye lads seem alright. Why don't ye join us? The cap'n might take ye on, if yer useful. Can ye haul a line?" Malachy asked.

Davy and John looked at each other and exchanged nods. This was their opportunity. John answered, "Course we can! We'd be honored to join ye."

A northwesterly half-gale filled the sails of a lone barkentine as it coursed through the open sea, leaving a creamy wake in its trail. The vessel had cleared the Bristol Channel four days ago, Wyn reckoned from the dark hold to which he was confined.

The iron shackles bolted into the deck limited his movement to just a few feet – enough to reach the bucket that served as his means of physical relief. The pirates fed him once a day, usually a couple of biscuits and water, thus he was fast losing weight. *They keep this up*, he mused, *and I'll slip me bones right through me bonds.*

A hatch opened nearby above him and a pair of men descended. He squinted at the blinding light. "Bit early fer me daily feast," Wyn rasped.

"Clap a stopper on it," growled one as he delivered a kick to Wyn's rib.

The other bent down and looked at Wyn, eye to eye. He tilted his head from one side to the other, studying his prisoner. "Ye don't look so well, old friend."

"Fuck you, stranger," Wyn answered. He glared at the other man, who stood with his arms crossed. "And fuck you, Shipwreck Tom."

The man in front of him scoffed. "That's no way to talk to yer old shipmate, Morgan." He sighed. "But ye always were a bit rough around the gunnels, so they say."

Wyn was silent. He knew they'd get around to business.

"Very well then, I'll get to it," the man said, standing up. "My name is Thomas Tew, and I lead this crew." He turned and began pacing back and forth.

"They say yer a man of William Kidd's company," Tew stated. "He hid his loot on some island, they say." He turned and looked at Wyn. "And ye are goin' to lead us to it."

"Don't know any Kidd. Don't know 'bout any treasure," Wyn answered. "I'm jest a poor fisherman. Ye got the wrong man."

Tew drew a deep breath and let out a long sigh. He cocked his head and glanced at Shipwreck Tom, who promptly delivered another kick to Wyn's side. As he lay on the deck gasping for air, Wyn managed to lift his middle finger in Tew's direction.

"I don't think so. My mate here says the two of ye go way back, before ye signed on with Kidd. Now stop yer foolin', or ye will find this to be a most uncomfortable voyage," Tew said.

Wyn knew he had little choice. They weren't likely to kill him, as long as he didn't give them all the information he'd memorized from the map, but he didn't relish the thought of spending the rest of his days in this dank compartment either.

"Alright," he replied. "I'll tell yer helmsman which way to steer his course, but ye ain't gettin' it all now. Besides," he added. "Only I know exactly where it's buried."

4

Davy's head was spinning, like a helpless ship caught in the jaws of a violent maelstrom. Awash in social lubricant, he stumbled out of the tavern, leaning heavily on John's shoulder. His unfocused eyes vaguely noted the darkness of twilight. A crisp, cool breeze entered his nostrils and blew away a few of the cobwebs that had formed in his mind.

Malachy and Cadfael guided them down the muddy street toward the docks. Davy suddenly lurched toward the gutter and spewed vomit. Malachy laughed and patted him on the back. "Come now, lad. Jest a bit further."

As they reached the dock, Cadfael called out to a dory moored nearby. The four carefully clambered into the boat and Malachy gave the oarsman a couple of coins. As the dory struggled against the tide, heaving up and down on the swell, Davy vomited again. Malachy chuckled and Cadfael rolled his eyes with disgust. "L-l-lubbers," he murmured.

For what seemed like an eternity later, the dory glided up to the sloped side of the 350-ton East India Company ship *Henry*. As the oarsman hooked onto the main chains amidships, Davy looked up at the huge vessel in wonder. In the dim moonlight he could just make out her three masts with sails furled on the yards. As the boat bobbed in the choppy bay, Malachy cried, "Let's go, mates!" and sprinted up the ladder. Davy and John looked at the tall tumblehome of the ship and then at each other. Cadfael grunted and gave them a shove. John waited for the rise of the dory on the waves before he reached up and grasped the ladder. Davy watched him awkwardly heave his broad body up and then waited for the next wave to bring the dory higher. He judged the rise and lunged for the ladder but missed his handhold and fell into the cold water. Cadfael chuckled and watched Davy flail in the water for a moment before he reached down and grasped the boy by his hair, holding his head above water. With his powerful arms he lifted Davy up so he could grab the ladder.

After Davy struggled up the side, he found John and Malachy stifling laughter as the watch officer glared at him in disgust. "Who," he said in a stiff, London accent, looking Davy up and down, "is this water-logged sea rat?"

"Sir, this here is Davy Jones," Malachy replied as Cadfael came up behind him. "An' the other one is John Roberts. They wish to sign on, sir, if you please."

"We don't need a couple of *squeakers*," the officer replied disdainfully. "That is, unless they can earn their keep."

"Oh sir," Malachy interjected, "they don't eat much and

they can heave a line. Why," he turned to John, "this one here is a regular bull. An' this damp one here, why, he is jest like a monkey. He c'n climb like he was born to it."

"Really?" the officer smirked. "One wouldn't know by the way he swam aboard." He gazed at the shivering Davy for a long moment. "Is there anything you can actually do, other than collect seawater in your pockets?"

Davy gaped at the condescending officer. John elbowed him in the ribs, startling him out of his shock. "Well sir, I could..."

"You could what?" the officer sneered. "You could fish the anchor? You could lay out on the yard and haul the topsail? You could swab the deck? Polish the guns? Just what can you do, little man?"

"I can pull an oar, sir. I can cook too," Davy replied timidly.

"I sincerely doubt you can pull an oar, even with a following tide," the officer scoffed. "But," he stroked his chin thoughtfully, "the captain is in need of a cabin boy. Perhaps, just perhaps, you can serve him and this ship after all."

He turned to Malachy. "Take these lads below. We'll read them in tomorrow if, and I say if, the captain will take them."

"Aye sir, we'll take good care o' them both," Malachy replied, grabbing John and Davy by their shoulders. They turned away and followed Cadfael down a ladder in the waist toward the crews berthing.

Davy smelled livestock, cordage, mildew, and unwashed men as they descended to the dim lower deck. As his feet hesitantly searched for the next rung, he heard muffled laughter coming from somewhere not far away. A sheep bleated, and the clinking of mugs made him feel less uneasy. A low light appeared below.

"This here is the crew's quarters. This is where we sling our hammocks," Malachy said. "We eat an' rest here, whenever we is off watch. Once the captain takes you on, o' course," he added with a smile. Cadfael made a strangled series of grunts that Davy supposed was the Welshman's version of laughter. "But since you don't have hammocks yet, jest rest yer heads here on the deck and try not t' get in the way. We'll see you two, bright an' early."

He stumped off into the dimness, Cadfael following.

John said, "Well, mate, here we are! Let the adventure begin!"

Davy said nothing.

"Ah, c'mon. It's gonna be jest fine. Let's get some shut-eye."

Davy lay down on the deck and shivered. His wet clothes stuck to him with the salt of the harbor. He was thirsty and needed to piss. He wondered about this strange ship and the men aboard her. He heard John lay down next to him and within a minute he was snoring. Davy envied the ease with which his friend seemed to adjust.

A shadowy form appeared out of nowhere and stopped next to him. It bent down and regarded him for a moment before uttering, "What in the 'ell does we 'ave 'ere? Stowaways?"

Davy looked at the threatening man with wide eyes.

"No sir, with respect sir, we jest…"

"Shut yer mouth or I'll shut it fer ye!" the man bellowed.

"Now calm down there, mate," Davy heard Malachy's

voice call out. "Them are lads we met in town. They gonna sign on. Leave off."

The dark form grunted. "Jest make sure ye stay under my lee, ye li'l shits. I hate fuckin' squeakers," he added as he left.

Davy let out his breath. His head was throbbing and he felt sick from the drink, cold from the harbor, and frightened by the crew. He wondered how many more men on this ship would despise him. As he laid his head down on the hard wood, he closed his eyes and prayed.

He was rudely awakened at dawn with a jab in his ribs. He let out a yelp and sprang to his feet. John was gone.

"Rise an' shine, lad," Malachy ordered. "Time t' see the master an' sign the book." He shoved Davy toward the ladder and they went up on deck. The cool morning air felt refreshing after a night in the smelly humanity below decks.

Malachy headed aft to the quarterdeck and Davy followed. They halted before an older, portly man who stood behind a capstan with a ledger. His tanned, weathered face featured sea-blue eyes, which regarded Davy with little expression. His empty left sleeve betrayed the lack of a hand.

"Hark at ye. Who's this, Ahearn?" he asked Malachy.

"This here is a willing lad we found ashore, sir."

"He means to sign on to the barky?"

"Yes, sir. Speak up, lad," Malachy ordered. "This here is Master Gibbs."

"Davy Jones, sir, if ye please."

Gibbs took off his cap, revealing a gray balding pate, and

scratched his head. With the Royal Navy presently at war, the EIC could use every man it could get, he reasoned, even if it was a young lubber. "He don't look like much. Don't expect a squeaker like ye served any time afore. Can ye haul a line?"

"I, I reckon so," Davy stammered. "I jest want a chance to serve at sea."

"An' serve ye shall. Cap'n Ross needs a cabin boy. Make yer mark 'ere," he said, pointing to the ledger. Davy slowly drew the letters of his name, earning a raised eyebrow from Gibbs.

"That's proper. Ye know yer letters, I see. If the cap'n likes ye, then ye will earn two shillings per month, plus food an' slops." He turned to Malachy. "Rated boy. Leave 'im with me. I'll see 'im to Cap'n Ross."

Davy watched Malachy bow his head and walk away. He suddenly felt defenseless.

"Stand o'er 'ere behind me, lad. Who's next?" Gibbs bellowed.

Davy saw Cadfael step up with John in tow. He felt relieved to see his friend again. Cadfael nudged John, who said, "John Roberts."

"John Roberts, WHAT?" Gibbs roared.

"This 'ere lad m-means no offense, sir. He don't know the ways o' the b-barky jest yet," Cadfael replied. He lowered his head and whispered something to John.

John nodded and bowed. "Me name is John Roberts, *sir.*"

Gibbs eyed him for a moment. "Ye look like a strong lad, although a lubber fer sure. Make yer mark 'ere."

John scribbled something unrecognizable on the ledger and stepped back.

"Rated landsman. Three shillings, six pence per month. Ye will work fer the bosun. An' mind ye, obey the bosun like 'e was yer father, lad," he added. "Take 'im away," he said to Malachy.

Seeing no one else, Gibbs closed the ledger and strode to the ladder. Davy followed him as they came to a door. Gibbs knocked and waited.

"Enter," a muffled voiced answered.

They entered the captain's cabin, their heads bent under the low ceiling. Davy saw an elderly man, sitting at a small wood desk. Gray light streamed in from the stern windows behind him as he scribbled away on parchment. Gibbs waited for him to finish and look up at them before addressing his captain.

"Sir, this 'ere lad signed on today. I figgered 'e might serve as cabin boy, if ye please."

Captain Ross removed his eyeglasses and squinted at Davy for a long moment. Davy shifted from one foot to the other, anxious to make a good impression. Ross finally spoke. "What's your name, lad?" he asked sternly.

"Jones, sir. Davy Jones," he answered in a high-pitched voice. He trembled and wished his stomach wouldn't hurt so.

"At least you can speak. Master Gibbs, make sure he is fed and get him some decent slops. His present attire is unfit for a ship of the East India Company. Then take him to the cook," Ross ordered. He donned his glasses and bent over his parchment.

"Aye, sir. Come lad," Gibbs said, grabbing Davy.

They left the cabin and Davy felt relieved.

As they made their way across the waist of the ship, Davy

saw John being beaten with a rattan wielded by a wiry, leather-skinned man. He noticed tears of rage in John's eyes as he submitted to the blows. John saw Davy approaching and looked away in shame.

"Don't stare lad," Gibbs said in a low voice. "Bosun Graves is teachin' 'im a lesson. There's nothin' ye can do fer 'im."

Shocked, Davy turned away and followed the master wordlessly. He heard John cry out as Graves mercilessly rained blows on his back. "Suffer in silence, ye grass-combing lubber!" Graves shouted. "Tis a simple nuff thing, blast ye! Flemish that fall proper like, or I'll have yer filthy hide!"

John coiled the block and tackle line again into a neat spiral. Satisfied, Graves reached into his jacket and pulled out a cigar and strode away.

The *Henry* was bustling with activity as the crew prepared to weigh anchor and catch the evening tide. Neither Davy nor John had time to take in the spectacle, as they were busy learning their new responsibilities. John was putting bars into the capstan, closely watched by the bosun's mate, whose stern gaze he avoided. He was grateful that it wasn't Bosun Graves himself, giving him the evil eye. Meanwhile, Davy was in the small ship's galley, learning to prepare supper from the cook, who'd introduced himself as Thomas Stoddard.

"Now wee bairn," Stoddard advised in a rich Scottish brogue, "jest ye heed the advise of Old Tom, an' ye will do jest fine." Davy noticed the cook's wooden peg leg that began just below his right knee, and looked up to see his piercing brown eyes fixed on him. He was an imposing figure, six feet tall and full of scars. Davy nodded mutely.

"We makes a fine fish stew an' plum duff for the crew, and fer the cap'n we make his fav'rites: Lobscouse, goose pie, and o' course, Spotted Dog," the cook announced.

Davy privately wondered what these dishes were, particularly Spotted Dog, but heeded Old Tom attentively as the cook taught him how to add just this spice and that vegetable to the fish stew broth, which was on the boil. Experienced at cleaning fish, Davy was assigned to a barrel of cod.

"Mind ye, lad, yer duties include cleaning this here galley and the cap'n's cabin, makin' good his quarter galley, an' servin' him whenever he calls. Ye will jump to at any time, watch af'er watch, an' heed me orders. Ye understand me?"

Davy nodded. "Yes, sir."

"Don' call me sir, lad, Old Tom works fer a livin'." The cook chuckled hoarsely. "Ye only call the officers 'sir'. When ye are done with them fish, go down t' the hold and fetch taters fer this here pot."

Hours later, after the ship cleared the Bristol Channel and headed into the Celtic Sea, Davy met John at the scuttlebutt in the waist. The mainmast towered over them, topsails taut with the northerly breeze, and the setting sun casting a golden glow over all. At any other time, Davy would have thought it a beautiful sight, but he was too tired to care.

"So, how do ye like yer first day?" John asked sarcastically.

"I jest tossed a crate full of fish heads o'er the side and then cleaned the head. Does it get any better?" Davy said.

John glanced around and lowered his voice. "If I survive that goddamned bosun, I may have fun yet."

As if on cue, a roar came from the forecastle. "Roberts, you scurvy dog!" Graves shouted. "Light along an' fetch a pot o' paint!"

John rolled his eyes and hurried off to the bosun's locker, murmuring under his breath.

Davy watched him leave then decided to go below before Graves could turn his ire toward him. He met Cadfael on the way up the ladder. The dour Welshman merely grunted at him.

He encountered Stoddard in the crew's berth. "Tom, what's the problem with the bosun? He's always got fire in his belly fer me mate John."

"Well lad, the bosun is a right hard case, but he'll make John a fine seaman...or drive 'im mad," he chuckled. He looked at Davy and put a hand on his shoulder. "Ye jest heed Old Tom an' ye'll stay outta trouble. Now, get ye some shut-eye."

The gibbous moon rose over the horizon like some great pale eye, unflinching in the twilight. The *Henry* sailed along in choppy seas with a steady breeze on her quarter and topsails and spritsail drawing every bit of cool air. Malachy was in the foretop crosstrees, scanning the horizon as the duty lookout. A thick, dark bank of clouds were approaching from the southwest, lightening occasionally illuminating the darker sea beneath. He spied a small sliver of white nicking the horizon to the southeast.

"Sail ho!" he cried. "On deck there, a strange sail, four points off the larboard bow."

Gibbs, who had the watch, acknowledged and sent word below to the captain. Ross presently appeared on deck and immediately climbed the larboard main shroud to the crow's nest. He carefully removed his spyglass and stared at the sail, hull-down and closing the *Henry*. He noted the colors flying from her main. Satisfied, he slid down the backstay and strode to the quarterdeck.

"Mr. Gibbs, steer two points to port and hold course. We shall presently be under the *Sapphire's* lee," he said. "Make our number and send word when she signals."

"Aye, sir," Gibbs replied. He turned to the helmsman and relayed the order. He then turned to the signal mate, gave instructions, and called up to Malachy.

The *Henry* cruised onward toward her rendezvous. Two hours later, the HMS *Sapphire* came within hailing distance and the *Henry* saluted the royal colors with a round of cannon fire. Captain Ross appeared on deck in his best coat, hat and breeches. He gave the order to back the topsails and lay to in wait. Davy, safely out of the way, watched from the forecastle as a boat was lowered over the side and oarsmen piled into it. Presently, Ross descended and the boat pulled toward the *Sapphire*.

Old Tom appeared next to Davy and lit his pipe. "Ah, there's our guard," he murmured, peering at the *Sapphire* in the moonlight.

"Is that a warship?" Davy asked.

"Aye, lad," Old Tom answered. "That there is a 28-gun, fifth-rate frigate. See her t'gallant sails? Only a man o' war carries them. An' that row o' guns on her lower deck are eight-pounders. She's got five-pounders an' three-pounders on the fo'c'sle an' quarterdeck. She carries a complement o' Royal Marines too. She'll keep us safe."

"Oh," Davy said with awe. He could just make out the dark gun ports as the ship rocked on the easy swell.

"Now, let's get below," Old Tom said. "Cap'n Ross will want his tea hot 'an ready when he comes back."

Davy glanced at Malachy in the foretop before he shuffled below with the cook. He thought about the warship, and the possibility of seeing her guns fire excited him. He wondered if he might one day serve aboard a sleek fighting ship of His Majesty's navy. But he knew he'd learn and see much on the good *Henry* – if he survived. More importantly, he fervently hoped, they were headed in the same direction he believed his father was going.

5

Bay of Biscay

N o matter what happens to me, keep this safe!"

Davy awoke with a start. Wyn's last words to him still rang in his head as he wiped his eyes and blearily climbed out of his hammock. He reached inside his shirt, first feeling the medallion and then the oilcloth map. Glancing around, he breathed a sigh of relief. Not a single snoring figure in the berthing compartment had noticed him. He made his way to the galley and reported to Old Tom to begin his chores as the cook prepared breakfast for Captain Ross.

Davy swept and cleaned Ross's cabin while the captain was on deck. He eyed the heavy saber hanging on a peg behind the desk. The scabbard and pommel were unremarkable for a man of such station; nonetheless Davy was impressed to see a real naval sword for the first time. He imagined swinging it and the sound it would make as it cut through the air. He dared not touch it, though. He regarded

Captain Ross as the closest earthly being to God, a superior being who would think nothing of tossing a lowly cabin boy overboard should he disobey him or desecrate his personal belongings with his unworthy touch. He sighed and moved to the captain's privy, the quarter cabin. *At least the cap'n shits like an ord'nary man*, he thought.

Meanwhile, John was huddling under the break of the poop deck as rain swept across the vessel like a waterfall. The squall passed over the ship and continued northeasterly, leaving a brief rainbow in its wake. He joined the hands as they climbed the rigging to shake out a reef in the topsails. As he moved out on the yardarm next to Malachy, he felt a sense of camaraderie with the men who seemed to accept his presence – except for Graves, who bellowed at them from below.

The *Henry* moved along at an easy five knots in company with the *Sapphire*, which led them by a half league. The ships proceeded south by southeast skirting the edge of the Bay of Biscay toward the northern Spanish coast. Two days out of port they met a Dutch merchant ship, a trader returning from West Africa. That evening Captain Ross returned from a dinner with the captain of the *Sapphire*, and Davy overheard him tell Gibbs the Dutchman had narrowly evaded a pirate sloop off the coast of Guinea.

"The seas turned dirty and she slipped away in the night from the bastards," Ross told the master. "We'll have to keep a sharp eye and heed *Sapphire's* signals. Apparently, the Dutchman was holed twice in the starboard hull and parted some rigging, but lost no men."

"Aye, they are desperate creatures to be sure," Gibbs said.

"I was a master's mate on *Deptford* in 1683 when we nearly captured a pirate brig just off the Canaries. We think it was Van Hoorn, but he ran away from us when a lucky shot parted our forestay."

"Well, we will serve them out if they come for us...with the *Sapphire* at our side," Ross concluded.

Davy turned away, fearful and strangely excited. He found Old Tom eyeing him disapprovingly. He knew the cook had been watching him eavesdrop on the captain. "Sorry Tom," he mumbled.

"Listen 'ere, lad. Ye know better than t' stick yer beak into the cap'n's business." He cocked his head and squinted. "Jest don't get caught." He smiled and chuckled. "Come now, let's get back t' work."

Later that night Davy met an exhausted John in the crew's berthing. He told his friend what he had heard and swore him to secrecy, lest the word get out. John smiled weakly and told him the whole ship already knew about the conversation, on account of the helmsman who had overheard them through the captain's open stern window. Davy sighed in relief.

"That damned bosun says the weather might turn dirty t'night, so we'd best git some shut-eye now," John said. "I fer one, am right foundered."

The weather did indeed turn dirty that night. A hard gale roared in from the west, causing the rigging to sing in a high pitch. Both watches were turned up on deck to set storm sails and extra hands, including Malachy, were assigned to the helm to keep the ship steady on course. The *Sapphire's* stern lamp was nowhere to be seen as rain came slanting in sheets. Davy felt like he was drowning every time he breathed as he tugged on lines with the other sailors amidst a deck awash with seawater that crashed over the gunwales and gushed out of the scuppers. John was out on the main yard arm with Cadfael and the other topmen, reefing the sail to reduce the press on the canvas.

Satisfied with the rig, Ross told Gibbs to send the watch below and a sodden Davy and John returned to their hammocks. They immediately fell into a deep sleep.

The next morning, Cadfael showed Davy and John how to splice the lines that had parted during the tail end of the storm as the crew repaired minor damage caused by the gale. The lookout at the foretop called down to the deck to report *Sapphire* fine on the port bow, about a league ahead of them. The crew was sent aloft to set the courses and topsails to catch up. By midday the *Henry* and *Sapphire* were in close company as they sailed down the Portuguese coast.

Davy and Tom prepared dinner for the captain, who liked to eat at two bells in the afternoon watch. Ross came down from deck, took off his coat and sat down at his desk to make some notes in his log as Davy set his table and Tom announced the captain's dinner was ready. Ross grunted in assent and finished his scribbling.

As the captain dipped into his fish soup, Davy waited

behind him to clear away dishes or serve more wine as directed.

"Boy, come here," Ross ordered. Davy approached and waited for his captain's command.

Ross sat back in his plush chair and looked Davy over from head to toe. "We don't have a schoolmaster aboard, but I expect you will learn what you need from Mr. Stoddard." His worn blue eyes bored into Davy. "Just remember to heed his word and keep yourself presentable and you'll be fine." He paused. "I know this is your first liberty port, but don't get mixed up with the type who drink and carouse on shore when we pull into Cadiz. I can't afford to have my own cabin boy embarrass me – or I'll have his hide, do you hear?"

Davy nodded. "Aye, cap'n. I'll mind me manners."

"Good. Now, tell Mr. Stoddard I'm ready for my main course."

Davy hurried away and notified Old Tom, who was already plating the captain's roasted fowl and lamb chops. He sent Davy below to fetch some of the captain's private reserve of port and entered the cabin.

"Here ye are, cap'n," Tom announced.

Ross nodded in approval and attacked the fowl. He looked up as the old cook was turning away. "Tom."

"Aye, sir?"

"How do you find young Mr. Jones?"

"He'll do, sir," Tom said stiffly. "He's been a good bairn. Show's up on time, keeps to 'is duties, an' e' don't talk out o' turn."

Tom watched Ross as he took another bite and chewed thoughtfully. "See to it," he said without looking up, "that he gets some time with the bosun and the master, he and his mate, young Roberts. I'd like to see them contribute to the working of the ship and become right seamen."

"Aye, sir. Will that be all, sir?"

"Yes. Dismissed." Ross resumed his meal.

Later that evening Davy was cleaning the small galley where Old Tom was enjoying his grog and smoking his pipe. The cook waved him over and Davy obediently put down his rag and stood before him.

"Now lad," Tom began, pausing to take a puff. "Ye need to t' learn the ropes, as we say at sea. I've asked th' bosun's mates to teach ye how t' knot n' splice."

Davy nodded. He dreaded being near the bosun's men, simply because he might run into the Devil's Bosun. He fidgeted nervously and waited for Tom to continue.

"Th' more ye make yerself useful around th' ship, the less hard men like th' bosun are likely to ride ye, an' who knows? Mebbe ye will be a right seaman someday."

Davy nodded.

"Now, make sure ye report to MacAfee, the bosun's mate, t'morrow after breakfast," Tom said. He paused for a moment, and then added in a cautious tone, "An' make sure ye get yer rest t'night."

Davy opened his mouth to respond but a piercing howl interrupted the night. It was followed by a chorus of shouts and the sound of a scuffle. He and Tom glanced at each other and quickly made their way to the main deck to see what was afoot.

They found John on the deck, held down by three men with a roaring Elijah Graves beating John with his rattan. His face was twisted in fury as he shouted oaths and rained blows down. Dozens of seamen gathered around the group.

"Avast!" shouted Captain Ross from the quarterdeck. Graves looked up, sneered at John and kicked him in the ribs.

"Enough, Mr. Graves! Pray tell, what is the meaning of this?"

"This here rat, sir, is drunk on duty," Graves proclaimed loudly. "He damned near killed a man with his stupidity, lettin' go of a line, causin' a block to fall. Simpson here near paid fer it." He jerked a thumb at one of the men holding John down.

"Aye, Cap'n, it came close to stovin' in me 'ead," Simpson said.

Ross climbed down the ladder and briskly strode over to the group. "Stand him up," he ordered.

He looked John in the eye and noticed him swaying slightly. "Take him below and secure him irons, Simpson. Mr. Graves, report to my cabin. The rest of you, back to work."

The crew murmured as they moved away. Davy watched as John was led below and a steaming Graves followed Captain Ross. "What do ye think the cap'n will do to my mate John?" he asked Old Tom.

"Most likely we'll find out t'morrow at the mast," Tom said. "It's against th' rules t' be drunk on duty. I'd hate t' be in 'is shoes. Th' cap'n hates that sorta thing. I seen 'im flog a man for less."

Davy pondered his friend's fate. Would he suffer the

wrath of the whip, or worse yet, be put ashore? He wanted to see John and try to comfort him, but he knew his friend was probably not allowed contact with anyone. He went below to his hammock and tried to sleep, but it wouldn't come. He kept thinking about the horror of watching his friend being punished and humiliated in front of the crew. His mind wandered to thoughts of Captain Ross's sword, fighting pirates alongside his friend and whether the crew would accept him as one of their own. The image of Elijah Grave's angry face briefly darkened his thoughts and he fearfully cast it aside. Instead, he concentrated on the rhythmic snoring of his fellow crewmen, which were interspersed with the creaks and groans of the ship as it steadily bore for the Spanish coast. Sometime during the night, he finally fell into a fitful slumber.

The next day, Master Gibbs presided over the noon observation and formally reported to Captain Ross, who nodded his assent. Ross gazed over the taffrail at the ship's wake thoughtfully. He finally turned and called out to his bosun to rig the grating. "Mr. Gibbs, call all hands to quarters," Ross ordered. He stood on the quarterdeck and waited, hands behind his stiff back.

The crew assembled in the waist of the ship and Graves appeared with a green velvet bag in hand. His mates brought John in irons to the front of the loosely formed ranks. John was sullen, but managed a hateful glance at the bosun. Graves glared at him with equal malice and patted his bag.

"Men," Ross began. "You know that although this is not a man o' war, we must maintain order." He paused, looking down at his mute audience. His eyes flicked across John, and then he continued.

"You all know the rules, and you also know that I abhor inebriation, especially on watch. Mr. Roberts, step forward. You are accused of being drunk on duty by Mr. Graves. Have you anything to say for yourself?"

John shuffled his feet and looked up. "No, sir."

"Then you admit you were in cups while on watch?"

"Yes, sir."

Ross studied him. The crew remained quiet. Davy glanced at Old Tom, who stared straight ahead. He looked at Captain Ross, then Graves, and finally at John.

Ross finally spoke. "You are new aboard this ship, but that is no excuse. You must learn to attend your duties in a sober and obedient fashion. You nearly cost Simpson his head. It may have been worse. The ship is a dangerous place in the calmest of weather, yea, even if all things seem peaceable. This had better not happen again, Roberts, or you *will* forfeit your pay and I *will* put you ashore. Mr. Graves, a dozen lashes."

The bosun cracked an evil smile and ordered his mates to release John from the irons and tie him to the grating. Still smiling, he drew a cat o' nine tails whip from the velvet bag and snapped it to the side. He rolled his shoulder and flexed his arm.

John stood at the grating and the bosun's mates stripped him to the waist. Graves looked at the captain in anticipation. The crew stared ahead, some venturing a sideways peep at Ross. Davy stared at the fearsome whip, wishing he could say something on his friend's behalf, but he knew he must not.

"Commence!" Ross ordered.

Graves leaned back and brought the lash down on John's back with a loud crack. Long, red welts appeared and Davy heard his friend cry out.

"One!" Gibbs called out.

Davy observed the punishment with horror and cringed every time the whip met John's bleeding back.

"Eight!"

John gritted his teeth and steeled himself. He issued something between a groan and a growl at the next strike. Ross stood impassively atop the quarterdeck and scrutinized first John, then Graves as the cat left its mark again and again.

"Twelve!" Gibbs bellowed.

Graves halted and grudgingly put the cat back in the velvet bag. He wiped the sweat from his brow and took a step back to the front of the ranks.

John sagged into the arms of the bosun's mates as they untied him.

"Now, Mr. Roberts, you have learned the laws of the ship the hard way," Ross said. He turned to the ship's surgeon, who was not a doctor, but in fact a barber. "Take him below, Mr. Grant."

Davy silently wept as his friend was helped down the companionway. He felt Tom's hand on his shoulder. "Come, lad."

The next morning the ship stood in the offing just outside the port of Cadiz, waiting for the making tide. Davy helped Tom clear the dishes away from the captain's table. Ross had already left for the quarterdeck, leaving the two alone in his cabin. As Tom drew the tablecloth, Davy asked, "Would the cap'n really put John ashore? I mean, he's jest a boy like me."

Tom nodded. "One thing ye must learn, lad. The cap'n's word is law, an ye must never disobey 'im. An' another thing," he paused and looked hard at Davy. "Stay clear o' that bosun."

Cadiz, Spain

The *Henry* sailed into the harbor of Cadiz under a clear blue sky, running before the westerly wind pushing her smoothly along at five knots. John and the topmen were out on the yards, ready to take in the sails, while the idlers were standing by the sheets and gawking at the passing commerce. One of those gawkers was Davy Jones. Old Tom came stumping up the ladder and joined him, his long, gray hair flying in the breeze.

"Ah, laddie, yer first port 'o call," he said with a grin. "Cadiz is a special place fer me. Lost this 'ere leg back in '69 scrappin' wit' Algerian pirates, when I was aboard *Mary Rose*, 48 guns. We served 'em out, we did."

"Ye fought *pirates?*" Davy exclaimed, wide-eyed.

"Aye. Sent a couple t' Hell meself, with me trusty musket."

Davy regarded Tom with an even greater respect. He never imagined the old sea dog fighting pirates, nor did he know the gregarious cook was formerly in the Royal Navy. "What was it like? I woulda been scared."

"Only a fool ain't scared in battle," said Tom. He gazed pensively at the brilliant blue water. "When men set about killin' each other, they know it may be their last day. But," he turned his hard brown eyes on Davy, "they muster up their courage an' do the job. Ye must look a man in th' eye when ye drive yer steel into 'im. Ye must turn yer heart t' ice, t' protect yerself when ye feel 'is hot blood on ye."

Mortified, Davy stared at the towering old man. His weather-beaten face, the scars on his arms, chest and neck...the look of sheer ferocity in his countenance made Davy take a small step back.

Then suddenly Tom seemed to shrink and his features softened. "There, there, lad. Didn't mean t' scare ye. Now look o'er there," Tom pointed toward the approaching city. Davy took a deep breath, realizing he'd held it for the last few moments, and followed Tom's gesture.

"Ye see that castle? It guards the offing," Old Tom said. "This here city 'as been at war many times, an' paid the price. Conquered by English, Dutch, Moors...even now th' Spanish is at war with the French."

Davy, now somewhat relaxed, admired his mentor, if he dared think of Old Tom as such. The man seemed quite a bit more than just an old, crippled cook of a merchantman. He cast his gaze to the bustling city, with its colorful red tile roofs and multitudes of people thronging the waterfront. He grew excited over the prospect of exploring this exotic place, but instantly felt a pang of guilt when he remembered his father was still in the clutches of pirates.

"Don't worry yerself, lad," said Tom, seeing his frown. "Every man must live 'is own life. Go an' see th' world, while ye are still young."

Davy met John in the crew's berthing, just as the first of the ship's boats put off for Cadiz.

"What's up, mate?" Davy asked.

"Graves says I canna go ashore," John responded sullenly. He tore his shirt off and threw it down on the deck. "That bosun is the Devil!"

"Well, if you canna go ashore, then I won't either," Davy declared.

"Bah! Ye go on liberty fer the both of us. Jest take care ye don't get in trouble like me. Go on." John turned his back on Davy and climbed into his hammock.

Davy looked at his gloomy friend. *It would be damned shame*, he thought, *to see this exotic place without John*. He donned his best outfit and headed out on deck to catch the next boat.

Hours later, Davy was strolling the streets of Cadiz with Malachy and Cadfael, who decided to take him under their wing. He was astonished at the foreign architecture, like the mosque with its minarets, and the shopping bazaars full of strange smells, shouting merchants, and colorful spices and silks. One stall even featured canaries and parrots with brilliant plumage. Another had roasted lamb on a spit, which he sampled courtesy of a coin from Cadfael. Overwhelmed by the sensory overload, he was almost relieved when his shipmates decided to duck into a tavern to slake their thirst.

It took a few moments for Davy's eyes to adjust to the dim light emanating from a few candles ensconced on the walls. The place was packed with foreigners jabbering in several tongues. Malachy smiled broadly and nudged Cadfael. "See there, mate?" He nodded toward the bar where two whores were attempting to charm a pair of rough-looking men. "I told ye we'd find some lovely comp'ny." Cadfael grunted in assent.

"Look 'ere lad," Malachy said to Davy. "This is the *real* Cadiz, in all it's shinin' glory." He ordered pints of ale and the three sat down at a table. They were soon surrounded by four women, dressed in provocative high skirts and low-cut bustiers revealing their ample assets. Malachy immediately commenced a negotiation with two of the 'ladies' while Cadfael sipped his beer. Davy fidgeted nervously.

A woman whispered something in Cadfael's ear. He nodded, grunted in assent, and then stood up. "Back later."

Malachy roared with laughter and then dug into his pocket. "Here lad, take these." He produced a small stack of coins. "Have yerself some fun, but don't leave without us." He departed toward the stairs in the back of the tavern, whores on each arm.

"How about you, young *sahib*?" the remaining whore

asked Davy in a thick Arabic accent. Her long black hair tumbled over her breasts as she leaned forward and fixed her black eyes upon him. "See anything you like?" He noted her alluring full lips, warmly colored with rouge, and her dark complexion.

"Uh, I um, I dunno," he stammered. He couldn't take his eyes off her. "I don't think I'm old enough."

The whore pulled out a chair next to him and propped her foot on the seat, lasciviously parting her thighs. She reached out and brushed his cheek with her brown fingers. "It is fine. We can have a good time. I will teach you," she added invitingly.

Davy felt his breeches tighten as he swelled in response to her touch. Embarrassed, he suddenly stood up darted toward the back of the tavern, looking for his shipmates. Her heard the whore giggling behind him as he wormed his way through the crowd. Feeling uncomfortably warm, he loosened the laces on his shirt and took stock of his surroundings. He searched, but was unable to locate Malachy or Cadfael.

He saw a loud group of men crouching in a corner and laughing uproariously. Curious, he made his way over to the men, who by now were shouting and slapping each other on the back.

At the center of the group, a wizened figure in Arabic garb was alternately pointing at and goading several men as they put money down. He then scooped up some dice and threw them down on a mat with several symbols. A collective groan went up, and the Arab collected more money. Fascinated, Davy hovered at the edge and peered over the shoulders of two men as they dug coins out of their purses. He watched the process repeat itself several times over the course of a good half hour, with the Arab winning more money than he surrendered. He knew what this game was.

Excited, Davy pushed his way between the men and gingerly put a coin down on one of the symbols shaped like a heart. The Arab glanced at him, and threw the dice. No luck. He scooped up Davy's coin and a few others and paid out two coins to one of the other players.

In a few minutes, Davy was out of money. He looked up to see the Arab studying him. "Luck leave, *shab?*"

Davy grimaced and prepared to leave. "Wait!" the Arab demanded. "You may still have something of value. He pointed to Davy's half-hidden necklace. "Let Hakim see."

Startled, Davy turned red and clutched his shirt. "No, I canna part with this."

Quick as lightning, Hakim darted his hand out and plucked the medallion out of Davy's shirt with a dagger. As it dangled, he eyed it closely. "Ahhh," he exclaimed, drawing in a breath through his crooked teeth. "You are right to keep it close." He stood up. "Come with Hakim," he commanded, sheathing his dagger. "We speak in private."

Hakim grabbed Davy's arm and led him to a dark corner of the tavern. When he was satisfied they were out of earshot of the other patrons, Hakim studied Davy closely. "Where did you get this?" he enquired.

"I, I've always had it," Davy stammered. "Me da said never to show it." He put the medallion back into his shirt, but Hakim plucked it out again, holding the medallion in his brown, leathery hand. He traced the ancient script with a crooked finger, mumbling in Arabic.

"It is special, Al-Lah be praised," he whispered. "Do you know what you have here, sahib?" Davy shook his head.

"This is a talisman of the ancient god of the Deep," he said, fixing Davy with his black eyes. "I cannot tell you more, but you must find your way home."

"What home? What ye mean?"

Hakim glanced around, as if concerned about eavesdroppers. "Go to the sea," he said in a hushed voice. "And you will find your true family." He swiftly moved into the crowd and disappeared.

Davy was swept with emotion. True family? Somewhere at sea? Confused more than ever, he stuffed the medallion into his shirt and wandered back to the bar.

The bartender eyed him suspiciously. "No freeloading, boy. Buy a drink or be gone."

Davy stepped away from the bar and looked around the room for his shipmates. He noticed the beautiful whore from earlier, catching her gaze. But this time she wasn't smiling. Instead, she looked frightened. She shook her head silently, broke off her stare and quickly scampered back into the crowd.

Just when Davy decided it was best for him to leave this strange place, Malachy and Cadfael appeared at his side.

"Ah, a right good day of lady comp'ny an' drink," said Malachy. He looked down at Davy. "Ye look like ye seen a ghost."

Davy didn't answer.

"Come, lad. Let's go see more o' the city." Malachy took him by the shoulder and led him out into the street.

Davy trudged along behind them as they explored Cadiz. He had no appetite for sightseeing, his mind preoccupied with trying to digest what the strange Arab had said.

Well, at least he didn't find the map, he thought. He needed to find Wyn and get some answers to the burning questions in his head.

6

"Salt. Salt is life, lad."

Davy blinked and nodded slowly, not sure what Old Tom was trying to say.

"Salt always helps, and for some, it hides a bad taste." He smiled and sent Davy to deliver the breakfast to the captain.

It was a bright morning, and the *Henry* coasted out of the harbor of Cadiz under topsails with the ebb tide. *Sapphire* led the way, about two cables length ahead in the fairway, flying her colors proudly.

"Good mornin' Cap'n," Davy announced after knocking on the door. He set the plate of fresh eggs and mutton on his table. Captain Ross was examining a chart at this desk and didn't bother looking up as Davy set out the silverware and cloth napkin. He took a sip of wine from the goblet Davy had just filled with some fine Madeira and finally leaned back in his chair. "Mr. Jones. I want you to see Mr. Phillips, the gunner, after breakfast. Inform Mr. Stoddard you will be spending time with him to learn the duties of powder boy."

Davy nodded. "Aye, aye, sir!"

"We will soon be off the coast of West Africa," Ross continued. "Even though the *Sapphire* will escort us through to the Indian Ocean, it never hurts to have an extra hand with the feeding of the guns. Also, he will instruct you in letters and numbers, if you are respectful."

"Oh, yes sir! I will do everythin' he says," Davy replied.

"That is all." Ross bent to his meal.

Davy hurried out of the cabin and stopped at the galley to talk with Old Tom. He told him what the captain said, excitement in his bright blue eyes.

"Very well, lad. I'll clean up," said Tom. He took a long drag from his pipe. "Take heart what Mr. Phillips teaches ye. The west coast of Africa is rife with pirates. They come out o' the coast o' Guinea, seizin' ships at the point o' the sword. Best t' have keen lookouts an' sharp gunners."

He noticed Davy's concern, and hastily added, "Oh, but I'm sure the *Sapphire* will protect us. Now, go on an' find the gunner. Look fer 'im down in the magazine."

Davy descended into the bowels of the ship and found the magazine. A heavy oaken door guarded the way into the powder room. He pulled the handled and tugged on the door with all his strength. It grudgingly creaked open, revealing a small room lit only by a single, large lantern with heavy glass panes. As his eyes adjusted, he saw a lone figure crouching in the shadows. Before he could cross the threshold, the dark figure commanded, "Stay! Remove your shoes before you enter."

Davy kicked off his rude leather shoes with wooden soles and slowly entered the magazine.

"Rule number one: no shoes in the powder room at any time," John Phillips commanded in a strange accent. "A chance meeting between your shoes and a nail, for instance, may make the spark that blows this here ship to Kingdom Come. When you are here, you wear these." The gunner threw a pair of velvet slippers to Davy, who missed catching them in the darkness. Retrieving them from the spotless deck, Davy muttered, "Aye, sir."

Phillips carefully unhooked the lantern from its peg and held it near Davy's face, studying him. The boy looked back at him. The gunner seemed to be in his mid-thirties, with bushy brown hair and mud-brown eyes. The lines in his face were few, but well established. Davy couldn't remember seeing him on the ship before this moment. After a few moments the gunner put the lantern back.

"Don't call me sir. I'm not an officer, although I have the King's warrant," Phillips said, sitting on a stool. Davy noticed the padding on its feet, although there was none on the seat. "And of course, no smoking below decks," he added.

"Rule number two: always do exactly as I say. A mistake here can be fatal."

"Sir, uh, Mr. Phillips..."

"Call me Gunner, boy."

"Yes, s...I mean, yes, Gunner. I was wonderin', where are ye from? Yer voice, it don't have the ring of the King's English."

"I'm from a royal colony called Maryland. It's across the Atlantic on a continent called America. You can ask geography questions to Mr. Gibbs or one of his mates," Phillips replied dismissively as he picked up a piece of slow-match and began chewing on it. "My task, according to the captain of this ship, is to teach you the task of powder boy, or as some say, powder monkey. I myself was a powder monkey for the English Navy when I was about your age."

Davy nodded, but held his tongue. He watched as Phillips reached for a keg on a specially built shelf with fenders that held it tightly in place. His lanky but powerful frame strained as he pulled it free of the tight rank of kegs and gingerly set it down on the deck. He pulled a handkerchief free and wiped off the top of the little barrel.

"See here," he pointed to some symbols stamped in the oaken lid. "This means the contents of this keg is priming powder. It's a fine powder used in the breech of a gun to ignite the main charge." Davy nodded and listened to Phillips describe the other types of gunpowder, their different grains, and uses. "Your job," Phillips concluded, "is to carry the charges that my mates and I create, up to main deck and deliver them to the gun crews as fast and as *safely* as you can. In the event of general quarters, you will report to me at once. Understood?"

"Aye, Gunner." Phillips dismissed him and returned to his work. Davy clambered back up the galley and checked in with Old Tom in the galley, but the cook had nothing for him, so he went up on deck, eyes blinking in the brilliant sun. Master Gibbs was busy with the noon observance, using his sextant to measure the angle of the sun to the horizon. John was with him, holding the ship's chronometer. When Gibbs was satisfied that it was indeed noon, he instructed John to ring the ship's bell four times in pairs. He handed a piece of paper to one of his mates and told him to report to the captain. Davy watched this odd naval ritual in fascination. Shortly thereafter, John came down from the poop deck to join him.

"Master Gibbs says we will reach Tenerife tomorrow," he said with a grin, knowing that Davy had no idea what that meant. He paused, relishing his friend's confused look. "It's one of the Canary Islands. That means we will be *officially* just west of Africa!"

"Ahhh," Davy exclaimed. "We is world trav'lers!"

The two slapped each other's backs and laughed aloud. The commotion caught the attention of the Boatswain. Graves angrily strode over and quickly whacked both of the boys with his rattan. "Clap a stopper in yer gobholes and git yer lubber arses off me deck!" he shouted.

Wincing, Davy and John ran for the ladder leading down to the crew's berthing. Nursing a bruised thigh, Davy said, "A right devil, that one." John rubbed the back of his arm and darkness came over his brow. "Well, he ken have his fun fer now, but his last day is comin', sooner than he knows."

Fair winds and seas pushed the *Henry* along at a leisurely pace of five knots. Malachy had endeavored to teach John his duties under the bosun, taking him under his care as they spliced lines, worked on the ship's boats, and manned the yard arms when it was time to change sail. His cheerful demeanor had little effect as John mutely went about the business, all the while plotting against Graves.

Davy spent his time split between learning how to cook with Old Tom and the ways of gunpowder and arms from Phillips. By the time the ship sighted Tenerife to the west, he could create a decent fish soup and understand the difference between the various great guns and small arms, including how to load them with just the right charge. He felt useful, like he was really part of the crew.

The ship anchored in the sparkling blue bay of Tenerife to top off their supply of wood and water. A few select hands went ashore for the supplies while Davy and John stayed aboard, glumly watching from the main deck. They observed the high cliffs and black pebble beaches, which gave way to lush green hills of myrtle and juniper, and finally pines on the higher reaches of the mountainous island. Santa Cruz, the coastal town on this northeastern part of the island, featured red Spanish tile roofs similar to those they saw in Cadiz. San Cristobal Castle guarded the bay, its stone fortifications bristling with cannon.

"So much fer world trav'lers," John remarked.

They watched the boats ply back and forth, from ship to shore until the sun set. Davy went below to prepare the captain's evening supper.

The next morning Davy and John helped the crew at the capstan weigh anchor and the *Henry* turned south.

The ship stayed a hundred miles off the coast of West Africa. As *Sapphire* led them deep into the Gulf of Guinea, the wind died and did not return for weeks. Davy passed the time serving the captain and learning to read, write and figure numbers from Phillips. The gunner was pleased with the results and complimented Davy on his progress. He had Davy copy his ammunition ledger and taught him how to load a pistol. Every evening he took him up to the main deck and inspected the great guns, explaining the different parts of the cannon.

"Now, this here is a 12-pounder," Phillips said. "It weighs close to two tons and requires six men to move her with these tackles," he pointed to the thick ropes that held the gun tightly to the bulwark.

"How does it fire?"

"First, the crew receives the order to loose the gun," Phillips began. "You must understand, the gun is to be secured at all times unless the captain directs it to be loosed. We can't have it rolling around the deck and injuring the crew. That would be what we call a 'loose cannon', ha, ha."

Davy smiled.

"Then they remove the tompion, here," he pointed to the knobbed disk that covered the muzzle. "The man removing the tompion will then grab the wad worm," he picked up a long pole with copper tines at the end. "He will insert and twist the wad worm in the barrel to ensure there is no debris left behind from the last firing. That same man will then dip this sponge," he grabbed another pole, "into the bucket of water and insert it into the barrel to ensure there are no hot embers remaining from the last shot."

"Do they have to do all that, even if the gun ain't been fired in a long time?" Davy asked.

"Yes. It's part of the routine the gun crews are drilled on, every time to make sure they don't forget," Phillips explained.

"While this is going on, the quarter gunner – that's the man in charge of the gun crew who actually fires it – takes this brass reamer and pokes it through the vent hole to ensure it is clear."

"It looks like a big needle," Davy said.

"Next," he continued, "A charge of powder – that's where you come in, bringing it to the gun crew – is loaded with this rammer, followed by a wad of cloth, then the 12-pound ball. Sometimes instead of ball the captain will order bar shot, or grape shot. In any case," he continued, "Another wad will go after the ball, and it's all rammed tightly in again."

"Why are these wads put in?"

The first one keeps the charge in place, and the second keeps the ball in place," Phillips explained. "The quarter gunner then takes the reamer and inserts it through the vent hole and punctures the charge bag. At this point he takes the charge powder from the powder horn and fills up the vent hole. As you know, the charging powder is a finer grain than the charge in the gun."

Davy nodded.

"The quarter gunner then takes this wedge, called a 'quoin', and jams it under the rear of the gun to adjust for elevation. The crew then grabs the tackles and runs the gun out through the port and it is ready to be fired."

"So many things have to be done," Davy marveled.

"Yes, and they *must* be done in exact order," Phillips said. "Finally, the quarter gunner grabs this linstock," he pointed to a long pole with a type of string attacked to the end. "He lights the slow match here at the end of the linstock and, upon command from the captain, touches it to the vent hole to ignite the charge and fire the cannon. The gun will recoil several feet, halted by the train tackles attached to the breech and run through these bolts in the bulwark and deck. It is critically important," he added, "that the quarter gunner ensure his crew stands free to the side before he fires the cannon, so as to avoid crushed feet."

The lesson complete, Phillips dismissed him. Davy admired the complexity of the operation and the gunner's obvious expertise. He decided he wanted to be a gunner someday.

More days went by and still the winds did not return. The ship slowly drifted south, carried by the current, but made hardly two miles a day. Davy noticed the crew had become noticeably nervous. He met John at the bow and asked him what was going on. They were less than 200 miles away from Accra off the coast of Ghana, John told him. Malachy had warned him to keep a sharp eye on the horizon, for what John did not know.

"Let's see if Old Tom knows," Davy said. They found the cook lounging in his hammock slung between beams in the galley. Davy sometimes wondered if he ever left the little nook as he greeted his mentor.

"Well, there's me bairn," he rasped. He cast a sideways look at John. "An' his mate."

"Tom," Davy began, "we was wonderin' what's got the crew all fidgety, an such."

"Och, is prob'ly nothin'," Tom said with caution. "I heard the cap'n say he twas expectin' Cap'n Swanson from the *Sapphire* fer dinner. That means we'll be busy fixin' dinner an' servin' the cap'n's best wine."

Davy relaxed somewhat and John nudged him. "See there? It's nothin' special, Davy."

"By thunder! Keep yer idiot tongue, lad!" Stoddard erupted. "It certainly is special. We is entertainin' an officer of the King's Navy – our protection! The reputation of the ship must be upheld."

John's face turned red and he turned on his heel. Davy watched him duck out of the compartment and stomp away. "Why did ye yell at me mate?" he cried.

"That ill-mannered lad has much t' learn," Tom said, calming down. "There's a darkness in him. Ye best be careful an' not follow his ways."

"John is me mate," Davy repeated defensively. "And he's alright."

Stoddard waved his hand. "Very well, then. Lookee here, go fetch me the plumpest duck out o' the pens. We gots a feast to prepare."

John ascended to the main deck and was immediately accosted by Elijah Graves. The bosun squinted angrily at him. "Well, what do we 'ave here? An idler? Where 'ave ye been?" he demanded. "Yer supposed t' be paintin' the gig! An' here ye are, stumblin' about like some lubber!" Graves cracked John in the thigh with his rattan, causing him to yelp in surprised pain.

"Ye didn't have to do that!" John retorted.

"Why, ye liddle whelp, I'll do more than that, if ye keep waggin' yer tongue!" He whacked John again, this time on his bare foot. "Now, git on with ye!"

John limped over to one of the ship's boats, muttering curses. He joined Malachy, who was scraping the underside of the gig. "Ye best be careful, mate," he said to John. "No sense in provokin' the bosun – it's a losin' battle."

John snorted derisively and picked up a brush and paint pot. He glanced over his shoulder and saw Graves glaring at him. "Does he always beat his mates?"

"Ye ain't a mate yet, lad," said Malachy. "Ye jest a new hand. He's always hard on the new hands, until they learn."

"Well, I don' give a damn what he says," declared John, his voice rising in anger. "Why, he's nothin' but a bully!"

Graves stepped forward and whipped the rattan across John's back, causing him to cry out in pain. He followed it up with another blow on his shoulder. "Stop yer gob! I'll not 'ave yer insubordination, ye lubber!" Graves cried.

"Bosun," Malachy interjected, "Go easy on him! He's only a lad!"

"Mind yer business, Ahearn!" Graves shouted. He saw Roberts' face twist into a snarl and responded by striking him across the face with his rattan. John howled and crumbled to the deck, curling into a ball. Graves rained several more blows down on his defenseless form. Finally, he stopped.

"Now! I'll learn ye the ways o' proper seamanship, or ye will feel me rattan again!" Graves declared. He gave John a kick in the ribs and strode away.

Malachy consoled the sobbing boy. "There now, take it easy. Don't let him git to ye."

John slowly rose to his knees, weeping tears of rage. He rubbed his bruised temple, grabbed the brush and silently went to work.

An hour later, Graves stopped by to check his work. "A lubberly job, if I ever seen it," he remarked disdainfully. "Ahearn, I hold ye responsible. Take him up to the fore crosstree an' let him think on it fer awhile." He jabbed a finger in John's chest. "An' don't come down until I tells ye."

John grumbled as he followed Malachy up the ratlines holding the foremast until they were far above the deck. He straddled the topmast yardarm and Malachy sat next to him.

"Look, lad. Ye need to keep quiet and not challenge the bosun like that," he said. "Ye jest cost me extra duties, fer sure. Not to mention, that bosun has ye marked as a troublemaker. Do yerself a favor and stay up here until he says come down. Besides," he added, "ye might jest enjoy a bit o' peace." With that he slipped his legs over the yardarm and slid down the backstay to the deck.

John sighed, still fuming. As he swung back and forth with the pitch and roll of the inert ship in the wave troughs, he quietly plotted his revenge.

At six bells in the afternoon watch, Captain Wallace Swanson and his first officer were rowed over to the *Henry*. John was aloft in the fore crosstree more than 60 feet above the deck and observed the arrival ritual as Graves blew his boatswain's whistle and Captain Ross and Master Gibbs greeted the English officer with salutes. After a brief series of handshakes, the group went below to the captain's cabin. With Graves' permission, John at last descended the ratlines and pretended to examine the ship's rudder as he eavesdropped on their conversation, which he could hear through the captain's open stern windows. He hoped to hear news, but was disappointed when the conversation remained cordial as the officers shared witty banter over dinner. He heard Stoddard come in and remove the dishes, while Davy withdrew the tablecloth and served more wine. Frustrated, he was about to give up when he heard Swanson change the subject to something more serious.

"Now gentlemen," Swanson began. "We are faced with a situation that requires our utmost vigilance. As you know, we are entering an area of the sea where two problems confront us: the doldrums and hostile ships."

"Ye mean pirates," interjected Graves.

"That is correct, sir," replied Swanson, his voice betraying irritation at being interrupted. "I've sailed this route many times and encountered them twice. The admiralty has issued a warning for all English shipping in this area.

"We will have our guns run out and ready to serve them for the next few hundred leagues," Swanson said. "I expect you to do the same, Captain Ross. God willing, we won't have to use them, but if we do, I want you to sail to the windward and stay within two cables' length at all times, unless I signal otherwise."

"We will certainly do that," replied Ross. "Mr. Gibbs is an excellent ship handler."

"Do not, under any circumstances, break formation and make a run for it. These pirates often work in pairs, and they may attack at night. If you spot them, send up a blue flare. I'm sure your gunner will have your small arms ready and boarding nets rigged in the event we need to repel boarders," Swanson said. He proceeded to discuss their route, special signals, and a few sailing tactics.

John slipped away and went down to the galley to find Davy and Old Tom cleaning the dishes. Fearing to step inside, he whistled. Davy greeted him, but Tom shot a dirty look. "Go on, lad," Tom told Davy. "But be back soon."

Retreating to the crew's berthing, John whispered what he had overheard. Davy was aghast. "Good gawd! I hope it's not true."

John hushed him. "I dunno, mate," he said. "But we'll serve 'em out if'n they dare."

That night, Davy couldn't sleep. He kept thinking about pirates, and the stories Old Tom had told him about how they murdered men and ransacked ships. He worried about his father, even now in the clutches of those fiends. He searched the dark berthing for John, but couldn't find him. He was about to give up when he heard the sound of a scuffle above him on the main deck. Shouting and curses followed, and then he heard a voice that was distinctly John's. He dashed up the ladder to investigate.

He found his friend, pinned up against the mainmast by two men of the watch. A third man was holding up a lantern, while another man struck John in the stomach with something that looked like a stick. John cried out in pain. Davy opened his mouth to say something, he wasn't sure what, but before he could he was shoved aside.

"By thunder! What is the meaning of this uproar!" shouted Master Ewan Gibbs. He grabbed the aggressor's shoulder and spun him around. "Mr. Graves! What is going on here, and why are you striking this man?"

Graves had a hideous grin on his scarred face, and a bloody stain was growing on the side of his shirt. "This here whelp tried t' stick me, with this." He pointed to a dirk, slick with red, lying on the deck.

"Is that so, Mr. Roberts?" Gibbs demanded.

"That there *bastard*," John jerked his chin toward Graves, "deserves it. He been ridin' me arse, tryin' his best to kill me!"

"I done nothin' out o' the ordinary, jest tryin' to whip this *lubber* inta a right proper seaman," Graves protested angrily. "An' this is what I git," he pointed to his ribs.

A voice came from behind them. "Mr. Gibbs, please explain this commotion." Davy turned to see Captain Ross, still in his nightshirt.

"It appears, sir, that young Roberts 'ere drew a blade on Mr. Graves and wounded him," Gibbs answered.

"Mr. Graves, see the surgeon at once," Ross ordered. "You two men fetch the master-at-arms and have Mr. Roberts clapped in irons. I will see both of you in my cabin tomorrow at noon."

Davy watched in horror as his mate was led away and Graves smirked triumphantly as he passed him toward the ladder. Davy saw him wince a bit as he slowly descended, holding his side.

Good gawd! Davy thought. *They will hang him, fer sure!*

7

Gulf of Guinea

The next day the bosun was seen on deck looking a bit pale. A large bandage was visible under his tight shirt as he instructed his mates in the day's work. As noon approached, he went below to the captain's cabin. Half an hour later, all hands were called to quarters on the main deck. John was brought up in shackles, escorted by the master-at-arms and the gunner, Phillips. Captain Ross appeared and addressed the crew.

"Mr. Roberts is accused of attempting to murder an officer, Mr. Graves," he began solemnly. "The law of the sea requires he be put to death if found guilty. Mr. Roberts, what have you to say for yourself?"

John said nothing for a moment, glancing around at the assembled crew and then finally holding the captain's stern gaze. "That bosun is the Devil," he began.

"You will address refer to him as Mr. Graves," Ross said

icily.

"Aye, sir. Well, he been drivin' me hard, whippin' me with that rattan," John accused.

"That's his job, lad," said Ross. "Do you have anything more to say?"

John took a deep breath and shook his head. "Nay, sir."

"Then according to the law, as captain of this ship I hereby sentence you to death by hanging," Ross said. "It's too bad, really. You might have made a good sailor."

John's jaw dropped. "But sir, I..."

"That's enough. The sentence will be carried out at noon tomorrow so that you may have time to come to peace with your Maker. Dismissed."

Shocked, Davy watched his friend be led away, catching John's fearful glance. Tom Stoddard leaned down and whispered to him, "This is what happens when ye lose respect fer the rules," he said. "I knew that lad was marked fer trouble when I first laid eyes on 'im. Ye know," he continued, "he damn near killed the bosun. Broke a rib an' put a big hole in his side. Made him bleed somethin' fierce. But that bosun, he's a tough one."

Davy barely heard him.

The new moon was nowhere to be seen, its shadow blending in with the sultry equatorial air, which failed to stir. Down below in the crew's berthing, Davy found the heat unbearable. He silently climbed out of his hammock and sneaked up the ladder. Avoiding the watch on deck, slipped down the tumblehome of the ship's hull for a swim. Immediately his irritated skin was soothed, and he swam underwater for quite some time before surfacing. He turned and his wide, fish-like eyes spied the *Henry* a half cable's length away. *Sapphire* was off in the distance, distinguishable only by its stern lamp. He dove again, his webbed hands allowed him extra push as he sped through the salt water. He enjoyed the freedom of the sea and forgot his woes, just for a while.

The two becalmed ships bobbed listlessly in the darkness, the sluggish current moving them at an imperceptible, snail-like rate. It was enough to lull a man asleep. Unfortunately, that man happened to be the after lookout, who didn't suspect a thing until the knife cut his throat. Rough hands pulled him over the stern and slowly lowered his body into the salt water. The fore lookout, gazing distractedly at the stars instead of the sea, met a similar fate.

Soundless shadows crept up the bow, stern, and main chains, slipping aboard like venomous eels stalking prey. Sawing through the boarding netting with daggers, they stealthily crept forward. Only one man of the watch remained to be silenced, and he was at the helm, stroking his patchy, two-day old beard stubble. The somber, stocky Welshman, known to his mates as Cadfael, had been in the service of the EIC for three years. In that time, he had learned to keep his stammering mouth shut and do what his superiors told. Now, at the mate of the watch, he was in charge. And he felt something amiss.

"Bill," he called to the bow. Only the starless sky answered. He turned to the stern. "Mick." Nothing. He held his breath and listened. He thought he heard something. Something like cat feet creeping on roof tiles. A sense of dread crept into his soul. He stepped into the alcove and grabbed a lamp. Lighting it with trembling hands, he turned and saw his worst nightmare.

Looming figures appeared out of the darkness, momentarily cringing as the lamp shone upon their evil forms, like so many cockroaches suddenly exposed in the light. Cadfael cried out in surprise and the nearest pirate lunged at him with a pike.

Cadfael instinctively leaped back into the alcove, his back against the bulkhead. He filled his lungs and shouted, "Ahoy, the watch! We're under att--"

He never finished his sentence as the snarling pirate drove the pike into his bowels. He dropped the lantern and clutched his gaping wound as the pirate jerked the bloody pike free. He slid to the deck, screaming in pain.

The pirates, now howling like a pack of wild dogs, headed for the hatch leading below decks and met the first *Henry* crewmember just emerging: Ewan Gibbs. The startled ship's Master paused, wide-eyed, as a pirate swung his boarding axe and split his skull. He dropped down the ladder, the axe still buried in his head.

As they dropped down the hatch, one by one, the invaders split up. Some headed forward to the crew's berthing while others made for the officers' staterooms. They mercilessly hacked down everyone they met, but one man stood in their way. Elijah Graves leaped from his stateroom, rattan in hand, roared an unearthly string of curses, and charged the pack of cutthroats. Swinging his cane like it was made of sharpened steel, he fearlessly kept several intruders temporarily at bay.

Captain Ross emerged from his stateroom, still in his nightshirt and armed with a pistol and sword. "*Henry!*" he called to his crew. "To arms! Repel boarders!" He charged forward and joined Graves in the fray.

John Phillips opened his armory door and immediately began handing out defensive weapons to crewmembers rushing in to arm themselves. "No time for pistols, men. We have a warm, close action on our hands," he remarked as he passed an armload of cutlasses and axes. His mates joined him and grabbed the pikes. When the last of the crew had departed, Phillips told his mates, "Now, let's prepare a little surprise welcome." He pointed toward a wooden crate stashed under the ledges of the powder kegs. It had three red X marks.

Davy surfaced a few yards away from the ship and pulled his long, black hair away from his face. He heard the cries and steel clashes of ferocious hand-to-hand combat and suddenly realized he wouldn't have figure out how to sneak back aboard to avoid discovery by the watch. He treaded water for a few moments, afraid and unsure what to do. Finally, he had an idea. He dived back underwater.

Below decks, the fighting continued aboard *Henry,* and it seemed the pirates were getting the upper hand. The crew was slowly driven back toward the chain locker at the bow of the ship below decks. The pirates pressed forward, when suddenly something exploded behind them, sending several to the deck in bloody heaps. The rest turned and saw the gunner and his mates, lighting *grenadoes*. Enraged, they surged to attack this new threat. The crew forward chased after them, hacking away at the nearest pirates. Two more *grenadoes* blasted them before they could reach the gunner. Beset on both sides, the pirates retreated up the ladder to the main deck and regrouped.

Phillips grabbed the master-at-arms. "We need every man we can get," he growled. They descended the ladder and found John Roberts. As he was unshackled, Phillips handed him an axe. "Better to die free than in chains," he said. John smiled wryly and hefted the blade.

By this time, a second wave of pirates had boarded the *Henry* to reinforce their comrades. The crew bolted up the ladder to see their enemy had them outnumbered three to one.

"Serve out justice to these savages!" bellowed Captain Ross. He pointed his pistol and pulled the trigger, but nothing happened. He cursed his misfire and raised his sword. "Attack!"

The *Henrys* charged forward and met the pirates near the main mast. Pikes lunged and blades swept through the air, but it didn't take long before the overwhelming number of pirates had driven the crew back toward the stern. Old Tom Stoddard, his cutlass knocked out of his hand, swung his crutch wildly, but two pirates managed to duck his fury and tackle him. One stuck a dirk into his ribs and another gripped him by the throat. Tom struggled like a trapped tiger, throwing off one and clobbering the other in the head with a stray wooden belaying pin. Before he could rise, a third pirate drove a pike into his chest. He gasped, and moved no more.

John suddenly appeared brought his axe down in a mighty blow on the pirate's shoulder, severing his clavicle. He glanced over to his side and saw the bosun driven back against the taffrail by two pirates. He was slumping against the bulwark, bleeding profusely from several wounds, but the wiry old salt was still holding on, slashing and clawing at his opponents like a trapped animal. John leaped forward and buried his axe into a pirate's back. He saw the other pirate raise his cutlass for a final strike and hurled himself bodily into him. They both fell over the side and crashed into the sea.

John emerged, finding the pirate gasping for breath next to him. He grabbed him by the shoulders and drove him under the water. The pirate struggled for a few moments, then went limp. John released him to the deep and looked for a way back aboard. He swam over to the main chains and scrambled back up the side. Sopping wet, he climbed over the rail and made his way through the torn boarding net. In the dim light, he was greeted with a grim spectacle. The remaining crewmembers, many wounded, were throwing down their arms in surrender. *No*, he thought, *it canna be!*

"Step aside, mate," a voice said behind him. John whirled around and saw Davy's head poke up from the side of the ship. He stood dumbfounded as first Davy, then a steady stream of Royal Marines and sailors from the *Sapphire* come up from behind him and charge past. More appeared from the bow and across the deck from the other side. A Marine lieutenant fired his pistol. Seeing a superior force, the bewildered pirates panicked and dropped their weapons. Falling to their knees and raising their hands, they pled for quarter in some strange African babble.

Davy walked over and greeted his astonished friend. "Ello, mate," he grinned. "Care fer a cup o' tea?"

John let out the breath he realized he'd been holding and chuckled. "Gawd, Davy! Good t' see ye!" The two hugged briefly and John asked, "Where did ye come from? I didn't see ye in the fight and thought ye was dead."

"Aye, well," Davy thought fast. "I fell over the side when it began, so I made fer the *Sapphire.*"

John looked at him in disbelief. "Ye swam that far? What is it, like a league?"

Davy just smiled.

As the *Sapphire* men loaded the pirates onto the boats and rowed back to the warship, their ship's surgeon came aboard with his mates to tend to the *Henry* wounded. Lamps were lit, and they painted a grisly scene of a blood-soaked deck and the prone forms of friend a foe alike. A familiar voice rose up in a wail as Malachy found Cadfael, almost disemboweled and bleeding to death from his ghastly abdominal wound. His left hand held the unlit blue flare. Davy and John rushed over to find him tending to his dying mate.

"S-sorry, M-Malachy," Cadfael gasped, his eyes rolling

back in agony. "I c-couldn't light it," he said, glancing down at the flare. He regained his composure briefly, looking at Davy. "Take care now, lad," he said. He closed his eyes, shuddered, and was still. Malachy wept and John mutely rested his hand on his shoulder. Davy was struck dumb with grief.

"Davy," John said quietly. He met his friend's watering eyes and jerked his head toward the taffrail. Davy followed his gaze and saw Old Tom crumpled on the deck. They rushed over and found him and found the pike still buried in his heart.

"No!" Davy cried. He knelt down and tentatively caressed his mentor's cold cheek. He recoiled in shock. John stood next to him, arms crossed. "That old cook may not thought much of me, but I know he was like a father to ye. I'm sorry, mate."

Their brooding was interrupted as Elijah Graves came limping up to them. "Well," he began, taking a long drag from a cigar, "this has been a hard night, lads. But ye fought like right seamen an' done the *Henry* proud." He looked down at Stoddard. "That man there was one o' the best I ever knew that sailed on His Majesty's ships. We will put 'im to rest t'morrow morn, with honor."

Davy and John stared at him, amazed at this almost sentimental aspect of the monster they'd endured. He was wounded in multiple places on his body, blood still seeping through the bandages of his ghastly wounds.

Graves looked John in the eye. "Ye saved me life back there. I owes ye a debt." He walked away without another word.

The 250 men of the *Henry* crew worked throughout most of the night, moving the injured down to the orlop, where the acting surgeon tended the suffering. Sixteen men with wounds ranging from fractures to lacerations rested on makeshift tables or lay about in the adjacent berthing compartment.

There was much work to be done to repair the damage to bulkheads and severed lines. John tended the rigging with the bosun's mates while Davy was ordered to put the captain's cabin to order and prepare breakfast. He went about his task in the galley, numb with shock.

The next morning, the bleary-eyed crew assembled on the main deck, where Captain Ross, his arm in a sling, read a passage from the Bible. Cadfael Hywel, Ewan Gibbs, and Thomas Stoddard were wrapped in sailcloth, with 12-pound shot inside the bag with them at their feet. Each was loaded onto a plank, covered with the English flag, and solemnly tipped overboard.

Davy himself had put the final stitch through Old Tom's nose and closed the bag, as was the custom explained to him by the ship's sailmaker. He found the gruesome task disturbing, but the sailmaker said it was his duty to perform, as he was the cook's closest mate. When it was done, Ross dismissed the men. Davy went below and tumbled into his hammock. He stared at the curved form of the sleeping man above him until he fell into a deep sleep.

The next morning, Davy rose early to prepare the captain's breakfast. As he laid the table with salted fish, biscuit, and fresh eggs he'd gathered from the chicken pens, Ross observed him in silence. His task done, Davy wordlessly withdrew to the galley. His tempestuous mind veered from poor Cadfael to John, who was back in chains, and then finally to his late mentor, Old Tom. He looked around despairingly at the blackened pots, carving knives, and assorted cookware, wishing he could bring him back. His missed his sea stories, cooking lessons, and affable nature. He saw Tom's favorite clay pipe and picked it up. A fairly plain piece made in Bristol by the famed pipe maker Phillip Edwards, it had a rather small stem and bowl. It was among Tom's treasures, and Davy decided he wouldn't mind if he kept it. He put it into his coat pocket.

Davy knew he wasn't ready for this new responsibility. Tom had so much knowledge that he had yet to pass on. The cook for the crew stepped in and informed him that he would be under his supervision until Captain Ross decided upon who would replace Tom, but for now the job was his. Davy wondered how he would please the captain with his scant culinary repertoire.

Later that day, signals from the *Sapphire* were seen by the lookout. Captain Ross ordered his boat lowered. He left Graves in charge of the ship and commanded Malachy and Davy to accompany him to the warship.

As they stepped aboard and saluted the flag, Captain Swanson greeted them. "Welcome aboard, sir," he said to

Ross. "I thought you might wish to observe our next proceeding."

Davy was impressed and intimidated by his first close-up view of an English warship. The differences between the man of war and the *Henry* were obvious. Brass cannon gleamed, the sails were furled tightly on the yards, the deck was spotlessly scrubbed, and the lines were neatly coated black with tar, the falls flemished in neat spirals on the deck. The ship's crew and company of Royal Marines were assembled on the main deck in straight ranks. Davy admired the how the Marines, in their perfect red coats and shiny boots, presented their upright muskets in precise unison.

Captain Swanson offered Captain Ross and Malachy refreshment in his cabin. Davy waited outside, unsure what to do. The crew remained in ranks. After a short time, the officers reappeared on deck and Malachy stood next to Davy. "Yer about t' see somethin'. Jest be quiet and respectful," he said.

The two captains ascended a short ladder to the afterdeck and Swanson motioned to his first officer. The ship's company and Marines were called to attention. From below decks, pirates appeared, chained to one another and led by an escort of Marines. Captain Swanson's eyes narrowed as he glared at them in disdain. He opened a large, leather-bound book and began reading.

"According to the Articles of War and the law of the sea, as an officer of His Majesty's Navy and captain of this vessel, I hereby charge you with piracy on the high seas."

Swanson turned to Ross. "Sir, are these the scoundrels that attacked your ship?"

Ross replied, "Yes, sir. They are indeed the savages that attacked us. Three of my men were killed and many more are suffering grievous wounds."

"Very well. Do the accused have anything to say for themselves?" He paused, giving the pirates just a moment to respond for the sake of legality. When they said nothing, he continued.

"So be it. I find the accused guilty. The punishment for piracy is clear and just. They shall be hanged by the neck until dead, dead, dead." He gestured to his first officer. "Carry out the sentence, Mr. Wells."

The pirates were herded to the masts, where thick ropes hung down. Nooses were tightened around their necks and hands were called to man the lines. The first officer gave an order and the lines were heaved up.

Davy watched in horror as the pirates jerked and twisted in the air. The lines were belayed and the gruesome spectacle continued for a few minutes before the pirates no longer struggled. Davy looked at their red faces, eyes bulging. One part of him was satisfied at this justice, but the other part was afraid. The process was repeated until all the prisoners were executed.

Captain Swanson dismissed his crew and bid Captain Ross farewell. They boarded their boat and rowed back to the *Henry* in silence.

Two days passed, and ships drifted westward on the equatorial current. Finally, a few puffs of wind heralded a breeze, which allowed the captain to call for sail. *Sapphire* led the way as they made for the Cape of Good Hope some 2,300 miles away. The mood of the crew changed noticeably, with some hands even laughing while they worked.

Captain Ross called all hands to quarters in the afternoon. Davy dutifully stood in his place among the ranks, wondering what could have prompted this occasion.

"Men," Ross began, "we've had a bit of a rough patch. We've lost some good shipmates, but we've come through it handsomely." He looked at his crew for a moment before continuing. "After some thought, I've arrived at a few decisions. Mr. Graves will assume the position of Master of the ship."

A wave of dread passed through Davy as he tried to imagine the power this promotion would give his nemesis. Before he could think further, Ross spoke again.

"I've also decided Mr. Ahearn will take over as the ship's Boatswain." Davy's dark thoughts fled and he cracked a smile. *Good fer ye, Malachy.* A murmur of assent went up in the ranks.

"And as to the fate of Mr. Roberts," Ross said, glancing at the master-at-arms, "his execution is stayed. His heroic actions during the recent battle were commendable. He is to be released at once and put in a probationary status under the direct supervision of Mr. Ahearn."

Now Davy grinned widely. He barely contained his joy, knowing his friend would be freed.

"Also," Ross continued, "I believe we owe our thanks to Mr. Jones for risking his life to swim over to the *Sapphire* and rally reinforcements. Three cheers for Mr. Jones!"

The crew huzzahed as Davy stood bewildered. Hands clapped his shoulders and Davy grinned stupidly. Ross dismissed the crew and John Phillips appeared at Davy's side. "Come lad, let's show your mate to the deck."

Still grinning, Davy went below with the gunner and met John, who was getting his shackles removed by the master-at-arms. He hugged his friend and they joyously ascended to the freedom of sunshine and a hot sun.

"Oh, I thought I'd never see it again!" John exclaimed as he took in the view of the azure sky and sparkling water. Davy nodded. They remained at the waist of the ship, quietly watching the waves go by.

Malachy appeared next to them. "Mr. Roberts, I am in short supply of qualified hands at the moment, so I'm makin' ye a bosun's mate," he said. Then, with a wry smile he added, "As long as ye ken behave yerself."

John looked at Malachy with feigned seriousness. "Well, that might be hard, but I'll surely try!" The three laughed and shoved each other about as sea gulls wheeled overhead, wondering at the commotion.

8

Cape Town, South Africa

The winds picked up and the ships made good time, approaching the port of Cape Town near the tip of South Africa in just over two weeks. Captain Ross announced the ship would pick up wood, water, and victuals at the Dutch settlement before rounding the Cape of Good Hope and proceeding to the Indian Ocean.

HMS Sapphire led the way as the ship's entered Table Bay on a cool, rainy morning and dropped anchor within sight of the settlement. Even though Cape Town was owned by the Dutch East India Company, the English were welcomed as allies – and customers. The two ships organized working parties and soon boats were lowered and the crews filled them with empty water butts and casks for provisions.

Captain Ross accompanied Captain Swanson as they paid a visit to the local Dutch Governor. Meanwhile, Master Graves let the crew know there would be a day of liberty, provided they accomplished the resupply and repair labors necessary to continue the voyage. Davy noticed the ornery former bosun seemed a bit more human, although he was still insisted on running a tight ship. He wondered how the man kept going despite his wounds, which were still many weeks from full healing. Meanwhile, Malachy took charge of the resupply effort. He allowed Davy to accompany the ship's cook to visit the town for needed foodstuffs. Captain Ross had given Davy money to purchase special items for his table, including wine and cheese.

Davy and the cook, Reynolds, bought livestock and had them delivered to the wharf. Next, they stopped at a wine merchant to put in an order for Madeira and Claret.

"All this wine is temptin' me dry mouth," Reynolds remarked. He eyed a tavern across the cobbled street. "Let us whet our whistles o'er there."

"Uh, Mr. Reynolds? We ain't got liberty yet," Davy said. "I don't want to git in trouble."

"Is fine, lad," Reynolds said dismissively. "We'll jest tip a pint an' be on our way." He ambled across the street, Davy tentatively following.

They entered the dim tavern and Reynolds ordered ale for them. Davy looked around the room. The locals were engaged in low talk. He noticed the lack of women and thought how different it was compared to Cadiz. Sipping his ale, he heard Reynolds strike up a conversation with the bar tender, who spoke English with a thick French accent. Surprised, Davy asked Reynolds why a Frenchman was here in a Dutch colony. "Huguenots came here jest a few years back," he explained. Davy wondered what a Huguenot was.

He shrugged it off and sipped his ale.

After what seemed like hours, Reynolds finished his beer and turned to Davy. "Let's go, lad." They walked out into the rain and searched for a place to buy flour and other staples.

"Did the Hu-hu...the bar man have any news?" Davy asked.

"Aye, he says the Cape storms are bad this time o' year," Reynolds replied. "Ye know, it used to be called the 'Cape o' Storms' a long time ago." There was a long pause. "An' he says some pirate in a Spanish man o' war has taken merchants near Madagascar."

"Pirates!?" Davy exclaimed. "I thought we was done with them."

Reynolds shot him a cold glance. "Nay, lad. Ye never know when they is gonna show. That's why we has the *Sapphire* fer protection."

The finished the errands for the day and went back to the ship. The crew continued to provision the ship throughout the day. That evening, Captain Ross returned from the governor's house and called a meeting in his cabin with Graves, Malachy and Phillips. Davy served refreshments, but Ross was silent while he was in the cabin. He left and stood outside the door for a few moments, but all he heard was low murmuring. The meeting didn't last long, and when the officers emerged, they were tight-lipped. Davy wondered what the big secret meant. He pulled out the oilcloth map he'd tucked away behind a sack of flour and examined it again. He knew the ship was getting closer to the place marked with an X, where he hoped to find Wyn. *That is, if we can avoid them pirates.* He rolled it up and stowed it carefully.

The next day he and John went ashore with Malachy. They explored the town, especially the taverns. Davy was too afraid to ask Malachy about the meeting with the captain, but he confided in John while the newly appointed bosun was taking a piss outside.

"I dunno what it means," John said without a care. He was happy to be free. "Figger they will tell us, if we need t' know."

Davy remained worried. "That new cook says there be pirates about, and I saw the gunner's mates sharpenin' the blades last night."

"They always do that," John remarked, taking a swig of ale.

Night descended on Cape Town and the three made their way back to the ship. Davy dutifully stopped by the captain's cabin to see if he needed anything, but he was studying a map and waved him off. Davy went to his hammock, still anxious. He fell into a fitful sleep.

The two ships got underway the next morning and headed south down the coast toward the Cape. The westerly wind pushed them toward the land, but Graves and his mates at the helm kept them well off the lee shore as the watch on deck trimmed the sails accordingly. At three bells in the afternoon watch, they turned east and the wind picked up and shifted from the south, creating swells that buffeted the ship. A cold, driving rain met them. Tacking, they managed to weather False Bay, and Ross ordered both watches on deck to reef the straining sails.

Davy met Phillips in the armory for his daily academic lessons, but the gunner had other ideas. "Take this," he said, handing Davy a sheathed dirk. "It's time you learned how to use a blade." Davy pulled it out and turned it over, admiring his first personal weapon. Phillips showed him how to thrust and parry with it, and how to move his feet.

"The key to defending yourself is keeping your balance and putting the other man off his," he explained. "There are vital spots on the body that when penetrated will cause a grievous wound. Here," he pointed to the inside of his thigh, "and the eyes. Since you are short, it is best to go for the lower target, then when your opponent collapses, take advantage and strike him in the face. If he turns, strike him here," he pointed to his kidney area. "Or his ribs. Finish him by cutting his throat."

"What about his heart?" Davy asked, nervously.

"It's protected by bone, and it takes considerable strength to drive a blade this size through it. Stick it in the vital areas and you'll do fine."

"Can I jest use a pistol?"

"Pistols are fine, but in a warm action you only get one shot. It takes experience," he said slowly. "We'll get to that later. For now, learn to master this. Practice with it every day after your duties are done." He dismissed Davy, who wasn't sure if he liked the idea of carrying a dirk.

A strong gale blew from the southeast, and the *Henry* struggled to make headway. The sleeker *Sapphire* fared a little better, signaling them with a gun to keep pace. As they passed by the Cape, the skies darkened and the wind rose to a howling pitch. The ship met the rising sea on the starboard quarter, pitching in a corkscrew motion. Waves crashed over the side, washing over the deck with great strength. The crew held onto the lifelines as they struggled in water up to their waists. Rain pelted them in their faces as the increasing gusts drove it sideways. They lost sight of the *Sapphire* as the squall demanded their full attention.

Ross, standing on the afterdeck in his foul weather attire, shouted orders to the crew to shorten sail. John climbed the ratlines on the foremast along with others to reef the topsail. He paused and tightened his grip as the storm tried to blow him off. Reaching the fore crosstree, he climbed out to his station on the port side, his feet finding the footrope and his arms hugging the long yard. He and the foretop men tugged on the heavy, wet sail, grasping for the reefing lines, which would allow them to tie the bunched canvas to the spar.

Men below worked the sheet lines, paying out just enough to keep some tension on the sail while the topmen slowly drew it in. A sudden blast of wind combined with a crashing wave knocked them down and the sheets loosed through the clews, causing the sail to flap wildly.

The ship yawed heavily and John lost his footing. He held on for dear life as the wind lifted him almost sideways. He looked down and saw the deck angle down, the port bulwark submerged below the sea, which rose and seemed intent on gobbling him up. The man furthest out fell, his scream cut off by impact with the merciless ocean. Then the ship plunged into the wave trough and the yard shot back up, nearly throwing John off the spar. He regained his footing and the captain of the foretop bawled at his men to keep pulling in the sail. They finally secured the topsail and carefully descended.

John came below, rainwater streaming down the hatch after him. He found Davy in the galley and his friend offered him a biscuit. John chewed, thankfully. "Is quite a blow," he remarked between nibbles. The ship lurched again.

"It feels like we're gonna capsize," said Davy, fear in his voice. "Are we doomed, John?"

"I dunno, mate, but at least I won't die hungry," John replied sarcastically. "I saw a man go over the side. Did ye ever think we'd leave home and suffer the likes of this?"

"All I know is the farther we go away from Swansea, the closer we get to my da," Davy replied. "If this storm don't drown us first."

The storm passed a day later and the *Henry*, crippled with a broken foremast and shredded sails, bobbed in the sea listlessly. Captain Ross scanned the horizon with his glass. He called impatiently to the lookout, whom reported the *Sapphire* was nowhere to be seen.

Graves and Malachy were busy leading repairs. As the sailmaker and his mates brought new canvas to the main deck, Malachy's men organized the watch in splicing stays and halyards. The carpenter and his mates caulked seams that had sprung open and replaced broken bulwarks. The cooper reported several broken water casks to Graves, who cursed violently.

"We are sitting ducks," murmured Captain Ross, as Graves reported the ship's condition and relative location. "We've got to get underway and make for Mauritius, since there's no way we can beat back to Cape Town. We need water and an overhaul, Mr. Graves. Fish a yard to jury-rig the foremast. I want new sails bent by sundown."

Graves nodded. "Aye, sir."

The entire crew worked all day, taking a break only for dinner. As sundown approached, they lashed a spare main yard to the broken foremast and set two spars on it. Before they could hoist a new sail, the lookout cried, "Sail ho, four points t' the larboard!"

Captain Ross came up on deck and immediately settled his glass in the northeast. The strange sail was hull-up, with a full spread of canvas, closing fast. He realized with dread that it wasn't the *Sapphire*. She was a Spanish double-decker, with what appeared to be at least 40 gunports. "Mr. Graves! Call all hands to quarters! Clear for action!"

Graves bellowed orders and the crew halted repairs and ran to their stations. Below, Davy scurried to the armory. He met Phillips, who immediately handed him a powder bag. As Davy climbed the ladder, he met John coming down. "What's goin' on?" Davy asked.

"Some ship comin'," John replied over his shoulder as he passed. "I been sent by the bosun to help ye."

Davy squinted as the low sun caught him in its glare. He hurried over to the number four gun and handed it to one of the crew. He saw several men taking muskets out of lockers and others strapping on cutlasses. He looked at the afterdeck, where Captain Ross was still peering through his glass. He followed his gaze and a ship, far off but definitely headed in their direction. John came up on deck, arms full with two charges. "Hurry up, mate!" John shouted. "The gunner is waitin' fer ye."

When Davy came up again with another bag, the ship was even closer. It seemed to be flying a peculiar flag from the main and another from the mizzen. He anxiously handed off the charge to the impatient gun crew. A puff of smoke erupted from the strange ship, followed by a hollow report, and soon a fountain of water arose in front of the *Henry*'s bow.

"Run out the guns!" Ross bellowed. "Musketmen to the top!"

The gun crews opened the gun ports and heaved the loaded cannon forward into firing position. Several crewmen climbed the ratlines to the maintop and primed their muskets. Malachy handed Captain Ross two pistols, which he checked and then tucked into his trouser pockets.

The intruder, just out of firing range, tacked and approached *Henry* from the bow. Ross grimaced and ordered the helm brought about in an effort to present his broadside to the attacker. The ship, with only the sails on the mainmast to help, feebly began to turn. He knew it wouldn't happen in time.

The warship, now passing within point-blank range of

the bow, some 200 yards away, began firing. Malachy turned to the anxious crew and yelled, "Git dow—"

Davy, who had just stepped to the top of the ladder witnessed Malachy disappear in a red mist, the cannonball pulverizing him into nothingness. Before he could cry out, another ball whizzed by his head, the force of the wind knocking him back down the ladder along with his powder charges. He hit his head hard on the deck, and all went black.

He awoke on deck and squinted in the glare of a nearby lantern. Night had fallen, and he realized his hands were tied behind his back. He struggled to sit up and was greeted with a blinding pain in the back of his head. He blinked, trying to focus at the blurry scene of dark figures before him.

"There, there, lad," a voice whispered next to him. "Be silent. Your life depends on it." It was John Phillips. Davy managed a nod.

He looked around him, noting the shallow tide of blood that ran back and forth across the deck as the ship wallowed in the sea. Dead men were strewn about the deck, some in pieces. He recognized some of them as crew of the *Henry*, including Graves, who lay in a bloody, twisted heap. Others were wounded and suffering. He could make out a few men that were bound like he was, sitting in the dim light.

He heard boot steps, and looked toward the source. A man came toward him, his confident stride signifying complete control. As he came nearer to the light, Davy could make out his white wig supporting a tri-cornered hat. His long coat was held together, not by the buttons, but a wide leather belt holding a brace of pistols, a scabbard, and satchel-like purse. His head was bowed, as if in thought, as he paced. Then he spoke.

"Ye might be wondering what's t' become of yerselves," he began, lifting his head. Davy noticed his cold grey eyes as they scanned the defeated crew. His gaze briefly rested on Davy, who looked away in fear. "I lost a man in this little skirmish," the man continued. "And a pair got nicked up. So," he paused, running his hand over the damaged foremast. "I require payment fer our losses."

A group of pirates near the stern chuckled as they fingered their weapons and winked at each other. The man smiled and turned slowly. "We will relieve ye of yer burdensome cargo, of course. But it's able men I need. The pay is good – better than what the damned EIC gives ye! And ye will live the life of *free* men! Who will volunteer to join my crew?"

"Free?" a weak voice croaked from the darkness. Davy saw Captain Ross, clutching his belly. He addressed the pirate in a weary tone. "Free until you're caught and hanged as a low, dastardly criminal."

"Aye, perhaps," the pirate returned solemnly. "But when the sun rises, I *will* be free. And ye will be dead."

"Tis yer own fault," the pirate continued. "Ye shoulda struck yer colors when ye saw me, but, ye had to fight. And now look at ye. Yer crew is hurt, and ye are dying."

"The English Navy will find you, sir," Ross threatened. "When they do, they'll hang you and the rest of your wretched, murdering thieves." He spat at the pirate's feet.

A thickset pirate from the group at the stern rushed forward and angrily seized Captain Ross. He leaned him up against the bulwark and put a dirk to his neck, leaning in close to the captain's face. A long scar ran from his scalp down the side of his face and ended at his ear, which was half missing. "Stopper that gob!" he snarled.

"Cap'n, meet Mr. Crakehall, my quartermaster," the pirate leader smiled. "He's been at this business fer nigh on ten years," he remarked. "He don't like merchantmen, and he's the main reason we are here on yer lovely vessel t'night."

"Aye, I've heard of you," Ross said in disgust. "You were tried at Cape Corso Castle for robbery, murder and rape, but you escaped from the Crown." He turned toward the pirate leader. "Judging by the company you keep and your stolen Spanish warship, I make you to be the infamous Henry Every."

"Guilty as charged," Every said with a sweeping bow. "Now that ye all know me name, ye must also know I'm a fair man." He looked at the crew again. "I offer any man here a life o' riches and adventure, but I only make this offer once. Say 'aye' if'n ye want to share our good company."

"Don't do it, men!" Ross shouted. "You'll be traitors to the Crown and hang with the rest of these devils!"

Every sighed and irritably waved his hand at Crakehall. The big man got nose to nose with Ross and slowly drew his dirk across the captain's neck. As blood spouted from the fatal wound, Crakehall laughed hoarsely, his wild dark hair flying back and forth. He shoved pushed Ross over the rail and a splash was heard a moment later. Davy's jaw dropped and terror washed over him. Then there was silence.

Every turned slowly, gazing at the forlorn group of men on the deck. "Anyone else? Good. As I was sayin', I'll take volunteers now. Come lads, be on the winning side," he grinned.

Finally, a familiar voice said, "Aye!"

Davy gasped, realizing it was his mate, John Roberts. Every smiled and walked over to him. "Now, this here is a fine, strong, young lad! Stand up."

John struggled to his feet. Crakehall moved behind him and cut his bonds. "Welcome to the crew, bairn," he whispered in a thick, Scottish brogue. He gripped John's shoulders and shook him.

"Very good," said Every. "Anyone else?"

Davy glanced at Phillips, who shook his head. "Don't do it, lad," he implored.

Every was suddenly standing in front of Davy. "What ye do fer this ship, young'n?"

"I-I jest cook fer, fer the cap'n," Davy stammered. He looked away from Every's smile.

"Well, looks like yer unemployed," Every chuckled. Now ye can cook fer all of us, seeing as how the man I lost t'night held that job, God rest his soul." He motioned and Crakehall lifted Davy up by his shirt. "Put him into the boat, Mr. Crakehall," said Every. "The rest of ye are free to go. I bid ye farewell."

Crakehall shoved Davy and John to the side of the ship and the pirates descended to their waiting boats. As they rowed toward the pirate ship, Davy looked back at battered East Indiaman and suddenly realized the oilskin map was still aboard in its hiding place. He tried to see John's face in the darkness and wondered how soon they would die.

9

Indian Ocean

enry Every, despite his somewhat genteel demeanor, was not a man to be trifled with. He sat back in his leather-cushioned chair in his cabin, sternly studying his two new crewmembers, closely watched by a swarthy pirate. With a wave of his hand, he dismissed the guard.

The boy on his right was rather tall and broad-shouldered for his young age. The other boy was diminutive and glumly stared at the deck. Every removed his hat and wig, revealing a balding pate with reddish-brown locks. He stood up and turned his back on the two as he reflected on the stars shining clearly through his window.

"I was once like ye," he said. "Bored with the town life, longing fer adventure at sea." Several moments passed before he resumed. "The sea is a beautiful, merciless companion, lads...and ye *must* respect her. What she gives ye, she can take back on a whim and fancy."

He turned back to them. "But this here life was meant to be lived without the tyranny of kings and their officers. On *this* here ship, we are all brothers." Every slowly walked around Davy and John, hands clasped behind his back.

"Ye can ferget serving the Company. They won't trouble ye no more. As long as ye can contribute to the working of the ship, ye will receive a fair share in whatever we earn through our labors – which is most likely more than they promised to pay ye, I reckon." He chuckled softly.

Every stopped in front of the boys and put his hands on his hips. He looked at them both, then settled on John. "What were ye duties?"

John met his gaze. "Worked fer the bosun," he replied with false bravado. "I ken hand, reef, and fight."

Every cocked his head to the side. "Is that so? Well, lad, we shall see. What's yer name?"

"John Roberts."

Every turned to Davy. "What about ye? Can ye do more than help the cook and sweep a deck?"

"Well, sir, I...I learnt some things from the gunner," Davy said with a shaky voice. "I run his powder to the gun crews, and know a little about the great guns and the small arms."

Every grunted with satisfaction. He turned back to his desk.

"The only rules here are the ones we as a crew of brothers have agreed. There's no thievin' from a shipmate, no fighting a shipmate. Ye take care of yer arms, keepin' them clean and ready – when we trust ye enough to give 'em to ye. All men in this crew will fight, when the time comes, and all share equally in the spoils." He looked at John. "Well, John Roberts, do ye agree to the rules?"

"Aye, cap'n."

"Good." Every turned to Davy, bending down to look at him eye to eye. "And what's yer name, lad?"

"Davy Jones, sir."

"Davy Jones, do ye agree to the rules of this ship?"

Davy knew there could only be one answer. "Aye."

"Alright then. Ye may claim a hammock in the crew's berth. We have a Dane aboard – goes by Soren Ostergard. He will get ye settled in and learn ye the ways of the *Fancy*. Ye begin work t'morrow. Roberts, ye will serve in the tops. Jones, ye will be me steward, work the deck when called, and serve the gunner during battle. That is all."

Every turned back to the window. Davy and John left his cabin and met their guard outside the door. The dark, fierce-looking man dropped his crossed arms and jerked his head toward the ladder. Davy and John glanced at each other and followed him as he swiftly clambered up to the main deck.

The former Spanish slave ship *Fancy* was larger than their old *Henry*. Not only was it broader and longer, it carried 18 guns on its main deck, including pairs of bow and stern chasers, and another 28 guns below. Several small swivel guns were mounted along the gunwales. Unlike the EIC ship, the *Fancy* featured a flushed deck without superstructure, such as a poop deck or forecastle, lending increased speed with less wind resistance. The three tall masts sported courses, topsails, and topgallants. She was clearly built to move fast and hit hard.

The found a wiry blond man in his late twenties sitting

on the capstan reading a small, tattered book. His blue eyes darted back and forth, taking in the text. His faint smile evidenced his enjoyment as he thumbed the next page.

"Soren," the guard rumbled. He grabbed Davy and John by the shoulders, shoved them forward and then left the two.

"Ah, de new hands," Soren said, putting the book in his jacket pocket. "I am Ostergard, ship's doctor," he said with a clipped Danish accent. He looked them over. "You must be tired and hungry...and maybe a little afraid? It's fine. Let's find you something to eat and a place to sleep in de berthing."

He led them down to the empty galley and grabbed a few biscuits. "Mr. Mayo won't mind," he remarked. He handed them over to Davy and John and rummaged through the cupboards until he found a pair of flagons. He poured them ale and stood while they devoured their meal. After they finished, he escorted them to the crew's berthing and handed them hammocks from a chest. "Rest now, but be up at de first light." With that, he sauntered off.

Davy and John stood in silence. Finally, John spoke. "Sorry I got ye in this mess, Davy."

"Why did ye offer yerself to these pirates, John? What were ye thinkin'?"

"I dunno," John admitted. "I suppose it struck me fancy to live the life of a pirate. Lookee, Davy, mebbe this is what we're destined fer – a life free."

Davy shot him an angry look. "Ye don't believe that crap do ye? Didn't ye hear Cap'n Ross? We're both gonna hang, fer sure!"

John scowled. "Nah. We'll be alright. This is what I've dreamed about, Davy. We ken ferget the past – all of it. That miserable town, Swansea, with it's shitty weather and shitty people. We ken be men o' fortune!"

"Men o' fortune! That's what ye think? Most likely we'll be dead men, mark me words," Davy retorted. He thought about how his prospects for finding his father were now uncertain. *No telling where this pirate ship will take me.*

"Bah!" John waved, dismissively. "Let's git some shut-eye, while we ken." They rigged their hammocks between the beams and went to sleep without another word.

The next morning, they were aroused by the thumping of feet as men got out of their hammocks. Davy sleepily rolled over, but suddenly he dropped to the deck, hammock and all.

"Git up, ye lubber!" croaked Crakehall. Bewildered, Davy saw the huge quartermaster leering over him, dirk in hand. "There's work t' do, an' if ye can't git out o' that hammock, ye git cut down. Now, git t' the galley an' make breakfast fer the cap'n." He stalked off, and Davy shakily rose to his feet as the deck swayed under him.

He found the galley and surveyed the contents, trying to figure out what he would serve Captain Every. Mayo, the cook, was nowhere to be found. There was hard tack, salted pork, a tin of ancient-looking sauerkraut, dried peas, and a few herbs. Davy went to the hold in search of livestock, and snatched a piglet from an ornery sow. He lit the galley fire and set a pot with fresh water to boil. He butchered the swine and set it on a spit next to the cauldron. When the water reached a rolling boil, he dropped in the sauerkraut, some peas, and a few pieces of the salted pork. He also threw in some pepper, garlic roots and sage. When the chunks of pig flesh were properly roasted, he heaped them on a platter next to a steaming bowl of the stew. Lastly, he fetched a bottle of rum.

Captain Every was sharpening his cutlass when Davy entered with the meal. He observed the boy as he laid the table. "Very good, lad," he remarked, hanging the cutlass on a hook. "I'll have a portion of this pig, and send the rest to the crew's mess. We all share, here on the *Fancy*." He took a few slices of the pork and scooted the platter away. Davy set the bottle down.

"Aye, cap'n," he said rather meekly. He grabbed the platter and quickly departed the cabin. He brought the pork to the crew's mess and set it on the suspended table, whereupon the crew immediately attacked it. Davy retreated to the galley.

Sitting glumly on a stool, Davy was thinking about his new life when John entered the small galley. Seeing his troubled friend, he thumped the galley stove. "Avast that sour face," he quipped.

"Bugger off," Davy mumbled. He couldn't get over how easily John seemed to take to the pirate life. It was one thing for his mate to want to travel the world, but it was quite another to become a sea-going brigand, he thought.

"Cheer up, mate. Let's go topside and get a breath o' fresh air. I could use a piss," said John merrily. He grabbed Davy by the collar and led his protesting friend to the ladder.

The warm, humid air struck them fully as the sun climbed the clear eastern sky. The ship was cruising along at a brisk ten knots, topsails and courses drawing the southeastern prevailing winds as the *Fancy* headed north, keeping within sight of the African coastline.

As they walked toward the bow, they beheld a strange sight. One of the pirates was straddling the bowsprit, holding what appeared to be a long spear with a length of line, and peering intently down into the water. Intrigued, they stopped at the head rail and followed his gaze.

Seeing nothing but water, John asked, "What ye doin'?"

The man lifted his bandana-covered head briefly, and without looking at them said, "Fishing."

John and Davy scratched their heads and continued to watch, alternating between the strange man and the water below. Then they saw it. A fish with wings flew out of the water, remaining airborne for several seconds just ahead of the bow. The man cast his spear and expertly lanced the flier. "Ah!" he cried.

As he pulled up his line and grabbed the strange creature, Davy asked, "What manner of fish is that?"

"'Tis a flying fish," the man replied as he secured his catch in a canvas bag. "You the new captain's steward?"

"Aye," Davy responded. "Davy Jones."

"Well, Mr. Jones, I am John Dann, coxswain. Here's a fish for the captain. You can fry this up for his dinner?"

Davy paused, thinking of the leftover fat from the pig. "Aye. This here is me mate, John Roberts."

Dann climbed down from the bowsprit, set down his bag, and stuck out his hand. "Pleasure to meet ya both."

Relieved at having met a somewhat amiable pirate, Davy and John shook his hand. He appeared to be in his mid-twenties, with green eyes and wisps of blonde hair. He was a bit short, but lean with tanned, muscular limbs. Dann offered the bag to Davy and then headed aft. The two boys shared quizzical looks, then shrugged and went to the ship's head to relieve themselves.

"See? It ain't so bad," John remarked, opening his breeches.

"Mebbe," Davy said thoughtfully. "That man Dann and Soren seem to be a good lot. I wonder how they got in with this bunch of villains?"

The *Fancy* anchored off Madagascar under hazy skies and a low swell from the southwest. Davy and John spent each day in the company of Soren Ostergard, and occasionally John Dann, learning how to read from the former and how the ship's boats worked from the latter. They dodged Bones Crakehall when they could. Davy continued to serve Every, who seemed to spend most of his time either reading charts or writing. The pirate captain rarely spoke more than a few words to Davy, but often consulted with Crakehall in his cabin or on deck.

The ship bought provisions from the local tribe, and the crew – except Davy and John, who were not yet trusted to be on their own – went ashore for rest and merriment. The African natives were generally agreeable and had traded with Europeans regularly. The crew loaded up on fresh water, fruit and coconuts, and sundry items. The carpenter's men repaired a few minor blemishes to the hull and gunwales caused by the recent action with the *Henry*. But certain stores were not to be found there, so a day later the *Fancy* sailed for Johanna in the Comoros island group north of Madagascar. This time, Every decided to allow Davy and John to go ashore under escort with Soren and John Dann.

Johanna was a lovely place with little in the way of civilization, but rather a beautiful stretch of beach dotted with a few huts inhabited with semi-retired pirates – those who currently didn't have a ship to call home. The men of the *Fancy* made bonfires and drank excessively from the rum and brandy they'd brought from the ship. Pigs were roasted and a score of native women provided music, dancing and intimate entertainment.

John basked in the light of the fire as darkness fell on the beach. Davy, sitting next to him, watched Dann and Ostergard dancing with the women. He took a sip from a pot of Gabonese honey and eyed his friend, who seemed to be enjoying himself.

"John, I still canna believe yer takin' to this pirate life," he began.

"Davy, Davy," John interrupted, waving his hand dismissively. "How ken ye be so stiff? Lookee where we is, on this here fine beach with them fine ladies...well, women, anyways. What's to complain about?"

"It's not always gonna be this way, John," Davy warned.

"Ah, clap a stopper on it," John retorted with a smile. He got up and tossed a piece of driftwood into the fire and took a deep swig from a bottle of rum. Swaying a bit, he held out his arms and grinned. "This here is the life!"

He spun around in circles, giggling like a schoolboy who

had gotten away with breaking some sacred rule. As he twisted around, his hand smacked a passing pirate right in the face. Davy didn't recognize him as a *Fancy* crewmember. The brute snarled and grabbed John by his shirt.

"Ye strikin' me, lad?" he hissed.

"Oh, um, sorry?" John replied shakily. Mustering up his courage, he said, "I dinna mean to hit ye, but yer big fuckin' beak got in me way."

The ugly pirate regarded him for a moment, scrunched his face in anger, and threw John to the ground. He jabbed his finger at him. "Ye best take that back, ye little worm, or I'll smash ye like the pile o' flotsam ye are!"

John shot to his feet, rage burning his cheeks. "Well, which is it, ye daft bastard? Am I a worm or flotsam?" he mocked.

The pirate roared and threw a roundhouse punch, but John ducked and drove his shoulder into him. They fell to the ground and grappled.

Davy, afraid for his friend's life, called out to him to stop, but John was heedless. A moment later, Soren and John Dann appeared.

"Avast!" Dann shouted. He moved toward the writhing combatants and tried to pull them apart. Unable to do so, he grabbed John and put him in a headlock. Soren grabbed John's arm and together he and Dann managed to get John disentangled. John flailed, still trying to strike the pirate. The big man stood and grabbed his dirk.

"I'll gut ye like a fish!" he screeched. He advanced menacingly, cutting the air in front of him. A loud report blasted the night air and his chest exploded with blood. He fell to the ground wordlessly. Everyone looked to the source of the smoking gun, held by the trembling Davy Jones.

The merriment on the beach ceased. Soren slowly took the pistol from Davy's outstretched hand. John Dann looked down and realized Davy had removed the pistol from his belt sometime during the tussle. "Lad, ye are in big trouble now," he said. He looked down at John. "Both of ye."

"Let's get back to de ship," the doctor said quietly. "We have to report this to de captain." The four tramped to one of the boats.

Captain Every was not amused by the story. He got up from his desk and stood in front of Davy and John. "So ye picked a fight," he said, jabbing his finger at John's chest. "And ye shot a brother-in-arms," he glared at Davy.

The boys said nothing and stared at the deck.

"First day ashore, and this is what I am to expect of ye?" Every shook his head.

Soren spoke up. "De scoundrel started de fight. It was a mistake, wasn't it, lads?"

John nodded. "Aye, cap'n. The lout came at me, and..."

"Silence!" Every shouted. "'Tis a good thing he wasn't a man of this crew, or ye would be digging yer own graves." He sat down behind his desk and folded his hands under his chin, studying the two boys. He looked at John Dann and Soren Ostergard. "Ye vouch fer these two?"

"Aye, cap'n," they said in unison.

Every looked down, thoughtfully. He looked back at Davy and John. "Ye best save yer tempers fer the action. Fer now ye will stay aboard the ship until I says ye can leave. All ye go, but Mr. Dann. I'll have a word with ye."

Davy sighed in relief and they left the cabin. The three retreated to the crew's berthing and slung their hammocks.

"John," Davy whispered. "I canna do this. I gotta escape somehow."

John looked at his friend wearily. "Davy, we canna go back."

Soren, overhearing them, came over. "Look, lads. You're part of de brotherhood now. Take this day as a lesson. There's nowhere to escape, and besides, we're all you have now."

Davy blushed in shame. The future looked dark.

After a few days, Every called the hands to the deck to make an announcement.

"Men, in our adventures we've seized brandy, wool, rice, silks and such, but little in the way of gold. Now, I've received certain intelligence that there is a good prize to be had, and after I consulted with our dear quartermaster, I come to set it before ye fer a vote," Every began.

A general grunt of satisfaction was heard among the pirates. Davy looked at John apprehensively, but his friend just smiled.

"Acquaintances of mine report the Mohguls be visiting the holy places by way of the Red Sea, and they be carrying riches back to Surrat – the kinda riches that are shiny and clink together in yer pocket." He paused while the crew laughed. "With your agreement, I intend to sail in consort with these friends – by the names of Captain Want and

Captain Faro – and attack the Moghul convoy."

Finding the sentiment among the pirate crew encouraging, Every put the proposal to a vote. The crew voiced their approval, and Every declared they would sail the next morning and join the two other ships.

Every searched the dispersing crew, his eyes finally resting on Davy Jones. The lad would bear keeping an eye on, he thought.

Northeast of Madagascar, Indian Ocean

"Yer sure that's the one?"

"Aye, a pretty little jewel, she is. This here is Silhouette Island."

Captain Thomas Tew lowered his spyglass and regarded his captive guide through slitted eyes. "Very well, Morgan Gwynn. I hope ye are right, or I'll be sendin' ye to hell meself."

The pirate brigantine had weathered the long trip around the Horn of Africa and past Madagascar to finally reach a group of uninhabited islands. Now, it was time to find Captain Kidd's long-lost treasure. Tew's men, suspicious by nature, had trusted their leader so far, but their impatience was growing. He needed results, or he'd be ousted for someone else – if they didn't kill him first.

Wyn felt the pressure even more, although he didn't show it. His gamble to stay alive had worked up to now, but his mind was furiously working to solve the end game. "Ye could search fer it yer whole blasted life an' never find it," he declared. "I'll take ye to it, but first I need a deal."

Tew smiled. "I'm all ears, Morgan."

"I claim my share – since it were part mine in the first place – and a guarantee I'll live to spend it."

"If there's as much there as ye say there is," Tew responded, "then I can part with a small portion. That is," he turned to his crew, who were listening with rapt attention, "if my brothers agree. What say ye, gennelmen?"

The pirates murmured to each other, some nodding and others shaking their heads. Finally, Shipwreck Tom spoke up.

"He ain't one of us, but he kept his word and led us here," he said. "But mebbe there's no prize ashore. I says," he looked to the men around him, "if he is true and leads us to it, we let bygones be bygones. He ken have his share and we part ways peaceably after we put him ashore somewheres. But if'n he is false, well..."

"I'll take ye swabs right to the very spot," Wyn answered. "All ye here will live like kings. I jest ask fer my share."

Tew spoke up. "Let's put it to the vote. All in favor of lettin' Morgan here have a share, say 'aye'."

A lusty chorus answered him. Tew noted the supporting votes.

"Opposed?"

Wyn closed his eyes and breathed deeply. He heard nothing but sea birds.

The crew of the *Fancy* had swollen to nearly 150 men with the addition of several marooned French privateers on Johanna. Along with Danes, Scotsmen, Irishmen and English merchantmen they'd picked up during their cruise in the past few months along the African coast, Every now commanded a sizeable ship's company. Although they had run down a Chinese junk, a few Arab trading dhows and a slave ship, Every refused to take a single dark-skinned man aboard, preferring the company of white Europeans.

Two armed sloops accompanied them, each sporting six guns and nimble maneuverability. The two captains, Richard Want of the six-gun Spanish brigantine *Dolphin* and Joseph Faro of the six-gun brig *Portsmouth Adventure*, came aboard and discussed plans. They decided to wait for the Moghul convoy at the mouth of the Red Sea near the island of Liparan. Under cover of darkness, they would sail into their midst and pick off the Grand Moghul's flagship. What they didn't know is how many ships would be in the convoy, nor how well they may be armed. But this didn't daunt Every, who figured his men would intimidate and overpower their dusky prey, just like they had easily taken the dhows.

As the ships cruised northeast to their rendezvous, Davy and John quietly learned the ways of the pirate vessel and her motley crew. John Dann took Roberts under his wing and taught him how to maintain and operate the boats, while Davy, between serving meals to Every, found himself apprenticed to the gunner, Angus Morgan.

Morgan was an enormous, hairy beast. Standing well over six feet tall, he was also the oldest man on the *Fancy*. Davy reckoned him to be near 50. Called "Iron Ball" by the crew, Morgan wore a goatskin vest over his furry chest and vast, black cowhide breeches. Like most of the men, he was barefoot. His shaved head was deeply tanned and littered with numerous white scars, as was much of his visible body. An enormous fleshy scar flashed angrily from his throat, perhaps the reason why he spoke with a hoarse rasp. Perhaps his most defining feature was his enormous arms, which hung like ancient tree limbs from his massive trunk. Clearly, he was a battle-tested veteran, a hulking menace among a band of nefarious men. Davy was scared for his life.

Upon meeting Iron Ball, Davy realized from his familiar Welsh dialect that he also was from the south of Wales, probably Cardiff – not that it seemed to matter to the gunner, who said nothing of his past. The big man spoke quietly, but with great authority and economy. Even Crakehall seemed to defer to him.

As they approached the armory, Iron Ball halted at the door and gently caressed a bird's claw nailed to the bulkhead. He motioned to Davy to do the same. "Fer luck," was all he said.

Davy learned where the small arms were stored and how the powder was kept. Iron Ball didn't say more than was necessary, seemingly protective of his realm. He did have one command for Davy. "Ye will carry not one, but two bags o' powder to my beloved great guns, lad, ye hear?"

Davy gulped. "Aye." He wondered how he was going to manage this feat. The bags were a considerable weight for his scrawny arms, and climbing the ladder thus encumbered seemed a daunting prospect. Understanding this, the gunner showed Davy a sling harness he had developed to carry cartridges around his chest and back like a yoke.

When Davy demonstrated his knowledge of gunpowder and small arms, Iron Ball nodded with satisfaction, apparently relieved he wouldn't have to begin from scratch with this new boy. They went up to the gun deck below the main, and Iron Ball presented Davy the row of cannons bowsed tightly to the bulkhead. He called to his three mates, who were tending another gun. The three pirates grabbed the train tackles on one side of the 36-pounder, and Iron Ball handled the tackles of the other side himself. Then, to Davy's sheer amazement, the four men hauled the cannon into loading position.

"How did ye do that?" Davy blurted out.

Iron Ball ignored his query and opened the gun port as the three pirates chuckled. The gunner waved the men off, and they resumed their work on the other side of the deck.

"Yer target is a two-decker merchant, veerin' away under full sail at nine knots an' presentin' her stabboard quarter as she crosses yer sight. She's at two hunnert yards an' reachin'." He picked up the quoin and handed it to Davy. "Double-shotted. Aim."

Baffled, Davy hesitantly bent down and peered along the length of the great gun. He realized the gunner was expecting a response, not an excuse, so he took a deep breath, briefly closed his eyes and envisioned his quarry.

"Two hunnert an' twenty," said Iron Ball.

Davy calculated the rapidly expanding distance, angle, velocity of the projectiles with the proper amount of powder, and specific aim point. He jammed the quoin below the breech and pounded it twice with a hammer. Then he tapped it gingerly and stood up. "Ready to fire, Gunner," he reported.

"Yer aimin' fer the mizzen top's'l yard at the crossjack," Iron Ball stated approvingly.

Davy nodded, astonished.

"Not a bad notion, to be sure," Iron Ball commented, "but if ye really want to cripple 'er, ye aim fer the rudder pintle. See 'ere." He bent down and grasped the quoin in his meaty fist. He wiggled it back about half an inch and the gun settled slightly. Still astounded at the man's strength, Davy looked along the sight line and saw how the great gun was aimed exactly where he imagined Iron Ball's calculation rested. He stood up, grinning.

"Very well," Iron Ball said. "Let's try another."

Hours later, Davy was in the galley preparing Captain Every's dinner. He opened the porthole to get some fresh air into the stuffy compartment when John sauntered in with wide smile.

"Hello, mate," he said cheerfully.

Davy regarded his friend with arched brow. "What ye been up to?" he asked. "Ye look like ye stole the cheese from the mouse."

"Oh, nuttin' much," John drawled in mock disinterest. "Jest duelin' with that man they call 'Bones'." He smiled again, unable to contain his mirth.

"What?! The hell, you say! And ye live to tell me?"

John nodded, waiting for his friend to take the bait.

Exasperated, Davy punched John in the shoulder. "Do tell, Mr. Roberts."

"He's teachin' me how to use the sword," John replied excitedly. He went on to explain that he and Crakehall practiced the art of close combat with the blade to a rapt Davy.

"And that's how it is," he finished.

Davy shook his head. "And here I thought he were the devil."

John shrugged. "That quartermaster ain't so bad, once ye git to know him." He ruefully rubbed his rump. "Of course, I spent half the time on the deck."

The laughed uproariously, until Davy remembered he had neglected the Every's dinner. They parted ways and Davy hurried to serve the meal.

Silhouette Island

Two boats put off from the *Amity,* Tew and Wyn together in one with six men, and Shipwreck Tom leading the other crew. Each was laden with picks, shovels, camp equipment and small arms. Although Wyn had said nothing about digging for the treasure, Tew wasn't taking any chances.

They passed over a submerged coral reef, coasted through the gentle, crystal-clear surf, and grounded on soft, white sand. Tew immediately jumped out and scanned the dense foliage. Wyn joined him a moment later.

"There ain't a soul here," Wyn remarked. "'Tis the reason Kidd chose this spot."

Tew grunted in reply as he took stock of the surroundings. The thick jungle, comprised mostly of palm trees, ferns, and various flower species, covered most of what he could see of the island. Kestrels flew overhead, drawing his attention to several mountain peaks well over a thousand feet high. He saw a giant tortoise sunning itself a few yards away among the large boulders that dotted the beach and made a mental note to have the men bring it aboard for supper when they left, regardless of whether they were done searching for the lost treasure. He loved turtle soup.

"Very well, Morgan, lead the way."

Wyn glanced at the mid-day sun and stumped off into the primeval forest, Tew and Shipwreck Tom close behind, with the rest of the pirates following in single file.

The ground became steep and the jungle more humid as they climbed through the dense vegetation. Wyn requested a cutlass and Tew reluctantly agreed when it became clear they would need to cut a path through the wall of plant growth.

Stinging flies, clouds of gnats and bloodthirsty mosquitoes descended upon them like a plague, causing the men to constantly slap and swat them away. After two grueling hours, Tew called for a break. The men immediately drank from their flasks – some containing water, others rum – and grumbled.

"Now brothers," Tew began, "I know it's a pain in the arse, but it'll be worth it when we're bathin' in gold an' jewels."

The pirates scoffed and grunted.

"How much further?" Shipwreck Tom asked. "These damned bugs are gonna eat us alive."

"Did ye expect it to be easy?" Wyn retorted. "Kidd had a king's ransom, and he hid it well."

A large red moth landed on Shipwreck Tom's shoulder. Startled, he jumped back and brushed it off, causing the men to howl with laughter. Cursing, he glared at them. "Bugger off, ye swabs!"

Tew smiled and cocked his head toward Wyn. "Where to from here?"

Wyn sighed and slapped away a mosquito. "We gots a ways to go. There's a gulley just over this here rise, and then it gets tough. I ain't sayin' no more, but I reckon by the time we get there we'll need to make camp."

Tew nodded. "Right. Well now, Morgan, I hope ye ain't leadin' us on some wild goose chase."

Wyn scoffed. "I ain't doin' this fer the fun of it."

"Aye, well then let's get to it," said Tew impatiently.

Hours later the pirates reached the bottom of a gully. A heavy mist clung to their clothes as they set up camp next to a small, meandering river. Fruit bats flew overhead and the air was thick. Tree frogs struck up a chorus of croaks, causing many of the pirates to gaze about in fear at this unfamiliar sound.

"This place don't feel right," said one of the pirates.

"Is they spirits?" another asked, glancing at the trees fearfully.

"Ain't nothin' but some kinda bird," Tew replied, a bit uneasily. "Now let's get a fire goin'."

Wyn sat on his haunches and watched the pirates gather dead wood and bark with a bemused smile. After several attempts to light some shavings, Shipwreck Tom complained, "Ain't no use. The wood's too wet."

Wyn guffawed. "Of course it is, ye idiots."

"That's enough outta ye, Morgan," Tew warned. "Make fast a line to them trees and rig the tarps fer shelter," he told the men. "We'll do without the fire."

The men grumbled as they set about the work. When it was done, they opened their packs and greedily dug into their rations of salt pork and ship's biscuit.

Tew ordered two men to set a watch, "Jest in case someone gets an idea of runnin'."

Wyn rolled his eyes. "Now where would I go? Ye think I'm gonna swim away?"

Tew leaned over and whispered to him. "Nah. I know ye wants this treasure as much as the rest of us. It's to keep them," he jerked his head toward the rest of the crew, "from bein' spooked."

Wyn regarded his captors with contempt. "Buncha pansies."

"Now ye stop that gob or I'll gag ye," Tew snarled. "Behave

yerself, or I'll lash ye to a tree."

Wyn scoffed and looked away. He studied the surrounding hillside and occasionally stole glances at Tew and his men. Satisfied, he closed his eyes and bided his time.

Long shadows quickly became night in the deep gulley. Soon, bats were seen overhead, flitting and whirling among the trees. Tew's men huddled under the makeshift shelters, some trading sea stories and others smoking pipes. Tew himself ambled about the campsite, making sure the two men on watch at either end were awake and alert.

Wyn leaned against a tree and pretended to sleep. He opened his eyes from time to time, noting the disposition of the pirates.

A couple of hours past sunset the men began to lay down and one by one, they descended to slumber. Even Tew, after ensuring Wyn was asleep, eventually found a spot under one of the tarps and reclined, keeping one hand on his flintlock pistol.

Wyn waited. A quarter moon shone down through small openings in the canopy of trees, but otherwise it was as dark as a ship's hold at night. One guard had already nodded off and the other seemed preoccupied with a piece of wood he was carving with a dirk.

Wyn slowly rolled over to his hands and knees and crept out of the camp without a sound. He'd barely made more than a few yards through the dense foliage when he heard a cry from the watch, alerting the pirates that he had escaped.

Damn my eyes, he cursed to himself. *If'n I'd waited a wee bit longer...*

Red Sea

Weeks later, the *Fancy* arrived at Liparan Island, and hove to in the narrow Bab al-Mandab Strait. As the sun went down and twilight commenced, a cry was heard from the masthead. The crew rushed to the main deck and listened as Every took the report from Crakehall. Three unknown sails were seen in the southwest, closing fast.

Every took up his telescope and trained it on the strangers. Satisfied, he snapped it shut and ordered the men to stand down, but be ready to go to battle at a moment's notice.

The newcomers turned out to be fellow brigands from the pirate haven in Libertalia, Madagascar. They hove to nearby and put off boats to the *Fancy*. Every stood at the side and welcomed aboard a group of rough-looking men.

They turned out to be Captain Thomas Wake of the 10-gun barque *Susanna*, Captain William Mays of the 16-gun brigantine *Pearl*, and Captain Thomas Tew of the eight-gun sloop *Amity*. All three ships were originally from the English colonies in America and together they had close to 200 pirates.

Captains Want and Faro also came aboard and together they crowded into the cabin for a conference. They agreed to partner in the attack on the Moghul convoy, with Every as the leader of the squadron. For now, they would anchor and wait off Liparan, with the Arabian land mass a mere mile or so to the east.

Davy and John kept busy. John had a relentless appetite for swordplay and close quarter fighting tactics. When he wasn't squaring off with Crakehall, he was learning how to dodge and grapple with Dann, who, despite his lithe form, turned out to be as slippery as an eel and twice as hard to pin down.

Dann also taught John the basics of the ship's boats, including the pinnace and long boat. He told him the differences between the two, and how the pirates used them in attacking prey at sea and ashore. John was enthralled as Dann regaled him with stories of cutting-out expeditions and sneaky attacks on ships at anchor during night raids.

Davy, on the other hand, was pulling triple duty. Three times a day he prepared and served meals to Every, who often merely pecked at them as he poured over maps and frequently paced the deck, waiting for a cry from the lookout.

Between morning and noon meals, Davy practiced musketry with Iron Ball. They set up bottles on the taffrail and shot them from a variety of positions on the mizzen and main masts. The gunner showed Davy how to load, aim, and breathe before firing. After a few dozen rounds, Davy began to hit the small, glass targets, much to Iron Ball's satisfaction.

In the afternoons, Davy met with Soren in the orlop, a place where the Danish doctor practiced his medical skills. Using his assistant, Thomas Hollingsworth, Soren demonstrated various methods of stopping blood flow to wounded extremities and how to properly suture and bandage. He also discussed basic anatomy and where the vital organs were located.

Davy enjoyed learning from Iron Ball and Soren. He felt, for the first time, he was a real member of the crew – villains though they were. Although he still missed his father, who was in the clutches of Tew (whom he didn't know had briefly come aboard for the meeting with Every), he began to feel – despite himself – kinship for these sea robbers. He had to remind himself these were the same men who killed the honest sailors of the *Henry*, including his friend Malachy.

Several days passed, and Every ordered Dann to take the pinnace north further into the Red Sea to discover the location of the Moghul convoy. John joined him and a half dozen other pirates as the boat put off. He waved to Davy, who watched him with dismay as he slowly faded into the distant haze.

Another two days came and went, with no sight of the pinnace. Captain Tew came aboard and met Every in his cabin. Tew had success in this same area three years ago, taking a richly laden and heavily armed Ghanjah dhow, and Every valued his wisdom.

As the two chatted amiably, Davy entered with dinner. Serving a suckling pig, tropical vegetables and Madeira wine, Davy nervously avoided the leering gaze of the guest, whom he still didn't know by name. The pirate captain was easily the ugliest man Davey had ever seen, worse even than the bully back in Swansea. As he finished pouring wine into Tew's goblet, the hideous pirate grabbed Davy's sleeve and pulled him close.

"What's a fine young lad like you doin' here?" he rasped. The corners of his crooked mouth turned up in a lascivious grin. Horrified, Davy pleadingly looked at Every, who furrowed his brow but remained silent.

"Ye plenty of men, Henry. Ye should let me have 'im," Tew drawled. "I be needin' a steward fer me cabin. I'm bettin' this little one knows how to keep it nice an' warm, eh?" he snickered.

"That's enough, Captain Tew," Every warned. "Ye ferget yerself. Let him go."

Davy's eyes widened in horror at the mention of Tew's name. *So this is the man who has me da!*

Tew's grin vanished. He turned his head toward Every while tightening his hold on Davy. "Consider it a gift in exchange fer me knowledge of this here seas. Besides," he added, his voice rising menacingly, "this one strikes me fancy and no harm done with one less scamp aboard yer fine, big warship."

Captain Every stood up and rested his hand on his sword hilt. "I don't think you heard me, *Captain* Tew. He's a member of *this* crew, and" he paused a moment, "experienced with killing."

Tew turned back to Davy, regarding him for a moment. "So not the virgin after all." He released his grip and Davy quickly retreated to the galley. He sat down on his little stool, trembling with fear and disgust. He soon grew angry and summoned his courage. He stood outside Every's door and listened to their conversation.

"Speakin' of killin'," said Tew, "I had to execute a mutineer last week."

"Oh?" Every replied, disinterestedly.

"Aye. An old shipmate by the name of Morgan Wynn. Quite the character," remarked Tew.

"So you had some problems with yer crew?"

"Nay, nay," said Tew hastily. "Jest that one. My crew is loyal, ye needn't worry."

"Very well. We need to work as a team for this attack," said Every. He went on to query Tew about his last encounter with the Moghul fleet.

Davy retreated back to the galley and unclenched his fists. He heard Tew depart Every's cabin moments later. Davy felt hot with rage. He took a deep breath and opened the porthole for fresh air. The encounter left him feeling nauseous. As he stood there, shaking, he heard Every call him. He took another deep breath and reported to the captain.

Every motioned to him to sit down. Davy plopped down in the chair, eyes downcast. Every studied him for a moment and said, "Take a glass of wine. I apologize for the rudeness of our guest. He will not dine at my table again."

Davy reached for the wine and took a big gulp. Every watched him carefully. "In fact, if you encounter him again and he makes unwanted advances, you have my permission to stick your dirk in his sorry hide." Surprised, Davy uttered, "Aye, captain."

Every dismissed him, and Davy went up to the main deck. The stars were glinting and the sliver of moon reminded Davy it was time for a swim. Davy looked around furtively. Only a couple of pirates were on deck, chatting away at the helm, so he slipped over the side and quietly climbed down into the warm water. It felt delicious. He ducked his head and swam underwater for some time, enjoying the feel of the salty sea. He felt like he could just bask in the embrace of the ocean, and part of him never wanted to come up again to the ugliness of the world on the surface. Eventually he did rise, breathing deeply while he treaded. A calmness descended on him and he closed his eyes to feel the fullness of peace.

Then he felt a presence and he looked around him. The darkness yielded nothing. Panicking, he realized he'd lost sight of the ship. He couldn't get his bearings. *O cach! Now here's a fine mess ye got yerself into*, he thought. His medallion began to vibrate and he knew something was happening, he just wasn't sure what. He whirled around in the water, vainly trying to find...what? He felt something like fingers brush his kicking legs and his eyes widened in fear. Was it a shark? The medallion grew warm and fairly hummed against his submerged chest.

He knew he couldn't stay in this spot any longer. He looked up at the sliver of moon, trying to remember where it was when he left the ship. When he looked back down, he saw a dark shape emerge from the water, only a few feet away. He couldn't be sure, but he thought it might be the head of a person. There seemed to be long, stringy hair, but he could not see a face. The medallion throbbed.

"Who are ye?" Davy whispered. The figure said nothing but remained where it was. Davy's fear began to subside when he realized the thing, whatever it was, didn't seem threatening.

"I'm lost. I canna find me way back to the ship," said Davy to the dark form. He didn't know why he felt compelled to confide to the form, but it cocked its head to the side in a gesture that seemed to mean that it was at least listening to him. "Can ye help me?"

The shape suddenly disappeared under the water and then reappeared a few moments later a few yards further. He saw its arm rise from the water and motion to him. Fascinated, Davy slowly swam toward it. The figure turned its head and Davy thought he caught a glimpse of a woman's face. Then she rose a bit further out of the water and he briefly saw a slender back as the creature dived into the water and a wide, fluked tail flipped up. It was shaped like a whale, Davy thought, but much smaller. But it too vanished beneath the waves and he was left alone. By impulse he began to swim in the direction the woman (or fish?) seemed to have been, and then he saw her pop up again, barely visible in the starlight. Now he knew he must follow her, wherever she was leading. He swam on the surface of the sea, keeping an eye open for her. He was relieved to see her rise again, look at him, and then dive beneath the waves.

He followed her for some time, and eventually when she rose again, she stopped. Davy paused as well, waiting for her to move. Then she lifted her arm out of the water and pointed. He turned his head in the direction of her outstretched finger and saw the *Fancy*, only a cable's length away. He smiled broadly.

"Thankee!" he cried, but the woman had disappeared again. He waited, but she did not return. A faint purple was visible in the eastern sky. Dawn was approaching, and Davy knew he had to get back under the cover of darkness. He took a breath and dived.

Davy was tired the next day, but he had his duties to perform. He served Captain Every's breakfast, cleaned up and reported to Iron Ball for his daily musket practice. But as they were sitting on the yardarm of the mizzen topsail, they heard a cry from the lookout. It was the pinnace! Iron Ball dismissed Davy – with a promise that he would return for his sharpshooting practice – and he promptly slid down a backstay to the main deck.

As the boat approached, Davy saw John heave in the sail. He waved and caught his friend's eye, who returned his greetings. Dann came aboard first and immediately reported to Every. They went below to the captain's cabin to debrief the mission. The rest of the boat crew came up the side and John smiled broadly as Davy embraced his sunburnt friend.

John told him they had stopped two fishing dhows and queried their small crews. According to the fishermen, the Moghul convoy had indeed departed Mocha and was sailing in their direction. Their quarry would be in range soon, perhaps a couple days.

Every came up on deck and ordered Crakehall to signal the pirate fleet to head west about three leagues toward the wider channel, where he assumed the fleet must pass. The *Fancy* crew, buoyed by the news, swung into action. Sails were loosed and soon the *Fancy*, followed by the other ships, was plowing along with a following sea.

Davy returned to the mizzen to resume his lessons with Iron Ball, who seemed not the least bit concerned when the excited boy told him the news. Three hours later Iron Ball dismissed Davy for the day, but warned him that should they encounter action, he was to report to him in the armory at once.

Davy met John on the main deck where he was caulking the seams of the hoisted pinnace with oakum. "Bloody thing leaked like billy-o," John remarked. "Spent half me time bailin'."

The two chatted as John worked, which Dann didn't seem to mind. They ruefully recalled how Elijah Graves would likely have caned them for such simple conversation. Inevitably, the topic of the impending rendezvous with the Moghul fleet came up.

"The coxsun says I'm to be with the boardin' party," John remarked. "What are ye doin'?"

"Iron Ball has me in the armory," Davy replied. "Gotta run the powder up to the guns. He says when the broadsides are done, I'm to climb the mizzen with a musket and shoot the enemy – until we win, I reckon."

"Well, I'm glad ye won't be down in the melee," John said. "But I won't mind if ye watch me back." The two chuckled a bit nervously.

"Don't worry, mate," Davy said reassuringly. "I'll be observin' yer arse."

They laughed again and then grew silent. They both knew that death lay just over the horizon.

Davy turned to John. "There's somethin' I needs to tell ye, John."

John recognized the somber tone in Davy's voice. He nodded. "What is it?"

"That man, Captain Tew, he's the one that kidnapped me da. I heard him say he killed him."

"Then that fuckin' swine must die," declared John through clenched teeth.

"Aye, mate," Davy answered. "I don't know how, or when I will get the chance."

"We'll find a way," said John firmly. "A lot of things can happen during a fight."

Red Sea

Two days passed and Captain Every ordered Dann to take the pinnace out again, this time to spy the exact route the Moghul convoy was taking. There could be only two choices: the fleet would either hug the coast and pass by the narrow strait east of Liparan, or they would choose the wider channel out of the Red Sea west of the island.

The pinnace returned two nights later. Dann reported the convoy was heading down, staying out in the middle. Every decided to keep his fleet where it was and wait under the cover of Liparan, windward of where he expected his prey in about a day or so. He told the crew their principal target was the Grand Moghul's ship, the 1,600-ton *Ganj-i-Sawai.*

"*Gunsway?*" John said.

Davy shrugged. "That's what I heard."

According to the Arab fisherman Dann interrogated a few

days ago, this vessel would yield the largest amount of treasure. Additionally, there might be important members of the royal court aboard, which would make for excellent ransom. Other ships would be snapped up as the opportunity presented itself, but Every knew there had to be at least one or two warships in escort. In discussion with the other captains, Every devised a plan to send *Amity*, *Portsmouth Adventure*, *Susanna* and the *Dolphin* after the escorts to distract them while the *Fancy* and the *Pearl* took the main prize. They agreed to share all spoils among the ships participating in the raid.

The tension among the pirates was palpable. Iron Ball continually sharpened blades with his grindstone and fussed over his great guns. He had multiple rounds of powder bags filled and ready, using the opportunity to teach the Davy the finer points of blast yield per type and measure.

Doctor Sorensen made his orlop ready for casualties. He and Hollingsworth set up chests as makeshift operating tables and prepared the instruments. Davy helped where he could, but the doctor was unusually curt and anxious, more often telling him to get out of the way.

John was busy working on the boats with Dann to get them ready for a boarding mission, should Every require it. They scrubbed the bottoms of the boats and checked every piece of equipment, from rudder to oars; even the masts were set up and then taken down. John also prepared his personal weapons for the assault. He sharpened his dirk, practiced loading his pistol, and swung his boarding axe against an imaginary opponent.

The long day turned to night, and the night eventually gave way to daybreak, but still no sight of the convoy. The pirates grew restless and began to murmur to each other. Various charms were produced from pockets and necklaces, which the pirates caressed or recited little prayers. None were particularly religious, but they all believed in luck and the spirits of the sea that might grant them the opportunity of their lifetimes. Even Bones Crakehall whispered a plea to the sea god Neptune to bring them fortune.

As the early morning sun began its steady climb, a cry went up from the masthead. A sail was sighted. Every immediately scanned the horizon with his glass, but disappointment was evident in his expression as he ordered a signal to *Amity* to intercept the unfortunate ketch. A few hours later, Tew came aboard and reported what he learned from the vessel: the convoy had passed the pirate fleet unseen during the night, probably going through the narrow eastern strait.

Clearly irritated, Every signaled the fleet to pursue. But there was a problem from the onset. Captain Want signaled that his ship had sprung a serious leak. Frustrated, Every convinced him to send his men over to the *Fancy* and burn the *Dolphin*. Commanding the largest and fastest ship, Every realized his fleet would not be able to keep up with him during the chase, but he needed *Pearl's* 16 guns and men to take on the *Ganj-i-sawai*, so he took her in tow. The others would just have to keep up as best they could.

The pirate fleet set off in pursuit of their quarry. Greed

got the best of Every and he ordered full sail, including stuns'ls, heedless of the other ships' lack of speed. After a day, Wake's barque had fallen so far behind she was lost over the horizon. The other ships struggled to keep up and straggled behind, except for the *Pearl* in tow. *Fancy's* masts and timbers creaked under the strain of the full, pressing wind and the *Pearl.*

The chase continued for more than a week. Finally, the lookout on the masthead spied two sails, hull down in the east. Every, pacing the quarterdeck, whipped up his glass and trained it on the distant skyline. He studied the strange sails for a full minute before snapping shut his telescope.

"Mr. Crakehall," he announced loudly to the quartermaster and breathless ship's company, "our prey is in sight." The crew gave a lusty cheer and immediately ran to their battle stations before Bones could even give the order. John clapped Davy on the back and grinned. "See ye in hell, mate!" He ran off to join Dann and other pirates crowding around the gun chests.

Davy had mixed feelings. On one hand, the boredom he had grown weary of had vanished, replaced with a strange elation. The knot in his stomach announced his dread. He was worried about John's enthusiasm too. He shook off his emotions and descended the ladder to the armory, where Iron Ball was already busy handing out boarding weapons.

After the pirates left, Iron Ball surveyed his powder charges, carefully considering his options. If Captain Every ordered shots from the bow chasers, which was likely, he'd need the charges for the long nines first. The broadside guns, which were heavier, would require different charges, especially if they were firing double shot. Bar and grapeshot would be next when they ranged close alongside their victim. He picked up two bags and handed them to Davy. "Fore'ard," he said curtly. "An' don't ferget the claw," he added emphatically.

Davy nodded, gasping with the deadly weight in his fore-and-aft sling, and proceeded with some difficulty up to the deck. Depositing his load at the feet of the gun captain of the two bow chasers, he glanced at the Moghul ships now hull up and getting closer before he headed back down. Automatically stroking the parrot claw on the bulkhead, he received the next pair of bags. His legs trembled as fear began to grip him. Iron Ball noticed his anxiety and grabbed his shoulder. His steely blue eyes fixed on him with intensity.

"Don't panic, lad. Do yer job, jest like I taught ye, an' you'll be fine," he said. Davy looked back at him, took a deep breath, then bobbed his head and left. *Tis jest a job*, he told himself.

Fancy closed within gunshot of the nearest ship a few miles south of Cape Diu, off the west Indian coast. Every cut the towing line to *Pearl* and she fell off. Tew's *Amity* and Faro's *Portsmouth Adventure* were just barely visible behind them on the horizon.

The warship escort was the six-gun *Fath Mahmamadi*, and it was prepared to fight. After a few shots from *Fancy's* bow chasers, the 600-ton Moghul ship turned to meet them. It fired a broadside from three guns, each shot finding its mark but causing little damage.

The *Fancy* yawed and responded with a full 23-gun roar, followed by a crackling round of musket fire. The broadside smashed into the Moghul ship, destroying rails, bulwarks and sent splinters flying. Musket balls fired by pirates in the topmasts found many of the massed men on deck. Disheartened by the stupendous firepower and deadly consequences from the pirate vessel, the captain of the *Fath Mahmamadi* immediately lowered his colors in surrender. The *Fancy* crew cheered and Every ordered the boats to put off with boarding parties, with himself at the head of the longboat.

Davy and John stayed behind on the *Fancy*, as ordered by Bones. They watched as the boarding party took possession of their prize, roughly shoving the Moghul crew into the waist and keeping them under guard as they searched the hold. After a while, Every motioned to Bones to send another boat over.

Chests and other items, including bolts of silk and a few barrels of powder were lowered down into the boats. The process took hours as the heavily laden boats plied back and forth between the ships, depositing their burdens of wealth aboard *Fancy*. It was a huge haul. Davy had never seen so much gold and silver. The pirate crew rejoiced as item after item was secured in the ship's hold.

"How much do ye reckon we got?" a wide-eyed Davy asked John.

"Oh, so it's *we* now," John chortled. "Seems one of us here has taken to the pirate life."

Davy blushed shamefully at his admission of greed. He left his friend and sulkily descended to the galley, plopping down on his wooden stool. He buried his burning face in his hands.

As the fiery red sun dipped below the horizon and twilight began, the pirates finished their looting and returned. A prize crew, comprised equally of *Fancy* and *Dolphin* men and led by Captain Want, took possession of the *Fath Mahmamadi* and made her ready for sailing. *Pearl*, *Amity*, and *Portsmouth Adventure* had caught up and rejoined *Fancy*. Captain Tew came aboard, furious that he'd missed the action – and a share in the prize. Alone in the fight, the *Fancy* crew was entitled to the entire haul, some 50,000 English pounds worth of gold and silver, along with other valuables belonging to the Moghul captain.

Shouting was heard in the captain's cabin as Tew vented his frustration. Every listened patiently and then told Captain Tew there would be more chances for wealth if they could catch up to the main treasure ship. He even promised Tew that he could lead the vanguard of the boarding party when the time came. Satisfied, Tew stalked out of the cabin, shooting a cold glance at Davy as he passed by, and left the ship.

The next morning, the pirate fleet and their prize made landfall and made ready to drop anchor to dispose of the Moghul men. They heaved the cannons overboard to render the ship toothless, while the *Fancy* carpenter and sailmaker gathered what useful spars and cordage they could salvage.

Every considered putting the prisoners ashore and burning the *Fath Mahmamadi,* since it would only slow them down in their pursuit of the rest of the convoy. But before he could give the order to John Dann to remove the prisoners, the lookout hailed the deck below with news of a sail due east, silhouetted by the rising sun.

Every took a quick look through his glass and immediately knew his principal target was within his grasp. He shouted orders and the crew, driven by the urgency of impending wealth, bustled about the ship, clearing it for action.

Want shouted over to the *Fancy* for instructions about what to do with the Moghul crew. Crakehall answered simply, "Leave 'em t' rot in their chains, an' git o'er 'ere!" Want hesitated a moment, then shrugged and ordered his prize crew abandon ship and row back to the *Fancy* with all haste.

While Every impatiently waited for Want's men to come aboard, he noticed the *Amity* make sail.

"Blast that little viper!" he cursed.

"Surely, 'e knows 'e canna take that little sloop inta action against that big Moghul," Crakehall said, shaking his head. "That man is a fool."

"Aye," agreed Every. "We need every gun we can get. Throw the towing line to *Pearl* and let's weigh anchor. I want to depart as soon as Want is aboard."

Davy made dinner for Every, who wolfed it down and immediately returned to the main deck. Davy cleaned up and reported to Iron Ball. The big gunner handed him two bags of powder and sent him to the bow chasers. On his way back down, Davy met John, who was carrying a pair of muskets and two powder horns.

"When did ye learn to shoot?" Davy asked.

"These here are fer the men in the tops," John replied. "Me, I'm gonna join the boarding party. I canna wait!"

Davy shook his head. "This ain't gonna be like them ships before," he said. "This one here, she's a big un, with lot's of guns."

"Bah," his friend snorted. "Them Moghuls are skeered of us. Wait 'til we send our broadside inta them, then ye will see." With that, he continued on his way to the main mast.

Davy watched his friend go. He knew it wasn't going to be easy taking the royal flagship, and he was afraid for John's life – and his own.

Tew's *Amity* got a good head start on the rest of the fleet, which waited for Every's order to move. By the time *Fancy* got underway, with *Pearl* in tow, the *Ganj-i-Sawai* had sunk the horizon and *Amity* was in hot pursuit.

As the day yielded to night, nearly the entire crew of the

Fancy was on deck, listening to the sound of cannon fire and observing faint flashes of light in the distant east. At first they heard only a few reports, then the ripple of guns firing consecutively. They understood the *Ganj-i-Sawai* had fired her 30-gun broadside at the little sloop. The staccato of a few muskets were heard, and then silence.

Soren stood next to Davy at the crowded gunwale and shook his head. "It's over. Either Tew pulled off de greatest upset in modern naval warfare, or *Amity's* gone to de bottom," he said solemnly.

Davy looked at the doctor anxiously. "Or mebbe she's run away?"

Soren glanced at him and didn't answer. He walked away, head bowed.

"The *Ganj-i-Sawai* is a slow ship, an' now *Amity* 'as bought us some time t' catch up," Crakehall remarked. Davy was startled by the quartermaster's presence next to him. "Don't matter, o' course. We will catch up wit' her soon enough. Stupid man, that Tew," he added bitterly.

Dawn arrived and the crew of the *Fancy* discovered Captain Wake and the *Susannah* were nowhere to be seen. *Pearl* was still in tow, and Captain Faro was just managing to keep up *Portsmouth Adventure*.

Every turned to Crakehall. "Full sail. Run out the stun'sls."

"Cap'n, we may spring a mast wit' that much sail," Bones warned. "Especially wit' the *Pearl* weighing us down."

Every thought for a moment. "No. We need her guns and men. Keep an eye on the masts and let me know if we need to shorten. Pass along to Captain Mays. I want him to put up all the canvas *Pearl* can handle."

Crakehall went aft to pass the word to Mays. Davy watched him go and then went down to the armory. He stopped at the door and dutifully stroked the parrot claw before entering.

"Cap'n says the *Gunsway* is right over the horizon," he announced. "He got every stitch of canvas spread to catch her."

Iron Ball grunted and handed him two powder bags. "Larboard guns. Light along there, an' come back fer more."

More than an hour later Davy had supplied the broadside guns with pairs of powder bags. Exhausted and soaking with sweat, he collapsed on the deck of the armory. Iron Ball studied him for a moment. "That's enough fer now. Cap'n's gonna give 'em a taste of both sides and then close fer boarding. Take a musket and go to the main top."

Davy struggled to his feet and complied. As he climbed the ratlines to the main crosstree, he hazarded a glance ahead and saw the *Ganj-i-Sawai* ahead less than a league. At present speed, *Fancy* would be upon her prey shortly.

The gun crews at the bow chasers were already in the process of loading their guns and running them out. Taking his position, he peered out over the rail and spied John standing next to Crakehall and two dozen other pirates. They were checking the priming of their pistols and passing out boarding pikes. Davy prayed his friend wouldn't get hurt in the upcoming engagement. He felt an ache in the pit of his stomach and grimaced.

Four other men crowded with him in the crosstree were busy loading their muskets. One, a man he knew as John Sparcks, turned to him.

"Lad, yer job is t' load the muskets," he said, pointing to the extras standing against the mast. "Jest keep loadin' as we hands 'em to ye, until I tells ye otherwise. An' stay down," he added.

Davy nodded and slung a pair of powder horns over his shoulder. A sack full of musket balls and a pouch with wads lay nearby. He went to work.

When the *Fancy* was within two cable's length of the *Ganj-i-Sawai,* Every ordered the red flag run up. The bow chasers barked as they sent ranging shots toward their target. As they moved ever closer, the pirates of the *Fancy* realized just how enormous the Grand Moghul's flagship really was. She was comparable to a large ship of the line, sporting 62 guns. Hundreds of soldiers crowded her weather decks, their fearsome *sirohi* scimitars and steel shields gleaming in the noon sun. Others strung double-curved *kaman* bows or hefted long *barchhah* spears.

Every seemed unimpressed. "A fine target they present," he commented. "Double shot the first two broadsides, then load grape," he ordered. Crakehall relayed the order to the gun crews and they went to work. The bow chasers fired again and then Every commanded the helm to yaw to the starboard in order to bring the larboard guns to bear.

The boarding party hunched down behind the gunwales or lay flat on the deck in preparation for the enemy's fusillade. John stared straight up at the main mast, but he couldn't see Davy. He waited tensely, fingering the shaft of his boarding pike.

"Steady. Full broadside on my command," Captain Every shouted, as the *Fancy* slowly swung around. "Fire!"

Both ships fired simultaneously, great clouds of smoke bellowing forth and obscuring the space between them. The *Fancy* rocked violently as heavy cannon balls crashed into the upper hull and whizzed by at head height past the main deck. Lines and rigging parted with loud snaps, but somehow the masts remained standing.

As a mild westerly breeze pushed away the bank of smoke, Davy peered over the side of the crosstree rail at the *Ganj-i-Sawai*. A bloody scene greeted his eyes. One of the Moghul's great guns had exploded, killing the crew. The ship's main deck was sprayed red and men were sprawled all over, some clutching wounds and bawling in agony. Others didn't move at all. The main mast had fallen by the board, crushing several more men. Davy tore his eyes away from the wretched mess and looked down for John. He was relieved when he saw his friend spring to his feet and join the boarding crew at the rails.

The *Fancy* surged ahead and yawed again, this time hard to the larboard, and the guns on the starboard erupted as the *Ganj-i-Sawai* was raked from stern to bow. Ranging up alongside, Fancy fired a round of grapeshot straight at the deck of their prey. Thousands of nails, musket balls, and assorted pieces of metal cut wide swathes through the Mohgul ranks, like a scythe through summer wheat.

Havoc and mayhem reigned as the Moghul gun crews fell and the ship's cannons were silenced. Every ordered grappling hooks and a general boarding. The men heaved on the grappling lines and brought the *Ganj-i-Sawai* within a few feet.

Crakehall led the charge as the pirates swarmed over the gunwales and leapt across the narrow space between the ships. The Moghul infantry put up a fierce resistance, despite their casualties. They met the invaders with a disciplined archery volley, cutting down several of the *Fancy* men in midair. The long *barchhah* spears pointed forward to ward off the attack, but the pirates thrust past them and engaged the *sirohi*-wielding Moghuls in the first two ranks.

John and Bones fought side by side, hacking away at the defenders like two berserkers. John's boarding axe found a vulnerable Moghul neck and nearly hacked off the man's head. Crakehall pounded a heavy mallet into the steel shield of his foe, crushing his arm. He swiftly followed it up with a kick to the groin and a dagger to the chest of the unfortunate man.

As Crakehall's boarding party continued their close quarters combat, Every and Want had gathered another force of men on the other side of *Fancy*. Unseen by the enemy, they boarded boats and rowed around the *Ganj-i-Sawai's* unprotected flank. They stealthily climbed up the side and engaged the enemy in a surprise attack on their rear quarter. Although they had superior numbers, the Moghuls were pressed into the middle of the ship by Every's pincer strategy.

From Davy's perch, Sparcks and the other pirates were firing down on the exposed deck of the *Ganj-i-Sawai,* picking off men at the helm, officers, and Moghul sailors in the tops. Davy reloaded several rounds and passed the muskets back to the sharpshooters. Satisfied, Sparcks turned to him, grinning. "Go ahead, lad, take a shot fer practice."

Davy hoisted a musket and peered down the long barrel. He spied John disappearing down the enemy's hold, following Bones. Satisfied that he was safe for now, Davy smiled and turned right to Sparcks, but just then something slammed into his face and his world disappeared in blackness.

12

Indian Ocean

He was having a nightmare, maybe. He was floating, above himself, above the others. Where was he? It was dim, but not completely dark. There was a lantern. He must be below decks. There was Soren! The good doctor was bending over a body...*his body!* From his position directly overhead, he couldn't see his own face. Soren was in the way, his bloody hands tugging on something. Then he pulled his hand free and held it up to the light. It was a broken stick of some kind, but something was stuck on the smooth shaft, just above the piece of triangular steel. Davy realized it was a broken arrow. He looked back at himself, sprawled on a chest. To his horror, he saw a gaping hole where his left eye was supposed to be. Another hole was nearby in his left temple. He looked back at Soren, who was putting the arrow into a small tray held by his assistant, Hollingsworth. The mangled remains of his eye still clung to the shattered arrow.

He instinctively tried to touch his face, but he couldn't. He couldn't find his face. In fact, he couldn't find his hand. He was invisible, or without form, he wasn't sure which.

Soren was packing the entry and exit wounds with wet rags while Hollingsworth began wrapping a bandage around his head. When he was done, the doctor bent his head down to Davy's chest, listening. "We're losing him," he said to Hollingsworth. Then the darkness closed in and Davy saw no more.

There was a voice. It sounded like singing. Beautiful singing. A woman, or maybe a girl. It was the sweetest sound he'd ever heard. He couldn't quite make out the words, but they seemed to beckon him. He felt so...rapturous. So loved. He wanted to find the heavenly source of this wonderful voice. He became aware of a dim light, getting brighter. The singing seemed to come from it. He willed himself to drift toward it, and as the light became brighter, the voice seemed closer.

Then there was another voice. A man's voice? It wasn't singing. It was talking to him. The singing faded away but the light did not. Now the man's voice invaded his mind, taking up all the room. *Damn it all to hell*, thought Davy.

"...and then I was aboard the *Gunsway*, hackin' and pokin' at them Moghuls. Ye shoulda seen 'em, all big white eyes, and brown skin! If'n I hadda been so mad, I woulda bust a gut laughin'!" John Roberts chuckled, then caught himself.

"Then I find out what happened to ye, and I came down

here straight away." His voice grew somber. "We almost lost ye, mate. When ye wake up, though, yer in fer a grand surprise!" He leaned over and whispered. "We is rich, mate! That Moghul was fat with gold and silver and jewels. I never seen so much wealth in me life! Never even dreamed that much loot was in the world! We is like kings now!"

Davy was confused. Was this all just another dream? He couldn't seem to open his eyes—or rather, his eye. His lips moved feebly, but no words came out. Then he became aware of an awful thirst. He licked his lips. They were dry, cracked.

John saw this movement and shouted for Doctor Ostergard. "He's movin', I tell ye!" he exclaimed.

Davy felt a wet cloth touch his lips, and he licked at it greedily. Drops of water coasted down his tongue, and he swallowed. Even his throat was sore from dryness.

He heard Soren. "Take it easy there, lad. You are seriously wounded. You need rest. Don't try to talk, just sleep for now."

His words were soothing, reassuring. John had finally shut up, shushed by the good doctor. Davy faded away into oblivion.

The pain woke him. A throbbing, excruciating pain that began on his left cheekbone and radiated outward toward his scalp and inward to his brain. That, and someone's damned whistling. *Bloody hell!* Davy's inner voice shouted. He opened his right eye and discovered Hollingsworth. Actually, *two* Hollingsworths. His blurry vision registered a double image of the doctor's assistant, rinsing rags in a bowl of water.

"Christ," said Davy. "Yer hurtin' me ears!"

"Ah! I see the patient is in fine spirits, doctor," he said over his shoulder.

Soren appeared and elbowed Hollingsworth aside. "Davy! Happy to see you did not give up de ghost," he remarked with a grin. "You've taken quite a blow to your noggin."

"What happened?" Davy asked. "And can I get somethin' to drink? I'm terrible thirsty."

"Yes, of course. Here's a sip of water," the doctor replied smoothly. He turned to his assistant. "Get him some broth."

Davy watched him go. At least the damned whistling had stopped.

"Now," Soren began, "let me catch you up. We boarded de Mohgul ship and after a bloody fight of nearly three hours, she struck her colors. However, in the process you took an arrow to de head." He paused. "You've lost an eye, Davy. De arrow punctured your temple and drove right through the socket. It's a miracle you didn't die."

Davy digested this for a few moments. "Is John alright? I had a dream that he was speakin' to me."

"Yes," Soren replied. "A few scrapes, nothing more. Unfortunately, de men with you in the maintop did not survive, except Sparcks. He got a bolt in the shoulder, but he'll live."

Davy thought briefly of Sparcks, but suddenly remembered his duty to Every. Who would cook for the captain?

"What's important right now is dat you continue to rest. You'll need time to regain your feet," Soren continued. "De captain is aware of your condition and agrees with me dat you need bedrest until further notice. You're under my orders now," he smiled.

"Can I see John?"

"I'll send for him when he comes off watch," Soren responded. Hollingsworth arrived with a steaming bowl. The doctor ordered him to feed Davy until he got his fill, and then departed.

Captain Every looked at the ledger offered by Crakehall. He felt the anxious stares of Captain Want, Captain Faro, Captain Mays, Master Ireland of *Amity*, and their quartermasters. He nodded and Crakehall beckoned the other men to take a look at the count of the wealth. As the pirates observed the figures for themselves, Every stood up.

"Captain Faro. Your ship, although it was present, did not come into the fight. Therefore, you receive no dividend."

"What do ye mean, we didn't come into th' fight?" Faro protested. "We are part of this fleet, are we not? We all swore to band together and attack the Moghul! Everyone there saw us."

"Tell me, Captain Faro," Every began. "Did your ship fire a gun? Did any of your men cross the threshold of the enemy and draw blood? No? Then you were not in the action." He looked across the desk at Faro and his brow furrowed, his eyes flashed. "I lost 16 men for this prize. Captain Want lost four, and Captain Mays lost seven. You lost nothing," he said, his voice rising. "You were there and did not participate. I say that makes you a coward!"

Faro looked up at him sharply and drew his dirk. "You'll retract that insult, Every, or I'll..." But before he could continue, Crakehall drew his pistol and levelled it at his head. Faro eyed the huge, daunting frame of the *Fancy* quartermaster and pursed his lips. He gulped and sat down. Crakehall lowered his gun but kept it ready at his side.

"Captain Mays, Captain Want," Every continued mildly, "your men fought alongside us and will receive their dividend. Naturally, each of you will get two shares and your masters a share and a half." He pointed to the ledger. "I'm sure you will agree with me that each man's share is equal to 1,000 pounds worth of gold and silver. In addition, each man will get his choice of a gemstone and either a bolt of fine silk or one of the other valuables on this list.

"Master Ireland, as you are now the leader of *Amity's* men – although your vessel was destroyed in a foolish duel with a greater foe at the behest of Captain Tew – you may also receive your share since your men rejoined the fight. Do we have an agreement?"

Ireland smiled and nodded.

Faro, clearly annoyed, left the cabin without a word. His glowering quartermaster followed.

The *Portsmouth Adventure* departed and headed west. Every watched the ship as it slowly disappeared over the horizon. He knew Faro wouldn't confront the heavily armed *Fancy*, but he suspected treachery at some point. He decided to avoid them as best he could. No need for senseless bloodshed among brothers of the black.

Want and his men were happy, and joined the *Fancy* men in taking game with the Moghul prisoners. It turned out the Grand Mohgul's vizier had a harem on the *Ganj-i-Sawai,* and the pirates took their liberties with the exotic women. A handful of the courtesans, including an elderly noble woman, actually committed suicide rather than submit to rape. The rest did not.

The surviving Mohgul soldiers and seamen were locked in the hold. Crakehall and a few of the pirates took turns torturing some of the Mohgul officers for information. They were looking for valuable personal effects they believed could still be hidden. The torture yielded few results, but Crakehall enjoyed it anyway. The wounded captives were dispatched and thrown overboard on Every's order. Just like his captain, Bones had little compassion for non-Europeans, and he carried out his inhumane duty without reservation.

Every resolved to go to the pirate haven at Libertalia on the northern shores of Madagascar. There he would share out the spoils among the crew and plan his escape into obscurity. It was only a matter of time before the navies of the world came looking for them – especially the forces of the Grand Mohgul himself. Accustomed to being the hunters, Every and his men would soon be the hunted, with rich bounties on their heads. He had achieved every pirate's dream: a lifetime of wealth. He reckoned he would like to live long enough to enjoy it. He began to plan his exit.

※

John visited Davy often over the next few weeks as the *Fancy* took a meandering course around the Indian Ocean to avoid ships of war, merchants, pirates, and anyone else who might report their location and course. Although his health improved, John noticed Davy's attitude grew worse. The once meek but hopeful boy had turned into an angry, sullen young man. He seemed to care little for his newfound wealth. John became concerned.

Soren released Davy to his duties after he was satisfied the lad was sufficiently recovered. Davy now sported an patch over the hollow place where his left eye once was. It annoyed him at first, but he got used to wearing it, and even took a kind of pride as the other pirates nodded appreciately when they passed him on the deck.

Whenever he wasn't in the galley preparing the captain's meals, Davy was applying himself with renewed vigor to the art of musketry and the great guns. Even Iron Ball noticed the boy's new intensity. The gunner was satisfied with his pupil, who seemed dead serious about perfecting the craft. Davy spent all hours of the day and night, sleeping very little, while he learned the intricacies of the profession of arms.

Soren urged him to do something else with his time. He was worried about the boy's preoccupation, but Davy paid him no heed and even began to shun his company in favor of his new obsession.

Fancy anchored in a wide bay in northeastern

Madagascar. The pirates, with purses and pockets jingling with coin, clambered ashore and strode into Libertalia, eyes glinting at the local whores and mouths watering for rum. They each had a king's ransom and intended to enjoy every bit of it.

Libertalia was a pirate haven, completely devoid of law and order. The town abounded with trading posts, shops and taverns. Davy and John entered one such tavern packed with patrons, and ordered their first round. As they relished their drink, John Dann stumbled up to the bar next to them.

"Bartender!" Dann bellowed, obviously drunk. "Set me up with another, an' a round fer me mates here." He sat down heavily next to John and Davy. "Well lads, we did it!"

"Aye," John agreed, grinning.

Davy sighed and sipped his rum.

John leaned over. "Listen, Davy," he said in a low voice. "I took care of that Tew problem fer ye."

"What?"

"Aye. I found him chained up in the hold with some of the *Amity* men," John said. "Bones let them all go so they could join us in the fight, but Tew stayed behind when the others left. It was jest the two of us. He asked me if'n I knew ye, and said somethin' nasty about ye, about claimin' ye as a prize of war when all of this was over."

Davy stared at his friend. "What did ye do, John?"

"Put me boardin' pike through his goddamned gut, of course."

"Dammit, John, I wanted to kill him meself," Davy cried in frustration. What he really wanted was to find out what Tew had done with his father.

"Sorry mate, thought I was doin' ye a favor." John turned back to his drink, a bit miffed.

Davy slammed his glass down and walked out.

After a few days, Every gathered what *Fancy* men he could find and held a meeting. He resolved to depart the area at once and flee to the Caribbean, seeking a refuge. He offered passage for those who would go with him. Many of his crew, after much discussion, agreed to accompany him. John Roberts was among their number.

For his part, John relished the action and excitement of the pirate life. John felt like he was just beginning a promising new career full of glory and riches. For him, the Caribbean offered new adventures instead of a life of retired ease, and he told Davy as much.

"Jest think of it, Davy," he said, "All the lands we'll see. The oceans we'll sail, and the ships and plunder we'll take!"

Davy stewed as he studied his dirk. "All ye want is gold."

"Aye," John agreed, "But there's also adventure, women, and the brotherhood. What else is there?"

Davy lapsed into a reflective silence. He thought about how far he had come. He thought about the woman in the water. He thought about his quest to find his father, now spoiled by his friend's careless act of revenge – *his* revenge. None of that seemed to matter anymore. John's enthusiasm ebbed and his smirk faded as Davy regarded him with a cold, almost menacing eye.

"The future ain't shiny coins and gemstones," said Davy

slowly. "It's the god of the storm, the sharp steel, and bloody decks." He raised his head and looked at John with his good eye. "And in the end, it's a ball in the chest, a hangman's rope, or perhaps a watery grave. That's what makes me feel alive. I ain't got no room in me heart fer friends anymore."

John looked at his friend thoughtfully. "Well then, I suppose we are partin' ways." He stuck out his hand. Davy ignored it and turned away.

John frowned and left.

The next day Davy struggled out of bed in the public house he was staying. He bent over a bowl of water and saw his reflection. He lifted his eyepatch. The hideous wound was healing, but it startled him still. He splashed his face and dried off, reflecting on the fact that he'd have to ignore the stares of curious townfolk the rest of his life. He adjusted his eye patch and put a bandana over his still-healing head. He shoved his boots on and clapped a pistol into his belt.

After breakfast he left the public house and winced from the glare of the blazing sun, already high overhead. He strode down the filthy street without any purpose or destination. He just needed to get away from the booze and clear his head.

His mind was so preoccupied with trying to sort itself out that he nearly collided with a huge man in front him. He looked up into the face of Iron Ball Morgan.

"Well now, fancy meetin' ye here," the gunner rumbled. "Ye look like ye been run over by a pair of oxen."

Davy nodded heavily. He could't find the words to reply.

"Come lad," Morgan said, taking Davy by the arm. They ambled up the street and entered a shop. Davy gazed at familiar equipment and rows of muskets and swords.

Iron Ball sat him down and handed him a cup of water. The gunner had chosen to remain behind when Every made his offer, and, he explained, he had established an armament shop in Libertalia. He figured the law would be looking for Every and his men just about everywhere except here, the most obvious hiding place.

"Ye could stay with me and continue yer craft," he offered.

Davy nodded indifferently. He had no plans, and his future seemed blank. *Might as well be here and do this*, he thought glumly.

Later that night, Davy walked down to the bay and shed his clothes. He waded out into the surf and then dived headlong into the warm salt water. The sea calmed him, as usual, but he was still despondent. He regretted what he had said to John and his lamented his lost father, but they both seemed to be in the distant past now.

Treading, he gazed up and reviewed the thousands of stars before his eye settled on the dim slice of waning moon. How easy it would be to just relax his limbs and let the sea take him down. He felt something pulse against his chest, and he felt the pendant. *What now*, he wondered. The pulse grew quicker, and even in the warm water he could feel strange vibrations spreading across and into his chest.

Something bumped his leg and he recoiled in fear. Soon he saw a shadowy object break the surface 20 feet away. He stared hard as it glided through the dark water. The wan moonlight glinted on its white-tipped dorsal fin as it slowly sank below and Davy knew at once it was a shark. As good of a swimmer he was, he realized it would be impossible to get away from it. He slowed his kicking legs as much as possible without sinking. *Mebbe it will leave me alone,* he thought.

He felt another bump, this time a little stronger, against his thigh. He broke out in a sweat. He whirled around, trying to look in all directions for his attacker. Then it came.

13

Libertalia, Indian Ocean

The white-tipped dorsal fin rose and now Davy could see the top of the shark's back just below the surface as it headed straight for him. He instinctively raised his webbed fists as his body shuddered with primal terror. The pendant was beating wildly in concert with his pounding heart. He gritted his teeth and then uttered an animalistic roar as the shark's head surged out of the water, revealing rows of sharp teeth bearing down for the kill.

Just before it could strike, Davy felt his entire body lift out of the water and he was flying through the air, arms and legs flailing. He fell backwards and crashed into the sea, the impact knocking the air out of his lungs. Disoriented, he struggled to the surface, gasping for a breath. After several attempts, his lungs relaxed enough to let in the precious air and he regained his senses. He heard a great clap and he jerked his head toward the sound.

The black fluke of a mighty whale slapped the shark, stunning it in mid-swim. Davy saw its triangular dorsal fin sink under the water and moments later the orca came up from underneath and savagely engulfed its prey. Its jaws worked rapidly, biting and chewing the helpless shark. Davy heard the shark's cartilage snap and pieces of its long body flew about. Finishing its work, the orca slipped beneath the bloody sea.

Thank you, Neptune, thought Davy, relieved. *Now, why did I think that?* he wondered. He mentally shrugged. *Best not press me luck. Time to get back.* Seeing no further sign of the whale, he fixed his gaze on the distant flicker of campfires on the beach and swam for shore.

Davy spent the next few weeks setting up the armament shop with Iron Ball. With their shares of the Mohgul raid, the two bought crude machinery, including a forge, and enough scrap metal and pig iron to produce all manner of small arms. They imported niter and other materials to make gunpowder for muskets, pistols and even cannon.

Morgan showed Davy how to grind and mix the powder, fashion blades from the forge, and even construct the small arms. Davy relished the work, especially the craftsmanship required for the fine parts of personal firearms. They often worked well into the night, absorbed by their task of stamping and engraving. Each musket or pistol was a unique work of art.

Under Iron Ball Morgan's tutelage, Davy wrought his very

own brace of flintlock pistols. Each 14-inch barrel was wrapped in a stock of fine walnut imported from the American colonies, oiled and polished until it gleamed. He scrolled the wood, adding a diamond pattern to the butt grip. The butt itself was capped with silver. A swimming mermaid sideplate made of silver was attached to the stock. Intricate leaves were stamped into the cock, the frizzen, flashguard, lockplate, trigger, and the silver guard. He carefully overlaid the patterns with gold. Next, he fitted a plate of shiny brass around the muzzle and attached a brass ramrod under the barrel. As a final personal touch, he stamped his initials and the name of the armament shop on the steel lockplate.

A man of dubious humor, the old gunner named his shop simply, 'Iron Balls'. His reputation as a master of the gunnery profession among pirates and privateers resulted in a steady flow of customers as ships put in to Libertalia for supplies. The two craftsmen made back their investment and the shop began to profit after only three months.

When the shop closed at dusk, Davy grabbed a small leather purse with a few coins and hit the streets for a bite to eat and entertainment. Unlike most of his former shipmates, Jones was more careful with his share of the Moghul prize. He husbanded his coins and never bet too much or too often. His days of poverty back in Swansea had taught him the value of money. Still, he frequently played dice games while guzzling pints of ale or flagons of rum, staggering back to his small quarters behind the armament shop in the wee hours of the morning. A young man had to do *something* in this remote part of the world. He had no different plans for tonight.

The warm, tropical rain pelted his exposed head and face as he navigated the dark, twisted streets. The only light available was the occasional lantern mounted below the eaves of taverns, but the jumbled sounds of humanity from various establishments pulled at him like a maelstrom. After these many months in the pirate town, Davy had grown accustomed to the confusion. He sauntered into the Leaping Leopard, a place he had yet to visit, and ordered a drink.

Leaning back against the bar, he surveyed the scene. The tables were full of the local underbelly: pirates and privateers, seedy merchants, tradesmen, professional thieves, gamblers, power drinkers, murderers, pickpockets, whores and passed out slobs. It was no place for the innocent.

Eyeing the crowd over the brim of his mug, he caught the passing glance of an auburn beauty. Her bored expression changed into a playful smirk. She was perhaps only a few years older than him. He looked away, embarrassed. The girls here never took him seriously.

Suddenly, he felt a tap on his shoulder.

"*Salut, beaute*," a velvety voice purred in his ear.

Davy whirled around and came face to face with the beautiful redhead. "Uh, hello." he stammered.

The woman flashed a smile and he couldn't help but notice her full, rouged lips. Her hand trailed down his arm and inserted itself in his. She pursed her lips in mock concern.

"Oh, do not be afraid. I did not come to pick your

pockets," she whispered. "I am Giselle."

He nodded, dumbly. She smiled again and leaned in, pressing her ample bosom against him. "And what is your name?"

"Uh, Davy." He was very uncomfortable, but at the same time quite enthralled by the gorgeous creature paying so much attention to him. He knew she was a whore – there were no other kind of woman to be found in places such as this in a town like Libertalia – yet he couldn't break free of her mesmerizing gaze. She had fantastic blue eyes, and the auburn hair framed her lightly tanned face perfectly. He felt her palm press against his crotch and he instantly rose to the occasion.

"Mmmm," she said, licking her lips. "You must be a sailor, judging by your main mast," she tittered. "One of Captain Every's men, yes?"

Davy nodded and took the opportunity to drink in the rest of her, noticing her small waist, bound up tightly in her black lace corset. His gaze fell to her shapely legs. Her thighs were hardly hidden by a skirt far too short for any civilized lady.

Giselle noted his wandering eyes and his full purse. "I think you like me, no?"

"Aye, I do," Davy replied with a husky voice. She was the most magnificent creature he'd ever seen.

"You want to see more of Giselle?" she asked lasciviously. Davy nodded, unable to find the words to reply to her magnetic voice. "Come," she commanded sweetly. Still holding his hand, she guided him to a narrow set of stairs.

They ascended to a balcony overlooking the bar and

walked along a passageway with a stained, red carpet. They passed a couple of closed doors through which Davy could hear creaking bedsprings and sounds of pleasure. She stopped at the third door and pushed it open. The musty room was just large enough for a sagging bed and a rickety wooden chair. She released his hand and shut the door. Smiling like a wild cat who has caught her prey, she stood before a mirror and began to unbutton her corset.

Davy nervously fumbled for his purse. "I, um," he stammered again. "How much should I, uh..."

Giselle finished unhooking her corset and let it drop to the floor. "*La, la, mon doux,*" she said soothingly. "Not now. Let us enjoy ourselves." She hiked a leg up on the seat of the chair and pulled up her skirt invitingly. "Would you please be so kind as to remove my *jarretiere?*"

Davy didn't know how much time had passed. He was bathed in glorious sweat. The bed sheets were a twisted mess at his feet and Giselle was curled up beside him. They were naked as newborns and in in sense, he felt born again. He stared up at the cracked ceiling and his nostrils drank in the scent of sex and perfume. This was the greatest moment of his life, he decided. His head swam with delight. *I am in love.*

Night gave way to morning, and Davy finally left the little room and his treasured vixen. His legs were a bit sore, as were other parts, but he didn't care at all. He whistled as he made his way down the winding streets to Iron Balls.

The old gunner was bent over a bowl and glanced up as

he entered. He shook his head slightly and grunted, "Mornin', young buck."

"Hello," Davy greeted him cheerfully. He plopped down on a bench across from his mentor and picked up an iron barrel. Twirling it nonchalantly with his fingers, he waited for Morgan to speak. Sensing his protege's attitude, the gunner finally spoke. "Good night?"

"Aye!" exulted Davy, barely able to keep his composure.

"Ye must 'ave run inta a good score." Morgan studied Davy with a cocked eye. Davy smiled and nodded. "By the look of that stupid grin, I'd wager ye got laid," the gunner pronounced.

"She's the sweetest thing alive!" Davy exclaimed. "I think I'm gonna marry her."

Iron Ball grunted. "Who is she?"

"Her name is Giselle, and," Davy began. "Well, she is a fine lass. I met her at the Leopard."

Iron Ball nodded and sighed. "Lookee 'ere, lad. Don't ye go fallin' in love with no French whore."

Shocked, Davy began to feel his temperature rise. "I only paid her a little bit, so she can eat and pay her rent. She ain't really a whore, jest down on her luck, is all."

Iron Ball chuckled softly, shaking his head. "That girl been around this 'ere town fer years. She's a favorite of just about anyone with money. She'll take all yers, and then leave ye. Ye canna trust whores."

Davy angrily shoved back from the bench and stood up, eyes blazing and fists clenched. Iron Ball drew a deep breath and his expression hardened. Davy knew that face. He'd seen it before, just before the gunner went into action against the enemy. He stuffed the words he wanted to say back down his throat, turned on his heel and stormed out of the shop.

He went back to the Leaping Leopard the next night, after he stuffed his purse with extra coin. He wanted to spoil his vixen.

He found her sitting at the bar, coaxing a rough seaman for drinks. Upon seeing Davy, she leaped up and ran into his arms. She received him warmly with a wet kiss and they sat. Her dazzling eyes captured him once again as they shared some laughs and drank away their cares.

Davy spent his money freely, attempting to impress her with his gamesmanship in dice games. He won no more than he lost, but it didn't seem to matter to Giselle. She maintained constant contact with him, draping her arm over his shoulder, pressing her thigh against his, and pecking his cheek encouragingly.

Hours later, she lured him, willingly, back to her room and repeated their previous night's pleasures. When he grudgingly departed in the early morning, he left behind a generous stack of gold coins.

As Davy entered the shop he nervously wondered if Iron Ball would judge him, but the old gunner said nothing about it and kept their conversation on the topic of business.

He introduced Davy to the forge and showed him how to temper steel and shape it into blades of all kinds. Davy made himself a dagger. It was a simple straight blade, double-edged and full tang with a grooved ricasso. The grip was wrapped in twisted iron wire and had a round pommel with a crab stamped into it. The crossguard featured two curved quillons to protect his hand. He engraved the ricasso with his initials in tiny letters. He sewed a leather scabbard and made a loop to attach it to a belt. Immensely pleased with his work, he showed his mentor. Iron Ball grunted his approval.

He visited Giselle every day after the armament shop closed, and every day he emptied his purse. She told him how she had come to Libertalia as a 12 year-old taken off a merchant ship by pirates. For years she had worked as a maid and sex slave to her captor, until he declared she was too old for him. Then he sold her to the owner of the Leaping Leopard, who allowed her to rent the room upstairs as long as she kept the pirates happy – and spending money. Naturally, he got a share of her profit.

Some days he had to wait and watch while she wagered at cards or dice. She was a good player and made some profit, but when she was down, she repaid with her body. It was aggravating to watch her go off with men, but Giselle hushed his jealous protests. She promised him that as soon as they both had enough money, she would marry him and they could live together in Calais, her hometown.

Within a few weeks, he had spent all of his fortune and was forced to wait for his share of the shop's profits. Giselle pouted and claimed she could not live with so little. She refused to see him until he could support her.

Depressed, Davy retreated to the shop. He decided he

would have to try harder to sell the wares of war, but it was difficult. Customers came and went with the tides.

Iron Ball began to spend less time at the shop. He'd developed a rasping cough and often shook with wheezing spasms. Davy became concerned when the old gunner took to his bed, often for days at a time. He brought him meals and made sure he was warm. Morgan refused Davy's requests that he been seen by a doctor. Instead, he simply told him to "mind the shop, and leave me be."

With the gunner abed, Davy had his hands full keeping up with customer demands. He spent most of the day filling orders for powder, shot, and custom-made weaponry. He squeezed in a meal or two while he worked, often just a hunk of bread and some salt beef. He labored well into the night creating parts for firearms or forging blades.

He barely had any time to see Giselle. He had reunited with her only after producing enough coin from the week's profits at the shop. Sometimes he even brought her presents of gold hoop earrings or silver pendants that he created. She rewarded him the only way she knew how.

Davy came back to the shop one morning after a night in Giselle's arms. He looked around for the gunner, but he was not there. *Still asleep, I suppose.* He went to his lodging above the shop and found the old man in his bed. Usually, Iron Ball was wheezing or coughing every few seconds, but today he seemed peaceful. Davy smiled and shut the door. *Best be gettin' to work*, he decided.

He thumbed through the logbook they used to record the customers' orders and settled upon his first task. It was a repair job for a musket. The stock was shattered and the butt broken off. *Musta walloped some poor bastard real good*, Davy mused. He carefully removed the remaining bits of wood and selected a fine piece of Turkish Royal Walnut to shape a new stock.

At noon he set his work aside and went to the pub next door to get some food for himself and the gunner. He came back with steaming bowls of lamb stew and went upstairs. The lone candle had sputtered out, giving the room a dim, cave-like feel. His nose twitched as it registered the foul, musty air.

Seeing the dark form of the old man still in bed, he cried, "Wake up, gunner. I got ye some victuals." Iron Ball did not respond. Davy set the bowls down and opened the curtained window. Bright sunlight invaded the room. Davy turned and saw his mentor's wide-open eyes staring lifelessly at the ceiling. He sat next to his mentor and watched him for a few minutes to see if he would begin breathing again. Finally, he buried his face in his hands and wept.

The next day, Davy found a few men at the pub and paid them to haul away the gunner on an ox cart. They took him outside the town and put him in the ground, on a hill overlooking the bay. Davy took Iron Ball Morgan's musket, pistols, and parrot claw and rested them on top of his massive chest before he covered him with the sandy dirt. Davy unsheathed the gunner's favorite cutlass and stuck it into the ground at the head of the grave and sent the men away.

He stood beside the grave in silent helplessness. He didn't

know what to say. *First, John left me, now you*, he thought mournfully. *All I got left is Giselle.* He sat down and stared at the bay, watching ships and boats moving about with the help of a humid breeze. He remained there until the fiery sunset cast its orange glow over the island.

Not knowing what else to do, he returned to the shop and began working on his musket. He finished the shape and sanded it down to smoothness. He found the work relaxing and restorative to his spirit. He stained the walnut and set it aside to dry. He decided to finish for the night and grabbed his purse.

Davy wandered through the streets aimlessly, his mind returning to the gunner. His footsteps instinctively guided him to the Leaping Leopard, where he found his love. Giselle was straddling a rough-looking patron, her arms wrapped around his neck. Davy felt his temperature rise as he saw her passionately kiss the man. He grabbed the hilt of his dagger and moved toward them.

"Giselle!" he shouted. "What ye doin' there with this scoundrel?"

The man turned his head and glanced at him irritably. "Bugger off, ye grass-combing lil' whelp." He buried his face in Giselle's neck and she giggled.

"Oh, Davy, do be a good *petit garcon* and go away," she said. "Can't you see I am working?"

Davy gaped in astonishment. "But, but," he stammered, "yer mine! Ye don't need to be with the likes of him." He waited for her to reply, but she ignored him and opened the top of her corset for the man. He responded with a grin and hungrily kissed the top of her breasts.

"Why, yer nothin' but a faithless whore!" Davy shouted.

The man lifted his head from her bosom and looked at Davy in wry amusement. "Of course she's a whore, ye idiot. An' she's me favorite." He roared with laughter and Giselle joined him, much to Davy's disgust. He turned away and stalked out of the tavern.

Outside, he stood in the street. His breathing became heavier as his rage seethed and then finally boiled over. He jerked the dagger out of its sheath and rushed into the tavern. Seizing the offensive man by the hair, he yanked his head back and drove his blade into the man throat and wrenched it out. Giselle shrieked as blooded spurted out like a fountain on her face.

Giselle tried to slap away the red that painted her, but Davy was not done. He grabbed her by her chin and leaned in close. "Ye ripped out me heart," he hissed. "Now I take yers!" He plunged the dagger into her chest and shoved her backward. She fell to the floor, her cries silenced by the blade sticking out of her breast like a gravestone.

Davy clenched his fist and screamed at everyone in the tavern, like some raging maniac. He seized his dagger, stormed outside and ran down the street, seeing nothing but blood red.

14

He had nothing to worry about, of course. There was no law to try him for his crimes in this pirate town. No governor, no constable. Men understood that sometimes blood had to be shed. Sometimes it was righteous. Sometimes it was needless. But it was a fact of life in Libertalia. Certainly no one would cry foul over the killing of a well-known whore. Sure, her customers would regret her, but there were other whores. The murder of a member of the Brethren, though, was something else. It demanded just cause, and barring that sacred motivation revenge was the order of the day.

Iron Ball had once told Davy why so many pirates made and abided by their own laws, as a group. This was the basis of forming articles or a code of conduct that every man would agree to or quit the company. Disagreements were handled by the community bound by those articles, and justice applied accordingly, he said. It was the closest thing they had to law and order.

Davy was close to losing his senses. Hate and rage flooded over him like a rogue wave, washing away his regard for decency. In one day, he had lost his love and his only remaining friend. His outright butchery of Giselle and her patron in full public view crossed a stark line. He was no longer just a pirate. He was a demon.

The man he killed was in fact a pirate, he learned – albeit a land-bound, unemployed one. His lack of affiliation with a company worked in Davy's favor, but what he did not know was whether the man had comrades who would seek to avenge him. He would have to watch over his shoulder, perhaps for years.

The news traveled quickly around town. Everywhere he went, people gave him a wide berth. Even the most hardened pirates glanced at him but would not look him in the eye. No one wanted to be the man who lit the match in the powder room.

After some days drinking alone in his little room, Davy resolved to go back to the shop and continue his work. There were orders to be filled. Maybe the engrossing task of creating and repairing would soothe his troubled mind. He picked up the stained wooden stock of the musket and began assembling the pieces.

He finished the work just after sundown and sat back to enjoy a cigar. He'd recently picked up the habit from Iron Ball and he felt like their evening ritual was a just tribute to the man who'd taught him his craft and, in the process, had become his friend. He was blowing smoke rings in the stuffy tropical air when the door opened.

The stern-faced man had short, dark, wavy hair. A pencil mustache and miniature goatee surrounded his thin lips. His thin frame was wrapped in a fancy red waistcoat and matching brocade jacket with a gold threaded design. A cutlass dangled from his hip and a pistol was tucked into the saffron sash at his waist. Black breeches and tall boots completed his stylish outfit. If it weren't for his penetrating, steely blue eyes, he might be regarded as a mere dandy. He strode into the shop with a confident gait, his gaze shifting to the left and right as he scanned the room.

He halted in front of Davy. "Good evening," he said in perfect King's English, without managing a smile. "Are you the proprietor of this establishment?"

"Aye," Davy replied.

His eyes narrowed as he contemplated Davy. "I was expecting Mr. Morgan."

"My partner has passed from this earth," said Davy. "Who might ye be?"

"My order," he began, ignoring the inquiry, "is under the initials G.B."

"Ah, the musket," Davy turned to the bench and picked up the firearm. He beheld it for a moment, taking one last look before handing it to the man. "The damage was considerable, but I think it's in a fine way now."

The man held it near the lantern on the bench and studied it. "Hmm. Yes. Excellent craftsmanship." He turned back to Davy and reached into his purse. He withdrew several gold doubloons and stacked them, one by one, on the bench.

"Is this satisfactory?" he asked.

Davy nodded and took a puff from his cigar. The stranger didn't make a move to leave, instead he observed Davy intently, as if he were scrutinizing a gold doubloon for authenticity. Davy began to feel uncomfortable, as the man's direct stare seemed to probe him for an answer to some unknown question. His handed drifted down to his dagger, resting on the hilt. Was he the expected avenger?

The man finally broke off his gaze. "I'm George Booth," he announced. "I've heard quite a bit about you, Mr. Jones."

Davy tightened his grip. Standing to face his client, he said "And what of it?"

Booth noticed his tense posture. "Do not be alarmed. I merely want to offer you a position with my crew," he said smoothly. "I'm with the *Dolphin*, 26 guns, Captain Samuel Inless and Quartermaster Nathaniel North. I could use a man of your talent as my gunner's mate."

Davy loosened his hand and let it fall to his side. He took a deep breath and crossed his arms. "Why would I be interested in joinin' yer crew?" he asked defiantly.

Booth smiled crookedly. "A man of your spirit doesn't belong on shore with ordinary mortals," he responded. "You belong to the sea, in the company of similar men. You are a predator, not a shopkeeper."

Davy didn't have an answer. He struggled to digest Booth's words, torn between the life he knew over the past year and the terrifying, yet strangely satisfying life of the pirate. Booth noticed his indecision.

"No need to respond now," he said. "Consider my offer. We sail tomorrow with the tide." He turned on his heel and left as purposefully as he came.

Davy closed up, left the shop and made his way through town to the shore. The waning moon reminded him of his monthly swim. He stripped off his clothes and waded out into the surf before plunging beneath the next roller. He surfaced about a cable's length away, mindful not to get too far out and take a chance of encountering another shark.

The pendant hung at his chest, humming with mild vibration, which he now knew meant all was well. He treaded water and thought about Booth's offer. *Mebbe it's time to move on*, he thought. *This town is makin' me angry.* He shook off his pensiveness and swam for a while, focusing on nothing but the feel of the salt water.

He returned to shore and dressed. He felt refreshed, as if the immoral slime of the past few days had washed away like so much filth. He didn't forgive himself for the murders, but decided it wouldn't do any good to dwell on them. He took a long look at the ocean before heading back to his room. For the first time in days, he slept.

He awoke at dawn. With a renewed sense of hope and urgency, he packed his sea chest. In it contained an extra shirt, breeches, a pewter plate and spoon, a silver flagon, a working knife and marlinspike, his 'housewife' sewing kit, and his old hammock.

He descended to the shop and selected the best weapons: an excellent French musket with powder horn, an Indian *shamshir* cutlass from the Mohgul raid, and his hand-made flintlock pistols. He strapped on his belt with the murdering dagger and filled his purse with the last few coins from the shop. Lastly, he threw on an old seaman's coat and departed.

He stopped at the public house next door and offered the

armament shop to the keeper for a cut-rate price, which the old man readily agreed without bothering to negotiate. His affairs now settled, he headed for the bay.

He found Booth among a group of men preparing to shove off in a long boat. "Ahoy!" he cried.

"Ah, there's my man," Booth responded. "Join us," he gestured to the boat. Davy handed him the chest and climbed over the gunwale, settling in near the stern. As the men rowed out to the *Dolphin*, Davy appraised her. She was a fine brigantine, clearly a former merchant of English origin. He noted her newly-stepped masts that raked backward and patched sails. They pulled alongside and Davy followed Booth and the others as they scrambled up the main chains.

They were greeted by Nathaniel North. A tall, lanky man in his late twenties, the quartermaster warmly shook their hands and invited them to the captain's cabin for refreshment. Davy followed, still carrying his chest.

The captain wasn't present, but North gestured for them to enter. He called for the cabin boy to bring drinks. Davy watched the boy as he brought a large bowl sloshing with red liquid and then hurried away, remembering how he began life at sea a few years ago. His reverie was interrupted by Booth handing him a glass of rum punch.

"Nat, this is Davy Jones," Booth said to the . Quartermaster. "I've asked him to join our company as my mate. He has experience serving under Iron Ball Morgan and is an excellent arms craftsman. Not to mention," he paused, "a fighting spirit."

North nodded appreciatively and removed his tricorn hat, revealing a mop of blond hair. "Very well," he answered with a clear, strong voice. "We could always use skilled hands with pluck, especially brave, youthful ones." He opened a drawer in the captain's desk and produced a scroll of parchment. "George here vouches for ye, so I would like to offic'ly offer ye a place with our comp'ny. These," he said, unrolling the parchment, "are our *Articles of Conduct* for this upcoming voyage. If'n ye agree to sign, ye may sling yer hammock and stow yer chest. But first," he raised his glass, "a drink to good health and prosperity."

Davy gulped it down. The punch was sweet and potent. A pleasant rush of warmth spread from his gut throughout his body. He licked his lips and handed his glass to North. Delighted, the quartermaster dipped his glass into the bowl and returned it. He grinned as he watched Davy throw his head back and drain the glass. Booth chuckled. "Easy there, lad, or you won't be able to focus on the Articles." He paused, furrowing his wide brow. "That is, if you can read. If not, I can recite them to you," he offered.

Davy regarded Booth coolly. "I can decipher the words," he said in a bitter tone. "And I prefer ye don't call me a lad."

Startled, Booth glanced at North and slowly nodded. "No. Of course not. No offense meant, Davy."

Davy leaned over the desk and read the parchment. He scrawled his initials at the bottom of the parchment below the list of the rest of the ship's company.

The ship sailed with the late morning tide and a Council of the Brethren was called to decide the target of their adventure.

Davy got his first look at the new captain, Samuel Inless. He was a short, balding man in his mid-forties, with a generous paunch and shrewd countenance. Davy wondered why the pirates would follow such a man into battle, until he learned Inless was fluent in Dutch and knew the Dutch East Indies quite well, having formerly traded in those parts.

After much discussion, it was resolved by the crew that they should sail to the Dutch East Indies and pick off the rich merchant ships returning to Europe from Java, Batavia, Shanghai and other Southeast Asian ports. Inless promised they should expect cargos laden with coffee, tea, sugar and exotic spices, not to mention bolts of fine silks, jade and gold-wrought jewelry.

North suggested that perhaps on the return voyage they would sail as far west as Ceylon, but their principal hunting area would be the busy Malacca Strait.

Since it was the end of the monsoon season, the *Dolphin* embarked on the shortest route possible straight across the Indian Ocean, using the easterly equatorial counter-current. Although it was hot, Davy found it not unbearable. He enjoyed watching the flying fish, whales, and sparkling sea as the brigantine flew along under full sail.

The days flew by, and within a month they sighted southern Sumatra. Entering the Java Sea, the pirates scoured the multitude of islands with telescopes, searching for viable prey. The area was filled with small boats, mainly fishermen and coastal traders. They stopped a few but let them go, realizing they carried little of value.

Captain Inless proposed they breach the Sunda Strait past

Sumatra and Java and venture toward Batavia, the capital of the Dutch East Indies. This the crew readily agreed, but North warned they might encounter well-armed Dutch VOC merchantmen.

"VOC? What's that?" Davy asked Booth. The gunner shrugged.

Inless overheard his query. "*Vereenigde Oostindische Compagnie*," he responded in a perfect accent. "It's the Dutch East India Trading Company."

Davy nodded. "But don't they have escorts?"

"Aye, but only a squadron based at Batavia itself, which comes and goes. That leaves us free to molest their shipping everywhere else," Inless continued. "Although some of them, as Mr. North reminds us, have teeth." He looked out over the assembled men in the waist. "We must be vigilant and prepared for battle."

The *Dolphin* cleared the strait and headed east along the jungle-lined Java coast. The myriad of small boats provided little incentive and they kept their course.

The next day they sighted Batavia. The port was crowded with shipping, large and small. As Inless and North scanned the area, they sighted five large merchantmen preparing to get underway. Unfortunately, there was also a squadron of three Dutch warships riding at anchor nearby. A strong breeze held them embayed, but Inless warned the offshore flow would soon return with the setting sun, and they would stand little chance if the warships came out to greet them, which they must surely do, having sighted the pirate ship prowling the coast.

North agreed, but offered the hope that if the only known naval squadron was here, then it wasn't anywhere else. The quartermaster ordered a course change to the north to skirt the coast of Sumatra.

Ten days went by without sighting a single ship worth pursuing. The crew became restless with Inless' promises of riches left unfulfilled. They complained to North, who assured them the next leg of the journey would provide more opportunity since it would be closer to European shipping routes. The *Dolphin* turned west toward Malacca.

Immediately upon entering the strait, they encountered a large three-masted Danish merchant. They swiftly overtook the vessel, which yielded without a fight.

Davy joined the crew as they swarmed over the side and herded the hapless crew into the waist at gunpoint. He held his musket at the ready as a score of pirates searched the quarters and hold. They emerged holding bolts of silk and casks of cinnamon, cloves and pepper.

North came from the captain's cabin, grinning from ear to ear. He whispered to Inless, who motioned to two other pirates to accompany them. They returned with two great chests, which they opened on deck for all the hands to see. The chests were filled with valuable Chinese porcelain, jade and silver plate.

"King Christian and your shareholders will not be

pleased, but we are quite so," Inless taunted the Danish captain. North whispered in his ear, and Inless nodded. "We shall require the services of your vessel for a while. Please make yourselves comfortable in the hold."

North and the boatswain supervised the transfer of cargo while Inless returned to the *Dolphin.* Davy and Booth kept the Dutchmen under guard.

It took two full days to move the goods, during which Davy took his turns on watch. At the conclusion, he was assigned to the prize crew with North in charge. The ships sailed the rest of the way through the Strait of Malacca without incident and Inless beached the *Dolphin* on one of the Nicobar islands.

Using the Danish ship to help steady the *Dolphin* as they careened her, Davy remained aboard. He explored the foreign ship, named *Flyvende Ulv,* noting how the Danes employed very old, bronze cannon. *Tis no wonder they didn't fight us,* he surmised. *These old things probably would burst if they attempted to fire.*

The *Dolphin's* hull was scraped clean and prepared for sea, using the *Flyvende Ulv* to haul her off the beach. Inless graciously allowed the Dutchmen to resume their voyage. The pirate crew, tired but modestly satisfied, voted to continue west to Ceylon.

A warm, tropical rain greeted them as they approached the island. Heavy clouds and mist veiled the horizon to the extent that they found themselves within gunshot of a fleet of Mohgul warships before they realized it.

Inless ordered a swift course change to the south, not before one of the ships fired a broadside, cutting through the *Dolphin's* rigging and main sail. As the fleet turned to pursue, Inless ordered the lanterns to be doused, stuns'ls set, and the bow chasers hauled to the rear.

The rain came down in sheets as a squall blew. North came down to the armory, dripping wet. "Booth! Time to earn yer keep. Ye and Jones, take charge of the stern chasers."

Davy and George hurried up to the deck and made their way aft. Six men waited next to each of the long brass nine-pounders, which were the pride and joy of the ship. "No use trying to load now, the powder will be too wet," shouted Booth to the quarter gunner. "Wait until the worst of the weather clears, then bring it topside."

Davy leaned close to Booth. In a low voice he said, "George, we can throw a tarp around de charges to keep 'em dry. Then they'll be ready when the squall clears and we can hit 'em before they know what's happenin'."

Booth regarded him coolly. "Alright, Mr. Jones. Make it so."

Davy motioned to two of the men and they rushed to the armory, returning a few minutes later with several wrapped powder bags. Booth ordered the pair of guns hauled back for loading, and then stepped inside the chart house. He lit a length of slow match and waited.

The squall passed through and was replaced with a light drizzle, which soon lessened to the occasional drop. Booth stepped out of the chart house and immediately issued orders for the gun to be loaded and made ready. He lit the other end, cut the slow match in half, and gave it to Davy. They hunkered down behind the breeches of the great guns and sighted down the barrels.

"Ten silvers from my share to the man who does the greatest harm to our pursuer," Inless called to them. Davy grinned and looked at Booth, who merely grunted anxiously.

The bowsprit of their enemy emerged from the squall line a half-mile away, followed by his towering foremast. They could see the Moghul captain standing along the forward rail, peering at them through his telescope.

Davy and George adjusted their aim and put the slow match to the touchholes. The two stern chasers barked and jumped backward. Davy watched the swift flight of the balls as they slammed into the Mohgul warship. Booth's ball holed the vessel well above the waterline. Davy's shot burst through the top rail and cut the captain in half, his legs flying through the air and his upper body falling into the sea.

The effect was instantaneous. The Mohgul ship veered away and tacked into the wind. As the crew of the *Dolphin* cheered, Davy locked eyes with Booth. The gunner chuckled and shook his head. Captain Inless appeared at Davy's side and offered a small bag. "I believe this belongs to you, Davy Jones."

15

Ile Aux Forbans

The *Dolphin* had an uneventful crossing of the Indian Ocean back to Ile St. Marie, known to the English as St. Mary's Island. The long thin strip of land lay about two miles off the northeast coast of Madagascar. While much of its eastern face was unapproachable due to shallow, rocky water and coral shoals, the western side provided a convenient little bay with a narrow entrance headed by an islet affectionately known by the locals as "The Rock". This bay was a mere mile wide, and if one was careful, a ship with a shallow draft and skilled pilot could enter it.

Sitting in the center of the bay was a tiny island within the island, one that pirates like Henry Every and Thomas Tew favored. It was called Ile Aux Forbans, or Pirates Island.

The *Dolphin* carefully navigated past The Rock and sailed into Pirates Bay, to the great joy of the crew. Davy leaned over the rail and took in the view. George informed him that St.

Mary's was a fine, lawless tropical paradise, conveniently located near major European shipping routes. The natives were friendly, and a former pirate captain named Adam Baldridge had established a fortified trading post on Pirates Island, where scores of gentlemen of fortune resided in wooden shacks. According to Booth, it was the perfect spot to rest, refit the ship, and fence their stolen goods. Davy's first impression was that it was a quaint more modest version of Libertalia.

After the crew took in the sails and dropped anchor, Quartermaster North called them all to the main deck to divide the Dutchman's loot. A committee of three experienced hands were elected to observe the estimation of wealth for each item, conducted by North and Captain Inless. One, a former trader in colonial America, was especially keen at assessing market value of cargo.

The crew milled around the waist, eagerly awaiting the result. When the estimation was complete, the total was divided into shares. Davy was pleasantly surprised to learn his share amounted to 400 British pounds sterling, more than a year's worth of earnings for the common man in Wales.

The illicit cargo was moved ashore by boat. Some went to Pirates Island, and the rest was sent to another trading post further north on St. Mary's run by some of Tew's former shipmates, led by his quartermaster, Byron Smith. The old pirate, like many shady traders in the region, had an agreement with an American businessman to import stolen goods into the English colonies at a reduced price. His agent in turn would sell the merchandise on the local market, thus avoiding heavy tariffs imposed by the Crown. Local buyers greedily snapped up the illegal goods, saving money in the process. Everyone won, except King William.

Davy was with the working party led by Booth that moved cargo to Smith's trading post, three miles away through the jungle. The road, an overgrown glorified trail, was cleared by men with axes and cutlasses to make room for the makeshift sled loaded with barrels of spice. Davy took his turn on the sled, alternately pushing and dragging with several others.

The pirates took breaks from their exhausting work every few hundred yards, allowing Davy the chance to take in the local flora and fauna. Wild orchids, lemurs, and exotic birds were just a few of the highlights.

When they finally arrived at the trading post, a slave took them to meet Smith. The old quartermaster quickly inspected the haul. Satisfied, he invited them inside his log blockhouse to have a drink and negotiate the price. Davy noticed the swivel guns mounted in cutout windows.

Several bottles of rum were passed around, and Smith asked them about their adventures. He was particularly keen on knowing if they had heard about Henry Every. When he learned from Booth that Davy was part of Every's crew, Smith grew excited. He questioned Davy about Every's whereabouts, and if he retired after the Mohgul raid, or whether the 'Pirate King', as he was now known, was still operating.

Davy pled ignorance, saying he was recuperating from his wounds in Libertalia when his old captain departed, destination unknown. Smith grew silent, and nodded. He took a long drag from his pipe and then began discussing the value of the cargo with Booth.

The men spent the night in the blockhouse before returning to Pirates Bay the next afternoon. They rowed over to Pirates Island and joined the celebratory festivities with the rest of the *Dolphin* crew.

Davy sampled some good Madeira wine, which cost him 15 times what he would have paid in a civilized port. He didn't mind, however, since he was flush with silver coin. He ate roasted pig, drank heavily, and played dice.

On the morning of the third day of debauchery, a signal cannon from The Rock was heard. The owner of the establishment, one Edward Welch, appeared with a telescope and trained it on the source of the gunfire. A rowboat put off from The Rock, pulling furiously toward Pirates Island.

Welch went down to the shore to meet it and swiftly took a report from the panting lookout. He sprinted back up to the outdoor tavern and loudly announced the presence of a squadron of English men-of-war approaching St. Mary's under a full press of sail.

Captain Inless immediately recalled the crew to the ship. The *Dolphin*, snug in the harbor, was at risk of being bottled up by the enemy fleet.

Davy staggered down the slope and jumped into a dugout canoe commandeered by some of his shipmates. They paddled back to the ship and clambered aboard. As they prepared to weigh anchor, the lookout high above in the main crossjack tree shouted to the deck below. The masts of four men-of-war were seen a league off the coast.

The bay erupted into chaos. One of the departing pirate ships ran aground in the east channel. Another pirate crew abandoned their ship and swam or rowed for shore.

Another gun was fired from The Rock. Soon, a cutter from the fleet sailed toward the harbor flying a white flag. The approaching boat hailed the *Dolphin* and halted just inside the west channel. Inless ordered a boat to be lowered and rowed out to meet it. When he returned an hour later, his face was ashen. He called the ship's company.

"Men, there's a 60-gun fourth rate out there with two frigates and a sloop," he announced to the tense company. "Commodore Warren offers a pardon from the Crown for any gentleman of fortune. The alternative," he paused, "is a hanging from the yardarm."

The crew instantly broke out into a furious argument. Inless glanced at the silent North and then held up his hand. "We can't get out without the English tearing us to pieces, and they can stand off and shell the bay at will." He saw only one option. Flee into the surrounding jungle and hope the Navy wouldn't send its Marines after them.

He put the question before the crew. "We have until sundown to decide," he concluded.

Davy looked at Booth, who in turn looked at North. The quartermaster grimaced and shook his head. "I ain't givin' meself over to the tender mercies of the Navy," he declared. "We stall for more time and wait til nightfall, then every man make his own way. Tis the only option, if'n ye value yer freedom," he added.

The crew murmured anxiously. Inless pointed to Booth. "Gunner! What have you to say about our predicament?"

Booth furrowed his brow and gave a sidelong glance to Davy. "There's a hundred guns out there, not to mention more than a thousand English sailors who would love to see us all dangle from the yard arm. Even if we sail the ship out under cover of darkness, they will be sure to anticipate that and have a guard ship nearby to catch us. However," he paused, drawing a deep breath. There may be a way out of this trap."

The pirates huddled closer. "Go on," said Captain Inless.

"We wait until sundown, then sail for the channel with a skeleton crew," Booth began slowly. "Everyone else slips away in the boats before *Dolphin* weighs anchor, and hauls them overland to the eastern shore. There they wait until they hear the signal, which will be one gun to leeward."

"The skeleton crew fires the ship in the channel and swims for shore," the gunner continued. "We'll leave two dugouts for them on The Rock. The rest of you make for the open sea. We can rendezvous at Libertalia."

"Canna we jest hide in the forest an' wait 'em out?" inquired a voice.

"Nay, they will land their men and scour the whole island to find us," North retorted. "We have to leave. Or take the pardon, if ye prefer," he sneered.

Several pirates voiced their agreement with North. Others talked in low voices. Captain Inless stepped forward. "Any man who wishes to take the pardon may go now, and fare thee well," he said. "I will remain aboard *Dolphin* and buy you the time you need to get overland. I'll need at least a dozen men to haul up the anchor and set the courses. After that, you can depart and I will sail her into the channel and make it look like we're making a run for it. I'll need two men to stay and fire her. Do I have any volunteers?"

"If anyone shall blow up *Dolphin's* magazine, it will be me," Booth announced.

"Anyone else?"

Davy gazed at the jungle. After a long silence he stepped forward. "Aye," he said quietly. "I'll do it. I, fer one, ain't gonna be taken alive."

"Yer all touched in the head, if'n ye think ye can git away," declared one man. "We've had a good run. I'm gonna save me hide an' take the pardon." A few other men voiced their agreement.

"Well then, begone with ye!" thundered North. "But don't ye tell them English bastards our plan!" he added with venom.

As the sun sank lower in the azure sky, fourteen pirates left the ship and rowed out to The Rock, waving a piece of sailcloth to indicate surrender. An armed cutter crowded with Marines from the men-of-war met them at the surf line and escorted them to the flagship.

Other pirates, including North, volunteered to stay long enough to get the *Dolphin* underway, while their comrades paddled away in dugouts for shore. Davy and George went below to prepare the ship for its destruction.

They transferred several kegs of powder to the main deck,

pried off the stoppers and inserted hollow wooden plugs filled with slow-burning gunpowder from grenadoes. Then they prepared the signal gun and lit a length of slow match, waiting tensely for the signal from Inless.

North led the remaining pirates to the ship's boats. "Good luck, gennelmen," he cried with a wave of his hand. Davy watched them go, wondering if he'd made the right decision.

The *Dolphin* crept forward, aided by a light offshore breeze. As the sun descended toward the terminus of its fiery path, Davy could see the silhouette of a frigate standing just offshore, blocking the escape path out of the channel. Light gleamed from the barrels of cannon and he could see the gun crews poised for action. He looked behind and saw not a soul remained on shore. Inless was manning the helm, stock still, as the ship neared The Rock.

"George, if'n we get outta this without bein' captured, first round's on me in Libertalia," Davy joked nervously.

Booth returned his quip with a smile. "Aye, and I'll set you up with the prettiest whore in the whole damned town."

"No thanks, already had her," Davy replied. Their laughter was cut short when Inless raised his hand.

"Prepare to fire the signal gun," he ordered.

Davy and George went aft to the stern chaser and looked back at the captain while the *Dolphin* slowly eased into the narrow channel, sailing against the incoming tidal current. The Rock was coming up on their starboard quarter, within pistol shot. Inless suddenly dropped his arm and cried, "Now!"

Booth put the slow match to the touch hole and the chaser roared its warning. Within moments the English frigate opened fire, peppering the *Dolphin*. Shots flew through the masts, rigging and sails. The fore shroud parted and a spar fell from the mainmast. Several holes were now evident in the courses and topsails.

"They're firing high to slow us down," Booth shouted to Davy. "Watch out for falling blocks and tackle."

They made their way to the main mast where the kegs of gunpowder awaited their final mission. Inless raised his hand again and paused for a few more moments, making sure the ship was well into the channel. He set a course to ram the frigate and tied the helm down. Then waved his arm and ordered, "Light it!"

George and Davy fed their slow matches to the fuses, igniting what they calculated would be a one-minute delay. Captain Inless rushed to their side as more shots from the frigate crashed into the foremast, causing it to teeter precariously. "Abandon ship!" he commanded.

The three jumped over the starboard side and began swimming for The Rock. Davy arrived well ahead of the other two, just in time to witness the charges go off and the main deck of the *Dolphin* explode, sending glowing embers into the lower decks, sails and surrounding water. Cannon were thrown clear of the ship and wood fragments rained down as Inless and Booth gained their feet and began wading out of the shallow water to The Rock. A falling timber smashed into the back of Inless and he fell face first into the sandy beach. Davy rushed to his side as Booth took cover.

"Cap'n! Are ye all right? Can ye walk?"

Inless turned his sand-encrusted face and blinked dumbly in shock. At last, he managed a feeble reply. "Nay. My back is broken and I can't move. Leave me." He closed his eyes and his breathing became ragged.

Booth had dragged a dugout canoe they'd hid earlier into the water. "Let's go, Davy!"

"Wait," Inless croaked. "Take my sword. I don't want the bloody English to have it."

Davy paused, then quickly fumbled at the captain's belt. He unsheathed Inless's fine French cavalry sword. "Fair winds, cap'n," he said, rising to his feet. He took one last look at his pirate leader and then dashed to the dugout. Booth handed him a paddle and they made for the far shore across the lagoon, the smoke of the burning *Dolphin* covering their escape.

They beached the dugout and had just reached the tree line when they heard an ear-splitting boom. Looking back, they witnessed the last of the *Dolphin* sink into the channel, blocking it from entry. It was just as Inless had planned. They shared a grief-stricken moment and then began running into the jungle.

They made their way to the path that led them to Smith's trading post three miles away. They arrived less than half an hour later, weary and breathless, at the clearing surrounding the blockhouse. The sun was down and the creeping darkness of twilight arose like a corpse resurrected from the dead.

"Get ye gone!" they heard Smith shout from within. A blast from one of the mounted swivel guns made them jump behind the trees. "I know ye had somethin' to do with the murder of Cap'n Tew, ye little shite!"

"That bastard!" Davy exclaimed. "I *knew* there was

somethin' fishy about him."

Booth motioned toward the shore. "We'll respond to his lack of hospitality by taking one of his boats," he replied. They rushed across the clearing to the shoreline. They heard the report of another swivel gun and sand kicked up beside them. George leaped into a small boat and grabbed the oars. "Shove off!" he directed.

Davy pushed the boat off the sandy bottom and jumped in. Another round from the swivel gun splashed next to them and now they saw four men emerge from the blockhouse, armed with muskets. Booth pulled hard and the little boat quickly gathered way. "Get down!" he shouted.

Musket balls whizzed close by as the boat moved further out to the surf line. Booth looked over his shoulder and timed his next pull to ride the rise over the cresting surf. The little craft's bow was airborne for a moment before it slammed down into the trough. Now they were out of effective range and the muskets fell silent.

Davy arose from his prostrate position and peered over the gunwale. The traders ashore watched helplessly as the two pirates made their escape. Squinting at the darkening figures in the dusk, he vowed, "That Smith is gonna pay fer his betrayal."

He loaded his musket and waited for the next crest. As the boat rose on the wave, Davy popped to his feet and instantly fired toward the beach. He fell back down into the boat as it descended into the trough. He had to wait a few more seconds before they were lifted on another swell to view his handiwork. The traders were gathered around a man lying in the sand.

"That's fer me da, ye rat bastards!" Jones gave a smirk to a gaping Booth.

"That was the luckiest shot in the world, Davy, or you're the Devil."

"Mebbe both," Davy replied.

They took turns rowing for several hours as night overtook them. The pale moon broke through low clouds in the east and shined brightly upon the pair in their little craft. Davy noticed the dark shape of a medium-sized ship about a cable-length away and three points to the north. It had three masts and a bowsprit, but didn't appear to be a man of war. The strange sail was on a line that would intercept their course. He pointed it out to Booth, who quickly decided it was a French polacre.

"She's a merchant, probably lightly armed with swivels. No great guns," he added, stroking his chin. "I say we take her."

"But there's only two of us," Davy objected. "How can we do that?"

"We stay on her bowline," said Booth. "When she comes near, we light along the mainchains and take the helmsman. The crew is likely asleep, with their arms stowed."

"Once we have control of the helm," Booth continued, "I'll seize the captain and force him to surrender."

Davy licked his parched lips and silently weighed the risk. He decided it was better than rowing about until they were dead of thirst or exposure. "Alright," he agreed.

Once aboard he crept up on the helmsman and put his pistol to the man's head and ordered him to remain silent. Booth went below and soon was back, with the sleepy, surprised captain in front of him at sword point. They altered course and set out for Libertalia.

As dawn appeared, the crew began to rise from their berthing and make their way out to the main deck. Davy stood on the slanted afterdeck, his musket at the ready as he watched the shocked crew gather at the mainmast. Booth spoke to the captain, who in turn addressed his men in French.

"Tell them we now control this vessel. We are sailing it to Madagascar," Booth instructed. The captain relayed the message.

"Now tell them if any of them wish to join us, we will not harm them. Any who do not will be marooned on the first island we see." The captain glared at him for a moment before telling his crew. Numbering a little over 200, the men winked and ribbed each other. One called out to the captain, *"Tuez les scélérats!"*

The French captain shook his head. *"C'est moi qui décide."* He turned to Booth. "The ship is yours. Release us when we arrive at your destination, *s'il vous plaît.*"

"Not before I get my crew," Booth replied. He scanned the ship's company and spoke to them in French.

The captain gaped at him. Davy also was stunned to learn that Booth spoke fluent French. The bewildered crew looked at each other before a score of them stepped forward. The rest grumbled in protest. But upon seeing several of their senior and popular seamen defect to the pirates, more decided to join them. Soon, only a few remained with the captain. Booth motioned to Davy to secure the rest in the hold.

"*Très bien*," Booth said. "Captain, please go with your men to the hold. I'm sure you understand. We will make sure you and your men will be fed and adequately disposed. We should only be a couple of days."

Davy learned the ship, a merchantman from Marseille, was named *Raconteur*. It was returning from India with a load of spices and gold-wrought dining pieces for the French court. Davy and Booth heartily laughed as they realized the French Sun King would never see his royal dinnerware.

The *Raconteur* sailed into Libertalia bay and Booth commanded his new French pirates to offload the valuable merchandise. He spent several hours that afternoon negotiating the sale of the goods and returned. He gave one of the ship's boats to the French captain and saw to it they were provisioned. Booth also gave them a compass before bidding them *adieu*.

Davy watched the boat depart as Booth joined him at the taffrail. "Ye shouldn't let him go. He'll report us to the first man-o-war he finds, like that English squadron out there."

"Some gentlemen of fortune have a little decency," George replied.

"Mercy then, is it?" Davy replied scornfully. "There's no place fer that in our business." He thought about Giselle and her betrayal. "I woulda carved him up, along with the rest of those dogs."

George stared long and hard at Davy. "You really are the Devil."

16

Libertalia

The French crew of *Raconteur* went ashore in Libertalia with their newfound wealth from the sale of the cargo, and promptly dispersed to explore the carnal delights of the pirate colony. Davy was relieved to see them go. His loathing for the French was mitigated only by their superior craftsmanship in firearms and ships.

He and Booth frequented the drinking establishments and whorehouses, as any red-blooded seaman was wont to do. Although he was initially cautious, Davy found that his reputation as a cold-blooded murderer drew many a wary glance, but none challenged him. He became more confident, even surly the more he drank.

After two months, Davy and George had spent much of their money and decided it was time for another cruise. They began to recruit the toughest and most talented men they could find. One such man was John Bowen.

Bowen was ashore after recently serving as sailing master of a brigantine. An experienced sailor, he was still new to the pirate business. After a few drinks, he agreed to sign on with the *Raconteur* as a master's mate. Davy took an instant liking to him.

When they had signed on a crew of sixty, the provisioned the *Raconteur* and armed it with ten guns. As the master gunner, Davy selected eight bronze 12-pounders and the best powder and shot, much of it from his old armament shop. He bought a pair of used long nine-pounders from a retiring pirate and had them brought aboard the *Raconteur* as chasers.

Booth was confirmed as captain by the new crew, and he promptly proposed a shakedown cruise of the inner channel between Madagascar and the mainland to search for merchantmen. "We'll meet new friends," he paused for effect, "and shake them down!" The crew roared in laughing approval.

The *Raconteur* sailed out of the bay and headed north, with Bowen at the helm. They passed the tip of Madagascar and headed southwest down the coast. Within three days they fell upon an English slave trading ship, which gave up without a fight. The 350 slaves were recently taken from a village known as Majunga, inhabited by Sakalava Malagasy. Some of the crew wanted to take them to a market to be sold, but Booth disagreed.

"We share this island with the natives," he explained. "It would do us well to continue having good relations with them. Setting them free may help us in the future, in ways we cannot foresee just now. Besides," he added, "we just began this cruise and fortune has smiled upon us. Now we have this fine vessel."

The crew agreed and voted to put the former slaves ashore and to send the Englishmen off in boats. Booth savored his first victory as captain and promptly put a prize crew on the large brig, the *Speaker*, with Bowen in command.

They sailed down into the inner channel for three weeks, but their luck seemed to dry up in the hot breeze. Booth declared they should turn north and patrol the African coast. After a few days, Bowen hailed *Raconteur*, claiming he was running out of fresh water. Booth agreed to put in at the island of Zanzibar for supplies.

As the two ships sailed north on the current, Davy spent his time ensuring the great guns were in working order. He exercised the gun crews with drills, but was careful not to overtask them. The men didn't mind a little training, but they loved their drink and Davy didn't want to risk their displeasure.

The *Raconteur* and *Speaker* navigated the archipelago and dropped anchor near Stone Town, the main port of Zanzibar, which was an island protectorate of the Sultan of Oman. Davy joined Booth, Bowen, and several pirates as they rowed past a fort overlooking the waterfront to negotiate with the Arabs for supplies.

The local commander of the Arab garrison greeted them. He was a tall, fearsome warrior, wearing a breastplate and carrying a large scimitar. Six troops with long spears waited in formation behind him.

"We have business with the Vizier," said Booth. "We wish to resupply our ship and humbly request his approval to trade."

The grim commander wordlessly motioned to them to follow him. They made their way through the narrow, twisted streets flanked by the guards. The locals scampered out of the way as the huge commander led them past the market stalls and small shops emitting fantastic, unfamiliar odors. Davy licked his lips as he passed a whole lamb roasting on a spit.

The vizier's residence was atop a small hill overlooking the harbor. Davy had never seen such a fine place. Mango and clove trees dotted the grounds. Leafy vines grew abundantly atop the low, white walls surrounding the palatial estate. Atop the house was a crenelated flat roof. A tall archway rose above a set of wide stairs leading to the entrance where two guards flanked a tall hardwood door with a great bronze handle. The Arab officer gestured for them to remain and he went inside. Four guards remained with the pirates.

Davy took the opportunity to examine the details of the beautiful house. The dazzling white stone walls featured windows with diamond-shaped glass panes in various colors, held together with stained wood. Arab writing was carved into relief above the enormous door.

The commander flicked his hand and the guards stepped forward to disarm them. Davy protested but Booth assured him that it was appropriate. "I feel naked," Davy grumbled.

A translator appeared and told them his name was Khalil. He bowed to the commander of the guards and motioned for the visitors to enter. The rather small, dark man wore a simple white robe, which had long sleeves and no collar.

The air smelled of rich incense. Flowers and potted planted abounded as they tread over tiled floors. There were small low tables surrounded by cushions and hookahs visible as they passed from room to room.

They entered a large chamber and Khalil held up his hand. "Please wait," he asked. He shuffled over to an important-looking man to a man resting upon several silk cushions. Khalil bowed, and whispered to him. The man glanced at them and nodded.

The translator stood up and announced, "You are in the presence of His Excellency, Vizier Badar al-Sur," his hand sweeping wide. "He is advisor to the Sultan of Zanzibar and manages his affairs." Seeing the pirates' uncertainty, he added, "You must bow before him."

Davy, George and John Bowen bowed deeply. As Davy began to rise, Khalil halted him. "It is not permitted to stand until His Excellency has acknowledged you," he said quickly.

Davy resumed his bow, staring at the ornate tile flooring of the chamber, marveling at the detailed craftsmanship.

"*Inhaad,*" said the Vizier.

The translator said, "You may arise." He glanced at the Vizier, who gestured to cushions on the floor near him.

"His Excellency would be pleased if you rested," said the translator. He motioned to a servant standing in the shadows and the dark figure scampered away.

Davy shifted uneasily in his seat. Something about this place, or perhaps this Vizier, made him uncomfortable. He glanced back at the towering Arab commander, who remained standing, his hand resting on his scimitar. The servant reappeared with a silver tray. Tea and sweets were offered to the guests as the Vizier stroked his closely trimmed beard and studied them.

Vizier Badar al-Sur appeared to be in his late forties, with a long, sharp nose and thoughtful, coal-black eyes. A striped light blue turban sat over his high forehead and bushy brows. A dark red satin robe framed his white robe, and a curved, gold-handled Arabic dagger sat squarely in the middle of his broad belt. Davy noticed the gold ring on his left hand. It was set with the largest ruby Davy had ever seen, clearly a sign of his important position as the chief administrator.

They sipped their tea in silence. Davy discovered he enjoyed the delightful plate of sweets, which included baklava dripping in honey, and a creamy wheat konafa. Al-Sur took note of Davy's pleasure and commented.

Khalil translated, "His Excellency gives thanks to Allah for his many blessings, and is pleased with your enjoyment of his hospitality. He also has empowered this humble servant," he gestured to himself, "to negotiate terms for any supplies or services you may require. He says you may stay here in his city, trade as much as you like, then depart in peace with his blessing."

Booth pulled out his leather purse and put it on the floor in front of al-Sur. "We offer this gift to the Sultan as a gesture of our friendship and gratitude for his kindness," he said, smiling.

The Vizier glanced at the purse and briefly smiled. Khalil spoke again. "This token will surely please His Most Glorious Eminence."

The Vizier dismissed the pirates with a wave of his hand.

Booth stood up and Bowen and Davy followed him as the hulking captain of the guard led them out. Once outside, Khalil turned to them.

"His Excellency the Vizier is interested in knowing if you have any slaves or women with which you would be willing to part?"

Bowen grimaced. "I told ye, we shoulda kept those slaves."

Booth glowered at him briefly, then smiled and addressed Khalil. "Our sincerest apologies to His Excellency. We just offloaded our recent slave cargo, but," he added, "should we obtain more during this cruise we will be sure to offer them to him for a special price."

"And women," Khalil reminded him.

"Yes, of course. We desire to supply our ships with fresh water and provisions for our journey. We understand His Most Glorious Excellency the Sultan is a generous man and a friend to visitors," he said. "Naturally, we are prepared to offer fair compensation...in gold," he added.

Khalil nodded and made arrangements to have water and provisions delivered to the ship, payable upon arrrival.

Bowen complained all the way back to the boat of how they could have made a respectable fortune selling the slaves. Booth ignored him for a while, but finally exploded.

"We do not take, buy or sell the Malagasy!"

"Oh, an' why is that?" Bowen retorted. "Is there somethin' special about 'em?"

Booth shook his head in exasperation. "Listen carefully. The Malagasy are different. They are not like Africans, or

Arabs, or Indians. We live on a huge island full of Malagasy tribes. We enslave a few and what do you think will happen?"

Bowen cursed and spat. "All I know is this here fella, this Viz-ear, is a buyer. We should keep any more slaves we find on this cruise and bring 'em back fer a handsome profit."

"So we shall, if the crew wants to do so, just not Malagasy," replied Booth. "Let's concentrate on the task at hand. You can have the boat crew offload the water casks. Davy, you're with me."

Davy and George spent the rest of the afternoon haggling with merchants in the bazaar. There were many interesting trinkets and wares to examine. They bought a few items and headed back to the ship. Davy noticed the Vizier's boats were already making deliveries of the items they negotiated earlier.

By evening their work was finished and the crew made ready to come ashore for liberty.

"And for God's sake," Booth said, as the men began to disperse. "Stick to the taverns. Don't get drunk in public or molest the women on the street. It is forbidden under penalty of death."

"A fine port 'o call," jeered Bowen in his Creole accent. "A man canna be a man? Well, I fer one, intend to have a good time!" The pirates climbed into the ship's boats, some grumbling under their breath.

"That Bowen, he's gonna be trouble someday," Davy remarked as he watched the boats make for shore.

"Yes," Booth agreed, "but he's quite popular among the men. I'm going back aboard to take a look at the charts and work out our options for the cruise."

"Aye, I'll take the deck watch," Davy replied. He went below, grabbed his French musket and tucked his pistol into his belt. Entering the armory, he chose a powder horn and ammunition pouch and slung them over his shoulder. His hand automatically felt the reassuring hilt of his dagger. Satisfied, he adjusted his eye patch and climbed back up the ladder to the main deck.

He relieved the watch and paced around the deck, watching the sea bird fly around and various fishing boats return from their day's work. The sun was setting, so he lit the ship's stern-post lantern. The dusk was always his favorite time of day. There was something about the transitioning colors of the sky and water that seemed almost magical. The waning quarter moon rose over the eastern horizon, huge and yellowish orange. It was a baleful reminder. Davy knew that in less than a week he would have to go for a swim.

Hours sped by in the quiet harbor. George appeared on deck at midnight and offered to take the next watch. "I can't sleep anyway," he explained. He leaned his musket against the mast and dipped the ladle into the scuttlebutt. The water was warm, but fresh, with a bit of a mineral taste. He took another sip.

A shot rang out. Davy and George rushed to the rail and

scanned the shore. Only a few dim lights were visible in the distant town. They might as well have searched the stars. Another shot. They heard faint echoes of shouts. George picked up his musket. "Stay here," he ordered. "I'm taking the jolly boat."

"What are ye doin'?" Davy asked. "That could be anyone."

"No," George responded firmly. "Only our men carry firearms on this island." He climbed down the stern and dropped into the boat. Untying the painter line, he grabbed the grabbed the oars and furiously pulled for shore.

Davy stood for a few moments, bewildered. He was alone on the ship. *What can I do?* he wondered anxiously. The shouts grew louder and more distinct. He knew he couldn't leave. He picked up his musket and began loading. When he was done, he set it on the rail and went below. He grabbed several more muskets and brought them up, loading each. Next, he loaded two swivel guns mounted on the starboard gunwale, which faced Stone Town.

The quarter moon and stars cast a weak light, but it was enough for Davy to see dozens of men sprinting to the beach, pursued by dozens more yelling furiously at them. It was obvious the pirates were on the run.

Davy picked up his musket and poured powder into the pan. He knelt behind the rail and waited as the pirates scrambled into the boats and shoved off. He thought he saw Booth and another man remaining behind on the beach. Booth appeared to be fighting some kind of rearguard action while the others escaped.

Davy could tell the pursuers were the Stone Town garrison because the unmistakably massive frame of the Arab guard commander was leading the charge. They were still out of his musket's range, but not Booth's. He fired, dropping a soldier, but they still came, howling like banshees. Booth retreated to the water's edge and helped the man with him shove the jolly boat off the beach. Davy squinted hard and discerned the features of Bowen.

Booth and Bowen strained at the oars as the little boat made way. Seeing his quarry fleeing beyond his grasp, the Arab commander seized a long spear from one of his men as he ran down the beach.

Then the world seemed to slow down. Davy positioned his musket on the rail and looked down the dimly lit barrel with his good eye. The commander was preparing to launch his spear at Booth. Davy aimed just above his head and squeezed the trigger. The pan flashed, temporarily blinding him, as the ball sped toward its target.

Davy lowered the musket and waited for his night vision to return. When it did, he saw the Arab commander on his knees, clutching his side as his men gathered around him. He looked at the dark water but couldn't see the little jolly boat.

Pirates swarmed over the sides of the *Raconteur* and *Speaker*. Davy shouted at them to get underway. The guns of the fort might fire at any moment. As the men climbed the rigging to loose the sails, he saw Bowen climb up from the main chains.

"Where's Booth?" Davy shouted.

Bowen jerked his thumb toward the side and turned away. As he shouted orders to the men, Davy leaned over the side and looked down. Booth was lying face up in the jolly boat. An eight-foot spear stuck out of his chest like the mast of a man-o-war.

Davy climbed down into the boat and quickly secured it to the ship with the painter line. He sat down next to George, who stared up at him with unseeing eyes. His expression was pained astonishment. Davy silently watched his friend until his final breath left him. He stood up, pulled the spear out of Booth, and cast it away.

The ship was moving. Davy looked up and saw Bowen staring at him. "Well, ain't ye gonna git aboard, or do we have to pull ye along?"

Davy rolled his eyes in disgust. He knelt down and pushed George over the side of the jolly boat. The body submerged briefly and then rose to the surface. Davy saw George's face, barely lit in the darkness. He seemed to regard Davy for a moment before slipping down to become lost in the sea.

Indian Ocean

T he two ships weighed anchor and skated away from the reaches of the fort at Stone Town, but not before the *Raconteur* was holed several times by its great guns.

As they progressed north by northeast away from Zanzibar, the carpenter reported he could not keep the ship seaworthy due to the damage in the worm-eaten hull. Bowen decided to transfer the crew to the *Speaker* and ordered *Raconteur* burned. As the ship went down in flames, Davy was burning too, with anger. He met Bowen in the captain's cabin aboard *Speaker*.

"Ye never related why there was such a fracas ashore," he blurted, barely able to control his rage. "I demand an answer fer the death of the cap'n!"

Bowen met Davy's fixed glare with consternation. "Ye demand? Lookee here, lad, this is a dangerous business we're about, an' sometimes things happen."

"Don't call me lad," Davy responded hotly. "I have a right to know what happened!"

Bowen looked away, pursing his lips. He slumped into his chair and waved his hand wearily. "It was a misunderstandin'. We paid fer our provisions, fair an' square. Then, when we was partakin' in refreshment, that big lug of a garrison commander comes tearin' inta the place with his gang o' soldiers an' demands a tax – a TAX!"

Bowen rubbed his chin ruefully. "I says, 'what tax? We done settled our accounts.' Then he says, 'ye ain't sent the tax on trade goods to the *Viz-ear*, as per local custom.' Well, I told 'im 'nobody said nothin' about no tax, an' we ain't gonna be shaken down by some *low official*.' So he says we gonna 'ave to be clapped in irons an' go to the stockade. So, I drew my piece on 'im an' says 'we ain't gonna pay no tax, we ain't gonna go to no prison, an' he can stop his gob."

Davy stared at him incredulously. "Ye challenged the commander? What, ye lost yer mind?"

"We is PIRATES!" shouted Bowen. "We ain't citizens, or mere traders t' be trifled with!"

Davy grimly shook his head. "And so Booth paid fer yer impudence with his life. That's a sorry tale."

"Bah!" Bowen retorted. "We got away, an' at least we ain't rottin' in that fort fer God knows how long. Ye should thank me – an' remember the crew backs me. They elected *me* cap'n, not you." He glared at Davy menacingly. "Why don't ye go back t' yer magazine, gunner, an' I'll ferget yer foul attitude."

"By the articles, I can challenge ye on the beach, if'n I am so inclined," Davy warned.

"Jest so," Bowen replied smoothly. "But we ain't gonna be on the beach anytime soon. Now, off with ye."

Davy stomped out of the cabin, breathing heavily and trembling with rage.

For the next few days, the *Speaker* followed the current north and east. They did not sight prey, only a few fishing dhows and small coastal craft. Davy used the time to ensure the cannon transferred from the *Raconteur* were well placed on the deck. He got the carpenter to cut openings in the ship's sides to accommodate the great guns, including his prize possessions, the long nine-pounders.

He supervised gunnery exercises, ensuring the quarter gunners and their crews were fast and efficient. He spent many hours getting the powder magazine and armory in shipshape condition as well. But mostly, he thought about George Booth. He resolved to get even with Bowen, somehow and somewhere, at a time of his choosing.

The crew had voted to attack Mohgul ships, hoping to recreate the luck of Henry Every's legendary haul. It was the pilgrimage season, and Bowen easily convinced the men they would be rich. Davy alone among them knew the peril of such a venture, but when the time came for objections, he remained silent. Truth was, Davy was itching for some payback for his lost eye.

It was a journey of some 2,000 nautical miles, and the brigantine covered it in two weeks of steady sailing before arriving in the vicinity of the Horn of Africa. Bowen proposed they lay in wait in the Strait of Bab el-Mandeb, similar to what Every had done a few years ago, but Davy said it would suit their interest if they instead posted themselves a hundred miles east, near the old port of Aden.

"They will be on guard in the strait," claimed Davy. "If'n we wait fer another day, they might relax watch, thinkin' they're safe." He explained the Mohgul convoys preferred to hug the coast of the Arabian Peninsula, so they couldn't miss. "We hide in the harbor and surprise 'em as they pass by. While we wait, we can get fresh water from the locals," he added with a glare at Bowen, "providin' nobody makes a fuss."

Although Bowen was clearly irritated by the remark, he put it to a vote and the pirates agreed to Davy's plan.

The *Speaker* arrived at Aden after sunrise and dropped anchor in the bay, which was formed by an extinct volcano. Bowen led a small group of men to the village and bartered for a few goods and fresh water. His main objective was to gather intelligence about the Mohgul fleet's whereabouts. As a precautionary measure, a lookout was posted on the headland to keep watch for the Moghul fleet.

Bowen came back to the ship and announced the Mohgul fleet was expected to return from Mocha and pass by Aden within the week. Since there was little to do in the poor town comprised mostly of huts, the crew loaded fresh water and took the time to clean their firearms and sharpen their blades.

Five days later, the lookout ran back from the headland to report sighting a large number of lateen-rigged sails a few leagues to the west, almost certainly Mohgul ships, and hugging the coast as Davy predicted. Bowen clapped his hands in delight and ordered the crew to weigh anchor and prepare the ship for sea.

The sun was just past its zenith when the first ships came in sight of the *Speaker* waiting at the mouth of the bay. A typical Mohgul convoy, most of the vessels were smaller, passenger ships guarded by a single large warship. Bowen ordered a full spread of canvas, and the *Speaker* weathered the headland and made a beeline for the main prize at the center of the convoy.

Davy took charge of the chasers and was the first to open fire from the ship's bow. The ball crashed into the mizzen boom, sending the huge lateen sail of the Mohgul ship to the deck. The impact created great confusion as Moghul warriors were scattered or buried under the lateen. Davy aimed the second chaser and sent a round through the ship's rudder, knocking its top off and jamming it awkwardly against the hull.

When the *Speaker* closed within point blank range, Bowen yawed the ship and the pirates let loose their broadside cannon. Several balls crashed through the upper works and one crippled the foremast. Pirates in the tops let loose with deadly musket fire, and soon the decks were cleared as survivors ran for cover to escape the onslaught.

Bowen ordered a general boarding as the *Speaker* came alongside. Grappling hooks were thrown and soon the pirates, Davy included, had clambered aboard the wounded vessel with pistols and blades. Bowen led a group toward the forecastle and engaged the Mohgul warriors who had taken shelter. Davy and others pried the hatches off and descended below.

The Moghuls put up a tenacious battle. With little light below decks, the pirates fought in close quarters with the enemy. Davy hacked away with his cutlass and used his dirk to finish off his opponents. After three hours of intense fighting and heavy losses, the Mohguls yielded.

Survivors were herded onto the main deck and guarded by pirates with muskets, backed up by the *Speaker's* swivel guns loaded with grapeshot. Bowen led a group of men as they systematically ransacked the ship from top to bottom. The ship's holds contained innumerable bolts of silk and casks of exotic spices, along with a modest sum of gold and silver coins.

Davy took charge of guarding the prisoners while Bowen organized the transfer of the precious cargo to the *Speaker*. The process took more than a day to complete. Meanwhile, the prisoners were questioned at gunpoint to ascertain if any were important enough to ransom. A sheikh was discovered, attempting to hide as an ordinary crewman. After some debate, it was decided the man was not worth the effort and he was shoved back into the crowd of prisoners.

The rest of the convoy had hastily departed when the pirates descended on the warship and were long gone over the horizon. It didn't matter to the pirates. They estimated the value of the cargo at close to 100,000 English pounds. The prize itself was too battered to be of much use, so Bowen ordered it released after the guns were pushed overboard.

As the Mohgul ship limped away under a jury-mast, Bowen considered his options. He put before the crew the idea of heading east to prowl the shipping routes around the Malabar Coast of India. With plenty of room still left in the spacious hold, the crew of the *Speaker* voted to continue the cruising.

The ship traveled 1,200 miles and on the morning of the seventh day the lookout at the mast reported a single sail, hull down, in the southeast. Bowen commanded the helmsman to steer a course to intercept. Davy came up on deck but was unable to see the strange sail due to the hazy horizon. Nonetheless, he went below and prepared cannon charges.

Hours later, as he and his mates were filling the last of the powder bags, another cry went up from the masthead. Again, he went up to the main deck and this time he spotted a tall, three-masted ship a league off the starboard bow tacking southwest. Bowen brought up his telescope and confirmed it was an Indiaman, precisely the type of prey they were seeking. He ordered the crew to pack on all sail and the *Speaker* gathered speed.

The pirates cleared for action and Davy took his position as captain of the bow chasers. His crew loaded round shot and ran out the guns. The chase had also opened its gun ports. "She's showing her teeth," he remarked to Booth. "Twelve guns. If we can catch her, we'll take her."

The prey seemed to match *Speaker* for speed. As the blazing sun proceeded on its arc across the sky, the distance between the ships remained steady. Bowen consulted the boatswain, Arnold, and the sailing master, Brown. They decided the best plan was to rig a kite sail and topsail stuns'ls while changing course slightly to bring the ship a half point closer to the wind. They would keep this sail plan as long as they could, but Brown warned Bowen that the masts might not take the strain for long.

As dusk settled and the light rapidly faded, the *Speaker* had closed the distance by half. The prey answered by heaving two of her guns overboard to lighten her and increase speed. As the Indiaman began to slowly pull away, an exasperated, Bowen again consulted Brown. The sailing master replied the only option was to lighten their load as well, and soon the crew was put to work throwing spare cordage and spars into the sea. Then the beef casks and extra barrels went over, much to the cooper's dismay.

The *Speaker* regained some of the lost distance, but couldn't close to gun range. Bowen called a meeting of the men to figure out what they could part with, under the circumstances. It became clear there were three things the pirates would never allow: their stolen cargo, the great guns, and their supply of spirits. It was the boatswain who finally presented a solution, although much to his regret. Soon, the spare anchor, which weighed two tons, was released into the sea.

As night fell, the prey was visible only by its battle lanterns on the main deck as men rushed about to prepare for battle. When the Indiaman was less than a mile off,

Bowen gave Davy the signal to commence fire. With little to aim for, Davy made a calculation and elevated his guns. He waited for the *Speaker* to rise with the swell and fired the port chaser. The shot fell wide of the target. He adjusted the angle of the starboard chaser and again fired when the ship reached the apex of the wave. The ball found its mark, parting the mainmast stay.

The pirates made encouraging comments to him as his gun crew prepared the next round of fire. Davy stood between the two long nines, holding slow match in each hand, and waited. He stared at the Indiaman's lights for a full minute then suddenly fired both cannons at once. The Indiaman's forecourse came crashing down as the yard splintered from the mast. Immediately the ship's progress was slowed and the pirates jumped for joy.

Bowen ordered the broadside guns to prepare fire. The helmsman yawed the ship to port and the *Speaker's* cannons thundered a fiery roar into the sultry night. The Indiaman managed to fire three ineffectual guns in return, but it was clear she was wounded. The *Speaker* closed in for the kill.

"We'll range up alongside, give 'er another broadside, then board from her bow," Bowen announced to the men.

Davy walked away from the chasers and went below to fetch his weapons. He tucked his pistol into his waist, strapped his cutlass and grabbed a pike before returning to the main deck. The *Speaker* was now sailing parallel to the Indiaman, and the two ships exchanged broadsides. Davy felt the rushing wind of a ball pass close by him and he involuntarily jumped to the side. Embarrassed, he raised his pistol and angrily fired at the prey.

"I don't think we're within pistol shot, Mr. Jones," Bowen cried, heaving with laughter.

Red-faced, Davy reloaded and grimly knelt behind the capstan, waiting for the signal to board. The *Speaker* cut across the Indiaman's bow and fired a third broadside down the length of the ship, leaving dozens of dead sprawled on deck. As the two ships ranged alongside each other, Bowen order all sails to be backed. Grappling hooks flew and soon the pirates were swarming over the sides.

Hot with rage, Davy joined the first group to land and immediately felled an English sailor with his pistol. He tossed it down and grabbed the pike with both hands, charging a group of Indiamen gathered at the forecastle. He snarled and thrust at an officer, who managed to parry and slash with his cutlass. Davy ducked and then threw himself back before his opponent could hack at him again. He drew his cutlass and with a blood-curdling scream, charged the mass of defenders.

The melee continued for more than an hour, the Englishmen giving a good fight to the zealous pirates. Men stepped on the dead and wounded strewn about the blood-slick deck as they viciously fought like animals.

Davy found the first officer standing near the foremast and called to him to defend himself. The shocked officer raised his cutlass in defense. An excellent swordsman, the officer slashed Davy across his chest and followed the stroke with a smash of his hilt to Davy's face.

Staggered, Davy ignored the searing pain and rushed inside the man's guard. Grabbing him by the throat, Davy plunged his dagger into the officer's side, again and again. The man's eyes bulged and he spit up blood. Davy held him by throat and stared intently until the life left his eyes. Releasing him, Davy panted and looked about.

The pirates were gathered around the deck, silently watching him. Some were stone-faced, while others openly gaped.

Bowen pushed his way through and he looked at Davy, from head to foot. "It's over," he said quietly. "They struck their colors a few minutes past. Ye didn't need t' kill 'im," he paused, then shrugged. "But ye did." He turned to his crew.

"Ye ever see fightin' like that, lads? Three cheers fer Davy Jones!" The pirates huzzahed, but Davy barely heard them. His head began to swim and the pain in his chest was overpowering his other senses. Two men grabbed him by the arms as he began to stumble backwards. The last image he had before he blacked out was Bowen with his arms crossed, nodding appreciatively at him.

He awoke in Bowen's cabin, thirsty as hell. He struggled to rise and felt something constricting his chest. He propped himself up on one elbow and numbly observed a wide, bloody bandage across his chest, which was completely wrapped around his midsection. His pendant was gone. *No! It's the only thing I have left from me da!* He resolved to find it, but first, he decided he must find a drink.

He glanced over and saw a jug and tankard sitting on a small table bolted to the floor. After a couple of attempts, he managed to roll over onto his side and swing his feet over the cot. His wound barked at him in protest, but the overpowering thirst demanded satisfaction. He steadied himself and then rose to his feet. His knees felt weak and he tasted iron in his mouth. He took a feeble step and then lurched over to the table, picking up the jug and searching inside.

He smelled, rather than saw the water with his one good eye. He tilted his head back and drank deeply. He lost his balance and staggered back, catching his hand on the desk. Then Bowen walked in.

"Easy there, mate," he cautioned. "Ye been out fer a day. Ye need yer strength before ye go walkin' about."

Bowen attempted to take him by the arm and guide him back to the cot but Davy jerked himself away. Davy glared at him and responded, "I'm not yer fuckin' mate." The pirate captain waved his hand dismissively and sat down at his desk.

"So, I see yer tongue warn't cut out. Twas a fine showin' ye made of yerself in battle. The men respect ye." He paused, waiting for a verbal response, but got an eye roll instead. "I wouldn't be surprised if'n ye were elected a cap'n someday."

Feeling a little dizzy, Davy slumped into a chair. He stared past Bowen and watched the ship's wake through the stern gallery. Finally, he croaked, "What of the prize?"

Bowen smiled. "She was carryin' 400 bolts a calico an' jest as many bars o' silver. We reckon about 70 thousand fer the lot; a handsome cut fer each man. An' since she's an Indiaman, we'll sail her inta port an' find a ready buyer."

"The prisoners?"

Bowen arched his brow and nodded. "Aye, the prisoners. Well, they had a crew of about 80. We done killed a dozen an' wounded almost twice that. Sixteen saw fit t' join us.

"The carpenter is repairin' their longboat, which we stove in with our guns," Bowen continued. "When he is finished t'morrow, we'll set 'em adrift."

Davy contemplated. They had to be hundreds, if not a thousand miles deep into the Indian Ocean. It would take the Englishmen several weeks in a small boat to reach land, presuming Bowen left them with a compass, water and provisions.

"Due to their brave defense, I've invited the cap'n to me table fer supper," Bowen announced. "No sense in bein' uncivil, even though," he eyed Davy, "ye were somethin' of a savage to the first mate after they surrendered."

"Ye ain't seen a savage," Davy retorted, "until we meet on the beach someday."

Bowen's jaw dropped, but he quickly closed it, not wanting to show fear. "Well then, Mr. Jones, when that day comes, I'll be ready.fer ye."

Davy rose to his feet and lurched to the door. "When that day comes," he said without turning, "Ye be ready to meet yer Maker, and tell Him the Devil sent ye."

18

The *Speaker* sailed southwest until it met the westward-flowing equatorial current. Its crew was in good spirits, having notched a victory against the English East India Company. The spoils of the combined captured cargos would set them up nicely for weeks, if not months, of drunken carousing once they made Libertalia. Captain Bowen, aglow in popularity, confidently strode the deck. With any luck, they might run into another ship or two on the way back.

Davy was not so happy. He spent much of the days in his armory, sharpening weapons and ruminating. Booth was more than a fellow brethren in arms; he had become the closest thing to a friend Davy had since old Iron Ball Morgan and John Roberts. Examining his dirk, he noticed a nick in the blade, probably from that first mate's rib. He pumped the grindstone with his foot and worked out the deformation. As the wheel turned and sparks flew, his mind whirled in concert. It was no use trying to kill Bowen now. The crew supported him, and besides, the articles dictated he must settle the dispute ashore. He decided he would challenge Bowen once the ship dropped anchor at the pirate haven. Until then, all he could do was prepare himself and his weapons – and find his pendant.

The humid night air wrapped the ship in its heavy, moist blanket as it cut through calm seas at a steady six knots under topsails and jib. The helmsman slipped a loop of rope over the spoke of the wheel and lit his pipe. The fore lookout wiped the sweat from his drowsy brow scanned the darkness once again before settling into crouch against the mast. His chin drooped to his chest as he completed his yawn and closed his eyes. The aft lookout was already snoring. He dreamed of the lips of a certain young saucy lass in Libertalia with which he was soon going to taste.

The mate of the watch, lounging near the dimly lit binnacle, noticed the last few particles of sand exit the upper half of the hourglass. He reached for the bell to announce three in the morning when he paused. He thought he'd just heard something, a raspy sound like a scrape. He cocked his head and listened. Nothing. Shrugging, he grasped the braided rope hanging from the clapper and drew it back to strike the bronze bell when he heard – and felt – a much louder scrape. Panicking, he raced to the side of the ship and peered down into the murky waves. Seeing nothing, he hallooed the fore watch.

Before the sleepy watchman could fully rouse himself, the ship lurched violently. The unlucky watchman pitched forward and over the rail of the crosstree. His scream was cut short when he crashed into the main deck. The mate of the watch picked himself up off the deck where he too was thrown and immediately shouted to the helmsman to seize the wheel. Despite the breeze still pressing against the topsails, the *Speaker* no longer moved.

Bowen was on deck in an instant. He ran forward and searched the water below the bowsprit. Sure enough, the dark outline of a coral reef was jutting out of the sea. As the dazed crew rushed up from below, Bowen commanded them to lower the sheets. He found the coxswain and ordered him to lower the longboat.

Davy arrived on deck and wiped the sleep from his eye. He saw Bowen waving his arms and bawling orders to the men.

"What the hell happened?" Davy asked.

"We struck a reef," Bowen explained, panting. "Need t' discover the damage. I'm goin' o'er the side t' inspect." He swung his legs over the gunwale and descended the main chains to the waiting long boat. The coxswain handed him a lantern and cast off.

Davy pulled a cigar out and lit it. The smoke relaxed his nerves and allowed him to think. He calmly watched the carpenter and his crew assemble their gear and go below decks. He listened to other pirates as they milled about the deck speaking in hushed tones, as if they were in the presence of the dead. A few minutes later, Bowen emerged from the side. His face was tensed in a grimace. The carpenter came from below and whispered in his ear. Bowen shook his head and then called out to get the crew's attention and cleared his throat.

"Men, as ye know by now, we done struck a reef," he began slowly. "We got six feet o' water in the well, an' it's rushin' in fast." He paused as the crew murmured. "The barky is lost. Gather what ye can in the way of yer personal effects an' provisions. We're abandonin' ship."

Davy sighed and nodded to himself. He turned away and headed for the ladder, even as other pirates began asking questions.

"We're in the middle of nowhere! Where we gonna go?"

"What about the cargo?"

"Should we split up fer a better chance of survival?"

Bowen held up his hands. "Hark ye, hark ye! There's enough space in the boats t' accommodate the lot of ye – but jest barely. The master will lead one boat, the boatswain another, an' I'll take the last. Each of us will 'ave a compass. Load as much provisions an' water as ye can carry. Bring yer personal arms. The gunner...where's Davy? Anyways, the gunner will bring an allowance of shot an' powder."

"We'll make fer Mauritius," Bowen continued. "Ferget the cargo. We don't 'ave space fer it. We'll lash up the boats an' stick t'gether. We will get t' shore, mates. Jest trust me."

Davy went to his cabin and collected what few things he needed: an extra shirt, his hat, brace of pistols, dirk, and cutlass. He adjusted his eyepatch and headed for the armory. He selected three kegs of powder for small arms and grabbed a bag of shot. His mates arrived and moved the ammunition up to the main deck.

The *Speaker* was now settling heavily, her bow leaning toward the surface, leaving the deck at a forward angle. The pirates scrambled over the side, one carrying a chicken, into the waiting boats. The two long boats and pinnace were lashed together with the pinnace in the lead, commanded by Bowen. Davy waited for the rest to settle in and finally climbed over the side, the last to leave the ship.

The pinnace raised its sail and pirates in the long boats began pulling on their oars to lessen the strain on the connecting line. And so the end of a long night began with a heavy labor. It wasn't long before the stern lantern of the *Speaker* winked out as the dark form of the ship slide beneath the surface.

The men took turns pulling on the oars and soon the dark blue glow of dawn painted the eastern sky. The pinnace charted a course south by southwest, its sail barely drawing as the breeze slackened in concert with the creeping light. The oarsmen in Davy's boat, led by the boatswain, grumbled as they strained. Davy squeezed past two men and took his turn.

As the rim of the sun pierced the horizon, the halting breeze died away completely. The men were now able to see enough into the water to realize they were traveling over a coral reef chain, much of which was just a few feet below them. Davy saw schools of brightly colored fish patrolling the crevices of coral outcroppings.

Bowen, ahead in the pinnace, called for breakfast and the men broke out their provisions. The boatswain, as captain of Davy's boat, cautioned them to eat sparingly and take just a couple of sips from their canteens. He produced fishing line and a hook from his pocket and tied it to his cane. He handed it to the man nearest him, who promptly attached a bit of hard tack and tossed it over the side.

"He ain't gonna get nothin' like that," said an old pirate sitting next to Davy. "Ho! Pull up that line, ye lubber." The fisherman glanced at him irritably and told him if he could do better then he could suit himself. The two bickered for a minute, then the fisherman handed over the cane.

"Ye gots to gets their attention," said the pirate, whom Davy remembered as Newton. The old man pulled a red silk handkerchief out of his pocket and tore off a corner. Davy watched as the man removed the soggy hardtack and impaled the cloth, settling it just above the eye of the hook. He removed his gold hoop earring and attached it to the eyehook.

Next, he cut a piece of hard tobacco for bait and lowered it into the water. He moved the cane back and forth to simulate a living aquatic creature. Within five minutes the line jerked and he pulled up a small bluefin trevally. Davy congratulated Newton, but the old man just shook his head.

"Tis a small victory," he said. "As soon as we move off this 'ere coral, we'll 'ave a devil of a time findin' any fish in shallow water." He quickly cleaned the fish and began handing out small chunks to his mates in the boat. Davy chewed thoughtfully, and wondered what would happen when they ran out of food, let alone the precious remaining water.

The merciless sun assaulted the pirates with oppressive heat. Davy felt like he had stood too close to a campfire, unable to draw back or turn away. He saw other men in the boat pull up their shirts to cover their heads, and thanked himself for remembering his hat. One man took a long drink from his canteen before the boatswain noticed and snapped, "Belay that! Are ye daft? We drink only when the cap'n says." The man sheepishly lowered his canteen.

Most of the men slept during the hell-hot day, covering themselves as much as possible. Their mates woke them when it was their time at the oars. As the sun lowered in the west, the breeze returned to relieve the stifling air and the men rejoiced. Bowen passed the word they had covered about 40 miles. The men groaned, knowing they had far more ocean to pass.

The next morning heralded the arrival of a tropical monsoon. Although there was little in the way of wind, heavy sheets of salty rain drenched the hapless men as they spent the hours bailing the seawater out of their boats. The downpour gave way to a steady shower of large, warm raindrops that impacted every surface like a small explosion.

The depressing weather lasted all day. Newton passed the time by telling stories of his youth and his far-flung adventures at sea. He regaled the men with tales of exotic food and women in East Asia, mysterious creatures of the deep he had glimpsed, and the towering waves and ice floes of the South Sea.

"When we was sailin' the Spanish Main, there was this one mate, went by th' name Israel," he said. "He was a strange lad from th' Dutch East Indies. His real name we couldn't make out. He barely spoke a lick o' English but was always readin' from 'is Bible, which was printed in some fereign script, maybe Dutch, I dunno."

"Anyways," Newton continued, "this 'ere lad was always recitin' the Old Testament, which we only figgered out cuz he would mention the names of folks like Israel an' Jonah. Well, we couldn't call 'im a Jonah, that bein' a bad name fer a fella, so we names him Israel, which he seemed t' take a fancy."

Newton leaned forward, as if confiding in a conspiracy. "Now this Israel, he was a sly cove. Whenever there was a scrape with some Spanish man o' war, this Israel would slip outta sight an' pop up behind 'em, takin' 'em by surprise. He wouldn't say what he did, but we soon figgered he was swimmin' o'er to the enemy ship an' climbin' up the side they weren't guardin'. That lad prob'ly killed scores o' Dons durin' that two-year cruise, back stabbin' and cuttin' throats. A right legend, he was."

"What happened to him?" Davy asked.

"Well now, that's the strange thing," responded Newton. "We was some 200 miles off Curaçao under plain sail. He had the watch one night, an' when it was time fer him t' be relieved, the mates couldn't find 'im. He jest disappeared."

"At sea?" one of the men gasped. "Was the weather foul?"

Newton shook his head. "Nay. It was like he jest decided t' swim away. To this day, I reckon that Israel weren't no mortal at all, but mebbe some creature o' Neptune."

The men gaped in shock. Satisfied with the reaction, the old man shifted his position and took an oar. Davy stared at him incredulously. *Neptune!* His hand drifted to where his medallion had once rested on his chest. He remembered his encounter with Hakim and the strange woman of the sea. And, of course he couldn't forget his own odd disposition. He hoped this boat journey wouldn't last more than a few days, otherwise he'd have to somehow explain why he went over the side for a swim to his curious, nay, *suspicious* fellow pirates. He began to sweat even more than the hot sun, now beating back the monsoon rains, inspired.

The men continued to pull their oars in the steamy aftermath of the storm. Many had drunk their allowance and were now licking their lips in regret. Newton continued to fish, but the deep water offered little to his short line, and in time he gave up. Misery was setting in.

Bowen, in an effort to buoy spirits, claimed they were nearly halfway to landfall, but he privately worried whether he was accurately guiding them. His frequent glance at the chart he grabbed before the ship went down told him that Mauritius was approximately 250 miles from their former position. His dead reckoning was their only hope. Then there was the problem of his gunner, Davy Jones. Although the young man was a talent with the gun and blade, it was his unbridled rage that really concerned him. Bowen decided he would use that emotion against him, when the time came.

By the third day it became apparent that one of the longboats had sprung a serious leak. The incredible heat had melted the caulking in the seams, and the sailing master ordered the men in his boat to bail the hostile water. The men used their hats and even their hands, but they were fighting a losing battle against a rising tide. The other boats had a similar problem, although not to the extent of the old longboat. They cursed the coxswain, whose shipboard job of maintaining the boats was often delayed by his excessive drinking. The hapless coxswain argued that all the caulking in the world wouldn't save them from prolonged exposure, but his fellow pirates retorted with accusations and oaths so profound that the sailing master was forced to end the bickering at gunpoint.

There was no room in the other boats for the men of the sinking vessel. An exasperated Bowen finally took down the sail of the pinnace and sent it to the longboat, with instructions to use it as a fother, or patch. Two men went over the short gunwales and pulled the sail with them. Others grabbed the other side of the sail and pulled it tightly over the gunwale, securing it to the locks of the oars. The sail was pulled up over the other side and secured in the same way. The suction created by the leaks drew the sail tightly against the hull. Then half of the men went over the side to lessen the weight in the boat, while the others bailed. In less than an hour, most of the water was deposited back into the sea and the soaking men regained their seats in the precious craft.

Bereft of their wind propulsion, Bowen considered the situation. Not only would it take longer to reach Mauritius – even if his navigation proved true – but they also had no other means to stop leaks in the other boats. The delay also meant more exposure to the sun, which would kill them faster than thirst or lack of food. Some men were already suffering ill effects, and it would only get worse as time went on.

The days passed at a tortoise's pace. For the men of the former *Speaker*, time had come to a grinding halt. Sunburned skin and parched throats took a toll. Some men became delirious from the effects of the tropical sun and dehydration, others succumbed altogether and drifted off to meet death in slumber. As they passed from the world, the boat captains directed the remaining men to slide their bodies over the side. Newton was one of them. The old man passed during midday, the men noticing when he fell backward from his oar and breathed his last.

Davy grabbed Newton by the shirt and suddenly noticed something underneath it. The pendant! *Why, ye old dog*, Davy smiled to himself. *He must've found it on deck after the bloody affair with that Indiaman and claimed it fer himself.* He jerked the pendant from the old man and stuffed it into his pocket. Then he helped two other pirates as they carefully passed his body over the side.

"Take care, old man. May ye meet yer old shipmates in the deep. Neptune and Israel be with ye," he said to the disappearing form. He took Newton's place at the oars and pulled with vigor, startling the others, who bade him to slow down and keep time with them.

The longboat with the fothered sail covering could no longer support its crew. Seeing that 30 men had already died and more were near death's doorstep, Bowen acquiesced to the plea from the sailing master and allowed the boat to be abandoned. He cut the line and eleven men boarded the two remaining boats, leaving behind a few who would not see another sunrise. The *Speakers* departed, some with a backward glance, and continued their long journey. Davy rested in the stern, staring at the forlorn longboat bobbing in the vastness of the sea and wondered if he would meet a similar fate.

Desperation set in. Hallucinating men began to drink seawater and swear at shades of long-lost associates. Despite Bowen's warning, those that feverishly drank the brine hastened their deaths. Some despaired of the battle for life and hauled their frail bodies overboard to relieve themselves of further misery. Few had enough strength remaining to pull the oars, and this they did in mechanical silence. Davy was weak and beyond hungry. Like most of the others, he gnawed on his leather belt for subsistence. It helped but little, and he, like the rest, began to resemble a skeleton. Bowen himself could barely rouse himself from a slump, his chart and compass now useless objects at his feet.

The current in its circular gyre slowly carried them south. After two weeks at sea, no one manned an oar any longer, nor had they the strength to dispose of the increasing number of lifeless shipmates. Resigning themselves to their fate, they awaited death's sweet release. Many hardly noticed when their boats slid to a halt.

Davy opened his eyes and stared up at the azure sky, unsure if he was actually still alive or perhaps delirious. He heard Bowen's cracked voice.

"Land!"

Mauritius

Th he island of Mauritius was once a bustling trading colony of the Dutch empire, but now it was little more than a decaying outpost with a nominal government and even less law enforcement. Still, there was some commerce in its small town and EIC ships sometimes came to lay in fresh water and provisions before continuing on to India, Batavia or the Far East. In short, it was the best place in the southern Indian Ocean for a weary pirate crew without a ship to quietly blend in with the European locals and rest.

Barely two dozen of the former *Speakers* survived their ordeal at sea. The kindly local townfolk, inspired by the Protestant God to help lost sinners, took them in after Bowen concocted a story about them being attacked by pirates and set adrift. The men were fed, clothed and tended by the zealous Dutch, who unceasingly plied them with scripture.

In a few weeks the pirates recovered and they hatched a clandestine plan. Bowen quietly instructed his crew to case the town for valuable seafaring supplies while he scouted the piers and harbor for a ship to steal. When they found the resources they needed, Bowen put together two parties to execute the devious conspiracy.

As night fell and the town was asleep, Bowen's group stole a pair of small boats and paddled out to a sloop in the harbor. Taking the lone watchman by surprise, they commandeered the vessel and quickly learned the rest of the crew was ashore. Bowen and his men prepared the ship for sea and sent the boats back to the pier.

Meanwhile, Davy's gang successfully looted several warehouses and shops of provisions, arms, and ammunition. They surreptitiously proceeded to the pier and loaded the supplies onto the boats Bowen sent. When all were aboard, the pirates cut the little sloop's cable and stole out of the harbor well before sunrise.

Satisfied with their victory, Bowen renamed the sloop *Content.*

Libertalia

Libertalia was a sight for a pirate's sore eyes, and the *Contents* wasted no time in selling the ship and going ashore. The shares of the sale weren't enough to last them more than a few days, but they'd had enough and disbanded to look for other opportunities. Davy Jones, however, had one last bit of business with Captain Bowen. He strapped on his sword and dagger, bought a brace of pistols, fresh powder, and shot from his old armament shop, and grimly searched the town.

Davy found the erstwhile captain tossing back shots of whiskey in, of all places, the Leaping Leopard. He was sitting at the bar, his back to the door. Davy stepped inside and looked around the room, his searching gaze halted and fixed on his target. His hand crept to his dagger and slowly withdrew it from the sheath. His breathing became heavy as he took a step, and then another, as a tiger stalks its prey.

Bowen ordered another shot, oblivious to the creeping death. Davy stepped closer. He was almost arms-length away from his intended victim. He drew the dagger to his hip, the business end of the blade pointed forward.

The bartender poured the drink while Bowen told him a joke. When he was ready to deliver the punchline, he raised his glass for dramatic effect. The bartender's eyes raised with it and darted to the left, over Bowen's shoulder, at the advancing assassin. The pirate captain noticed his distracted glance and caught a reflection in his whiskey glass. Bowen spun around and whipped out his pistol and found himself face to face with his former gunner, Davy Jones.

Before he could pull the trigger, Davy thrust the dagger forward into the barrel of the flintlock pistol. Flustered, Bowen cried, "Ye mean t' stab me in the back, like some common cutthroat?"

The patrons of the bar fell silent and witnessed the confrontation. Davy regarded Bowen with cold malice. "I mean to deliver ye a challenge," he retorted. He turned his furious gaze to the audience and raised his voice for all to hear.

"This scoundrel caused the death of me mate, George Booth, a profess'nal gennelman of fortune. Hell, this, this, *coward*," he sputtered, turning back to Bowen, "damn near got the whole ship's comp'ny killed!" He leaned in close and locked eyes with the pirate captain. "And so, I challenge ye to a duel."

"Ye liddle viper!" Booth snarled. He withdrew his pistol and stuffed it into his belt. He puffed out his chest, as if daring Davy to drive his blade into him in front of the patrons. "Name the place, an' I'll meet ye at sunrise."

"Show yer rat-face at the beach at dawn, and I'll conclude me business with ye," Davy responded. He spat on Bowen's boot. "And if the sun rises and ye ain't there, I'll find ye, no matter where ye run."

"Oh, the lad is a big man now, is he?" Bowen laughed harshly. "Well, boy, I don't run from tit-sucking whelps. Ye 'ave a good time t'night, fer surely it will be yer last." He turned his back on Davy and resumed drinking.

Davy sheathed his dagger and clenched his fists. He glared at Bowen for a moment longer, then stomped out of the bar.

A panoply of colors stretched across the morning sky. Orange and pink blended into light blue and indigo as Apollo's blazing chariot peeked over the saucer rim of the ocean. The incessant cries of sea birds punctuated the steady roll of the surf as it noisily crashed and skimmed across the sand. A lone figure stood on the beach, intruding on nature's timeless glory like an unwanted guest.

Davy had paced the sandy expanse all night, imagining how he would kill John Bowen. A pistol would be too easy, too quick. No, it would have to be a blade. Having seen him fight, he knew Bowen was handy with a sword, perhaps better than himself. It didn't matter. Davy had hate in his heart, and that, he reckoned, would be enough. He'd find a way to get past Bowen's thrust and take him down. Then he'd have the distinct pleasure of cutting his heart out and offering it to George Booth's spirit as compensation. He impatiently kicked a rock and kept his inner fire burning.

Bowen clambered over the dune and paused, taking in the scenic canopy. He took a deep breath of the salt air, noting the southwest breeze. It helped clear the whiskey cobwebs from his head. He yawned and searched the beach. Spotting his adversary a hundred yards to his left, he pulled out his pistol and check the priming. Satisfied, he trotted down the dune and strode across the hard pack at the water's edge.

Davy heard the approaching footsteps and turned to face his nemesis.

He was swimming. No, he was drowning. He felt a familiar thumping against his chest and realized the pendant was drumming wildly. His back was pinned to the sandy bottom, and a pair of hands were clenching his throat. He opened his mouth but no words would come out and no air was coming in. Nothing but the acrid taste of salt greeted his tongue. He looked up and saw Bowen's blurry face, contorted in hateful effort as he pushed Davy down and slowly pulled his life out.

He grabbed Bowen's arms and tried to pry his grasp loose, but it was no use. The pirate captain's arms were like iron pillars weighing upon him. His lungs were burning, the used air unable to escape. A darkness began to close in. With one last effort, he punched his hands toward that hateful face, but Bowen merely raised his chin out of their path. His arms felt heavy, and fell back into the water, settling beside him. *This is it*, he thought. The darkness crept in further, until only a narrow hole of light remained. His anger subsided and a gentle peace engulfed him. He no longer felt his arms, his legs, or the iron grip on his throat. He began to close his eye.

Wait, he thought. *Why am I holdin' me breath?* He fought back against the darkness and focused on breathing through his neck. Sure enough, the gills formed. He felt energy flood through his body as the precious air did its work. He opened his good eye and saw Bowen above him, a shocked expression of horror on his face.

Bowen suddenly loosened his grip and fell back, mouth gaping, as he witnessed what no other living man, save Wyn, had ever seen: the bulbous, black fish eye of Davy Jones.

Davy struggled out of the water and sat up. The two regarded each other for a moment before Bowen cried, "What the hell are ye?"

As Davy's face reverted back to its human form, he lifted his submerged web hand out of the water and slapped Bowen, sending him reeling backward.

"I'm the Devil," he replied.

Davy pulled out his dirk and jumped on top of Bowen. Stunned, the pirate did little more than raise his arm in defense before Davy buried his blade into the throat of his enemy. Air bubbled mixed in a watery cloud obscured Bowen's face as Davy held him down with one hand and stabbed him repeatedly with his other hand. Finally, his energy spent, Davy released his grip and crawled to the shore. The sun warmed his scaly arms as he passed out from exhaustion.

Something sharp was tapping his forehead. The blinding light made him squint until he could accept the imperious sunshine. He coughed violently, spitting up sea water. He reflexively rolled onto his side and coughed again. Gulping deep breaths of air, he looked straight into the beady eyes of a large, greenish yellow crab. He reached, but the crab scurried away into the surf and buried itself in the sand.

Davy sat up and looked around him. He saw Bowen's body, pushed and rolled by small waves, red with his blood. He stood up, trying to maintain his balance against the rush of dizziness. He searched the sand and found his pistol and hat laying nearby. His cutlass was shattered, evidently from some great blow Bowen had delivered during their fight. Then he remembered his dagger. He went over to the pirate captain's body and pulled it out of his chest. He wiped it off on Bowen's back and gave him a kick for good measure, then slowly walked back to town.

Arriving at the Leaping Leopard, Davy ordered a drink, a

whore and a bath from the smiling bartender. As he stood waiting for his rum, patrons approached and clapped him on the back in congratulations for his victory over Bowen. Davy responded with a simple "thankee" and threw back his shot. A pretty little brown-skinned whore sidled up to him. Davy gave her glance and took her outstretched hand. They climbed the stairs and proceeded to a room, whereupon he roughly threw her onto the bed and slammed the door shut.

Davy awoke the next day with an incredible headache. He rolled over and commanded the whore – a whose name he hadn't bothered to ask – to fetch him a bath. As he relaxed in the steaming water, the young Portuguese whore caressed his aching body with a wet rag. He closed his eyes and smiled as her hand ventured beneath the water. He was in the process of deciding whether he would take her again now or after breakfast when she gave a little shriek.

"What's the matter with ye?" Davy demanded.

"Oh, she's just a little surprised," a familiar voice responded behind him.

Davy jumped to his feet and held his dagger, which he'd kept in the tub. Stark naked and dripping wet, he flushed red and cried, "I'll be damned! If it ain't the quartermaster himself!"

Nathaniel North stepped forward and extended his hand in greeting, a broad smile painting his face. The two clasped hands and shared a hearty laugh. Davy dismissed the woman and quickly dressed himself as North caught him up on his latest adventures.

"There's a brigantine looking for volunteers," North said with a sly look. "Captain Halsey commanding. He's asked me to be his quartermaster, and I sure could use a reliable hand as gunner. Know anyone you could recommend?"

"Sure," Davy replied with a grin. "There's this fella named Davy Jones I hear is lookin' fer work."

They laughed like old school chums and went below for a celebratory drink.

Captain John Halsey welcomed them aboard his 10-gun sloop, the *Charles*, along with his other recruits. He shook Davy's hand, complimenting him on his reputation as a fine gunner and fierce fighter. Although he had worked with Bowen in the past, he respected Davy's challenge and the result.

Halsey and North recommended a cruise to the Red Sea to catch ships transiting the Bab el Mandeb strait. The spot had proven lucrative, as Davy well knew, and the crew agreed. They wrapped up provisioning the ship and set sail two days later.

The *Charles* made good progress in fair weather and late in the afternoon of the eleventh day, North informed Halsey the ship had made landfall near Oyster Island at the mouth of the Strait. The captain nodded and directed his quartermaster to seek an anchorage nearby for the night.

The next few days saw the *Charles* sail up, down and across the lower Red Sea awaiting prey. One morning in a dead calm the lookout on the masthead reported more than two dozen sails creeping down the coast. Halsey felt his moment had arrived, but North was skeptical. He trained his spyglass on the distant ships and shook his head.

"They're pulling at sweeps," he reported. "Making four, perhaps five knots. At least two warships in the van, could be more." He lowered the glass. "We should lay low and let 'em pass."

Davy, who stood nearby and listened to this conversation, asked "Can't we jest wait fer the men o' war to pass? We could pick off the stragglers."

Halsey shook his head. "Nay, Gunner. They could signal the warships upon spyin' our approach. With sweeps manned by God knows how many slaves, even one o' those hefty men o' war could turn around an' blow us out o' the water before we could escape. All we can do is pray fer a breeze."

But the wind didn't come and the Mohgul fleet passed by in the night. However, the next afternoon the wind did return, and they weighed anchor to pursue the Mohguls. As they secured the anchor to the cathead and prepared to sheet home, the lookout spotted a two-masted small ship heading down the coast from the direction of Mocha. Halsey decided to snap up this prey and gain intelligence.

The ship was rigged like a brig or snow, perhaps 150 tons, and an oddly-shaped prow. As they approached, the little vessel began to tack into the wind to avoid them.

"Tis nothing but a gurab," said North. "She's a modified galley without the sweeps. Hideous design," he remarked.

"Mr. Jones," Halsey called over his shoulder. "Please be so

kind as to say hello to our little friend."

Davy ordered some men to load one of the guns and run it out. He adjusted his aim with spike and quoin, then timed his fire with the rise of the swell. The 12-pound shot snapped the fore halliards of the gurab, causing it to momentarily lose way as its foresail came tumbling down. The vessel struck her flag and lowered her main sail to lay to and wait.

"By God, Jones, your gunnery is better than I expected," Halsey cried. "Quite efficient. Mr. North, lower a boat and find out what she knows."

North and his boat crew returned two hours later after confiscating nearly 200 English pounds worth of silver coins, baskets of fish, and some spare cordage for boatswain. He also brought news. The captain of the gurab reported seeing four armed English merchants preparing to leave Mocha. He estimated they would be in the vicinity within a day. Halsey let the vessel depart and the *Charles* got underway.

As twilight set in, the lookout spotted the four ships and hailed the deck.

"Douse the lanterns. We'll fall in with them in the dark," Halsey announced. "When morning arrives, we'll see what we're up against."

The ships passed close by, faintly visible in the starlight. The *Charles*, well hidden behind Oyster Island, waited until the last ship was a league off before venturing out under courses. Trailing the convoy, the pirates quietly prepared for battle.

Dawn rose up and Halsey ordered all sails to be hoisted. The speedy *Charles* caught up with the nearest ship, a sixteen-gun brig, in less than half an hour and engaged her. Davy directed a broadside which dismounted one of the brigs guns and crippled her gaff. He then climbed up to the mainmast crosstree and began picking off men on the deck of the brig with musket fire, beginning with the helmsman.

Halsey ordered North to bring the ship alongside and the pirates boarded. The action lasted 45 minutes, during which several of the Englishmen died, including the first mate, whom North slew with his cutlass.

The merchantman in the vanguard turned to fight the pirates and bore down on their position. Halsey trained his glass on the approaching vessel and determined she was a 24-gun brigantine. As North secured their new prize, Halsey called over to Davy.

"Mr. Jones, receive our new guest."

Davy climbed down the ratline and directed a gun crew to ready the long nine-pound bow chaser. He observed the approaching brigantine as it headed straight for them. When it was less than 200 yards away, he carefully aimed the brass piece and fired. The shot shattered the bow bulwark and raked the ship from fore to aft, ball and splinters killing several men clustered on the main deck. Dismayed, the captain of the brigantine signaled a general retreat and the three remaining ships peeled off in different directions.

The prize was named *Rising Eagle*, from Bristol. Halsey interrogated the captain and learned which one of the other ships was carrying the most money. The captain, fearing for his life, told Halsey the lead brigantine, named *Essex*, was carrying pay for an English garrison in India. Satisfied, Halsey left North with a large prize crew on the *Rising Eagle* and ordered both vessels to pursue.

The *Charles* and *Rising Eagle* swiftly caught up with the *Essex*. Halsey raised the red flag at the masthead, which meant 'surrender or no quarter', and ordered Davy to fire a shot at the quarry. Davy complied and sent a ball through her main topsail. The *Essex*, outnumbered and wanting no more of this implacable enemy, immediately struck her colors in surrender.

The chase proved fruitful, as the pirates discovered 40,000 English sterling pounds in the hold. The ship's captain, who knew Nathaniel North, was spared of his belongings and those of his gentlemen passengers. Halsey amiably invited the captain, whose name was Punt, over to the *Charles* for dinner.

During the dinner, which Davy attended along with North and Halsey, Captain Punt told them the English Crown was searching for specific pirates roaming the Indian Ocean. "In particular, men of Henry Every's crew are named in the warrant," he declared. "Mr. Jones, you are one of them."

"What? How the hell does King William know of me?" Davy cried.

"Queen Anne," Punt corrected. "Some of Every's men were captured attempting to sneak into Ireland. I suppose Her Majesty's court discovered your identity from one of the crew. The man himself, Every I mean, apparently escaped."

Davy's face turned ashen and he excused himself from Halsey's table. Later that evening, Halsey sent Punt and his ship on their way.

The pirates rejoiced with their haul and celebrated with a night of drinking the *Rising Eagle's* captured stock of Madeira wine. The next day they agreed with Halsey that their cruise was successful and they should return to Madagascar to distribute the shares. Davy was not so sure he wanted to go back to the pirate haven, especially since it would be one of the first places the Royal Navy would look for offenders named in the warrant, such as himself. He dreaded capture and death by hanging, just as Captain Ross had warned so long ago.

The *Charles* and *Rising Sun* sailed on a southerly course for Madagascar, and with each passing day Davy became more anxious. His encounter with the Royal Navy at St. Mary's Island informed him of their deadly earnestness in capturing wanted men. A squadron of frigates would wreak havoc on piracy in the area until they found what they were seeking.

As he sat on the capstan brooding, Halsey squatted next to him. "There's a storm comin' up from the south," he commented. "It appears t' be directly in our path, and I'll wager it will come on t' blow pretty strong."

Davy looked in that direction and saw the blackening sky. "Aye, that's a bad un," he agreed. "I'll secure the guns." He called his mates and they bowsed the cannons tightly with extra lashings.

That evening, less than a hundred miles from Madagascar, the hurricane struck. The two ships lost sight of each other as mountainous waves rose from the water and complete darkness engulfed them. Sideways rain beat hard upon the men as they struggled to reef the sails. More than one man aloft was carried away by the wind or washed over the side as the sea swamped the main deck. Below decks, men prayed.

Halsey ordered the spritsail set and determined to ride out the storm, but the men understood the odds were long against them. As they made peace with their God, a surging wave smashed into the side of the *Charles*, bowling it over onto its beam. The ship quickly turned over completely, keel exposed.

In the armory, Davy was tossed onto the bulkhead. Shaking his bruised skull, he rolled with the deck until he found himself laying on the overhead. That's when he knew the ship was going down. He forced open the armory door and crawled toward the hatchway on the upside-down deck. Seawater poured in so fast he couldn't get through, so he waited until the flood was up to his neck before he took a deep breath and plunged.

He felt his way through the dark turbulence and finally freed himself of the ship. Breaking onto the surface, he observed the bottom of the *Charles* riding like an upset canoe. The driving rain pelted his face as he tried to get his bearings in the tempest. He latched his arms around a broken spar and prayed to Neptune to make it stop.

He wasn't sure how much time had passed when he awoke to bright sunlight. It could have been hours, or even days for all he knew. Pain in his feet told him he'd cut himself on some coral rock. The spar was gone, he noticed, but he was atop some sort of rocky outcropping. A reef, he groggily concluded.

He stood up and scanned the choppy ocean, but there was no sign of life, or even floating bodies. Debris from the *Charles* littered the area. The *Rising Sun* was nowhere to be seen. He spied a chunk of wood and thought he could make out the shattered husk of one of the boats in the distance, too far damaged to be useable. He coughed and realized he'd swallowed a great deal of seawater. His stomach roiled in protest. Davy sighed in despair and sat down, wondering how long it would be before he died.

A few hours later he observed sharks circling the reef. He pulled himself up a little further to avoid the rising tide, but it came nonetheless. Would it wash over the rock and leave him defenseless against the maneaters? He spied an oar floating nearby and made a grab for it, but stumbled and scraped his hands across the sharp coral. Bleeding profusely, he grabbed the oar and prepared to fend off the malevolent predators. The water now lapped at his ankles.

There was a splash behind him and he whirled around, prepared for battle. But instead of a shark, there was a woman's head poking out of the water. She had dark green hair like seaweed, and huge blue eyes like a fish. As a flabbergasted Davy watched, the eyes contracted to human size – just like his did after a swim. Then she spoke, in a beautiful voice. "Come home."

"I seen ye before, ain't I?"

She nodded.

Who are ye?"

"I am known as Pallas," she responded melodically.

Davy pursed his lips. "What do ye mean, come home?"

"Leave this place, and come with me," she responded. She rose out of the water enough to reveal her voluptuous naked breasts. Davy stared at her inviting form and tentatively took a step.

"Yes," she said, stretching forth her arms. "Come with me and reunite with your father."

"Me father?" Davy gasped. "But he's dead."

Then the mermaid whipped her head to the side and a frown came across her lovely face.

Davy followed her gaze and spied a ship's mast breaking the horizon. When he looked back, she had disappeared. He searched the water and waited for her to reappear, but in vain. Disappointed, he turned back and saw that the ship was headed straight in his direction.

The *Reine de la Mar* was a French pirate ship. Captain Emanuel Costeau welcomed him aboard and declared he was heading to the Caribbean. The present sea, he said, was too dangerous for gentlemen of fortune since the Royal Navy had showed up in force. Davy readily agreed.

"And sir," Costeau asked, "What is the name by which you travel these seas?"

Davy looked down at his bloody hands. Surely Neptune, that great God of the Deep, had a plan for him. The pendant quickened with his heartbeat. He lifted his eyes, now full of belief, and smiled grimly.

"Israel. Israel Hands."

Epilogue

The sea rushed past the bow of the fishing vessel as the old man stared at the foamy wake. The wind whipped through his long, gray hair, as a reminder that here, in this place, he was a powerless object to the forces of nature. He hardly noticed, as he struggled to gather his thoughts. Plans had to be made.

The years he spent on Silhouette Island came to an abrupt end yesterday when he came upon the landing party quite unexpectedly. Although he knew nothing of their language, his savage appearance was easily identifiable as a castaway and he was invited aboard their little trading vessel.

Some hot soup and biscuit restored his body, which was much depleted from living on what little fish and geckos he managed to scavenge. The old wound from a musket ball was already scarred over when they found him, but he was nearly delirious from the agony of solitude. He shook their hands and kissed their feet, rejoicing in his salvation. The merchants were astonished when he offered them pieces of eight as payment for his passage.

Imminent peril was no longer a consideration, for now. It was the future he must consider. There was a boy to be found. A boy with a secret that must never be discovered. He bent his head in silent prayer to the sea god. *Oh Neptune, let me find our son, whom I have cared for all these years.*

The sun was setting as a lone figure watched the ship sail away. With a flip of her tail, she disappeared beneath the endless sea.

Coming Soon, the second book in the
Legend of Davy Jones series:

Davy Jones
and the Raging Main

About the Author

Scott D. Williams is a native of Indiana and resides in San Diego. He served in the US Navy for more than 20 years and has written several works of fiction. He loves to watch baseball, smoke cigars, and catch up with his pile of books.

Note from the Author

Word-of-mouth is crucial for any author to succeed. If you enjoyed *The Pirate Davy Jones*, please leave a review online—anywhere you are able. Even if it's just a sentence or two. It would make all the difference and would be very much appreciated.

Thanks!
Scott D. Williams

Made in the USA
Columbia, SC
05 May 2022

59981623R00152